The List

"*The List* contains all the must-haves of the thriller genre—danger, intrigue and suspense. Powerful villains. Exciting action scenes. Anticipation. . . Tom Wallace excels is in his ability to make his characters come alive. As with Wallace's previous thriller, *Gnosis*, I ended up finishing this book in less than two days. This book makes for an absorbing and enjoyable read, the kind that had me incessantly turning the pages."

--Mary Fan

"*The List* is a fast-paced, thrilling read. It takes the reader on a journey of intrigue immersed in political and corporate greed. Detective Jack Dantzler's quest to solve the mystery behind his parent's deaths thrusts him into a world of international crime. It has graphic detail but it is perfectly balanced as the story of death, fear and reprisal unfolds. Not a book for the faint of heart."

--Patricia Day (Readers Favorites)

Gnosis

"A page-turner. *Gnosis* is a book that's virtually impossible to walk away from."

--Mary Fan

"The book features cerebral challenges for readers who like their murder mysteries served Kentucky-style."

--Kentucky Monthly Magazine

Heirs of Cain

"Quite simply, one of the best novels of 2010."
--Gelati's Scoops

"Wallace raises interesting questions about moral relativism and how trained killers can adapt to civilian life."

--Publishers Weekly

"Powerful and compelling. This story is so intense . . . that you will still be breathing it and thinking about it for a while after you've turned the last page."   --Night Owl Review

"*Heirs of Cain* is graphic, chilling, exciting and thoroughly worth the time to read. For those who are daring enough to step out of their typical reading genre, I invite you to check out *Heirs of Cain*. For all others . . . enjoy!"

--Sabrina Marino,

FreshFiction.com

The Devil's Racket

"BRAVO!! By far the best book ever. Jack Dantzler is a complicated man and a unique detective with a long shelf life, reminiscent of Michael Connelly's Harry Bosch. *The Devil's Racket* grabbed me from the beginning and it held me to the end. This is a book that you will want to read and pass on to your friends and family. What we have here is a winner."
--MyShelf.com

"Central Kentucky's stunningly beautiful horse farms are the picture of serenity and refinement, but who knows what evil lurks beyond those four-board fences? Enjoy the ride, although it's bumpy and bloody. It just might give you a shiver as you drive past the next pretty horse farm—so pretty, it's, well, scary."
--Lexington Herald-Leader

What Matters Blood

"A masterpiece of murder. Jack Dantzler is a complicated man and a unique detective with a long shelf life, reminiscent of Michael Connelly's Harry Bosch. I suspect Dantzler will be around for quite a while. HIGHEST RECOMMENDATION."   --MyShelf.com

"Tom Wallace delivers a wallop of a thrill with *What Matters Blood*. With masterful characterization, his portrayal of the serial killer is chilling, as well as authentic, enough to elicit goose bumps. The story is fast-paced, the dialogue realistic, and the search for the killer intriguing. One galvanizing read that will hold the reader's interest throughout."   --Midwest Book Review

The List

The List

Tom Wallace

Hydra
Publications

Hydra Publications | Madison, Indiana

Hydra Publications
337 Clifty Drive
Madison, IN 47250

This book is a work of fiction. Names, characters, places, and incidents either are
works of the author's imagination or used fictitiously.
Any resemblance to actual events, locales, or persons, living or dead,
is entirely coincidential.

Printed in the United States of America

www.hydrapublications.com

This book is dedicated with great love to Sarah Small, who is without question the smartest one in the family.

PROLOGUE

Laos, September, 1970

The rain was relentless, golf-ball size drops of water striking the red mud like bullets fired from heaven. It had been this way since what seemed like forever, and based on those thick, gray clouds blanketing the morning sky, the deluge showed no sign of easing up anytime soon. This was a monsoon in all its soggy glory.

Terry Jackson lifted one hand from beneath his poncho and swatted at the mosquito buzzing near his right ear. The cagey insect dodged the strike, flew a few feet away, and then launched a bold counter offensive that located the new landing zone squarely on Jackson's cheek. Jackson slapped his face hard, drew back his hand and looked at the decimated attacker's blood, wings and crushed body in his palm.

"Damn mosquitoes here are so big you could pick 'em up on radar," Jackson said, wiping bloody remains from his hand. "Damn little bastards."

"Damn rain," Damon Russell said. "Never seen this much water in my entire life. This is the kinda shit Noah had to deal with."

"Noah was lucky," Kenton Mullins pointed out. "He only had forty days of rain. We've had it for almost three months now. Ain't that right, Scholar?"

"As always, you are right on the money, Mr. Mullins," Jackson said. "The heroic dove Noah sent out from the ark on the world's first recon mission would still be searching for dry land if he were here today."

Jackson, a corporal, was wedged between Mullins and Russell, both PFCs. The trio was huddled beneath a makeshift tent—four blankets loosely tied to bamboo stakes—in an effort to avoid being drenched by the incessant deluge. They were barely succeeding. The blankets sagged at the center, thus allowing water to cascade in from all sides. Mud splashed from the ground onto the men with increasing intensity, changing what had once been olive-drab ponchos into a shiny rust-red color. They had been here for three hours, since a few minutes past daybreak, sitting quietly, getting soaked to the bone.

Their being together, *anywhere*, was one of those twists of fate rarely experienced outside the military. Three men, two white, one black, from different parts of the country, complete strangers until only a few months ago, thrown together by blind chance. Under no other conceivable set of circumstances would these three men meet each other, much less become friends. It simply would never have happened. Yet, here they were, ten-thousand miles from home in a god-forsaken country, bound together by fear, uncertainty and an overwhelming desire to stay alive. The only thing each of them wanted was to get back home in once piece. Back to family, friends, girls . . . the safety of familiarity and routine. To achieve that end, they would protect themselves and each other, no matter how dangerous or deadly the situation. Not long ago they were strangers; now they were brothers. Survival was the bond that held them together.

Jackson, from Ft. Lauderdale, Florida, was known as "Scholar" in honor of his two semesters at a junior college. It was a moniker he neither sought nor rejected, although he was pleased to have it. Being viewed as intelligent was important to him. His big dream was to return to school, earn a degree in journalism and become a sportswriter.

Mullins, a big raw-bone blond-haired kid with shoulders as wide as goal posts, grew up on a farm outside of Lincoln, Nebraska, the youngest of six children. Quiet, shy, and not given to introspection, he was one of those rare individuals who accepted whatever came his way, good or bad, with the belief that this was simply how things were supposed to be. He also possessed that awe-shucks, good-old-country-boy charm that tended to cause people to underestimate him and his abilities. That was their mistake. Mullins was strong as a bull, tough, and the finest marksmen of the trio.

At nineteen, Russell was the youngest of the three, and the one with the most intriguing background. Born and raised in Los Angeles, Russell was a superb baseball player and a solid student in the classroom. Baseball scouts saw him as a can't-miss Major League prospect, and top-name universities courted him from seventh grade on for his academic prowess. A golden future lay in front of him. That all changed three months before his sixteenth birthday, when, according to his mother, "Damon was hijacked by one of the worst gangs in South Central L.A." Baseball and academics gave way to street crimes and brushes with the law. Several arrests followed, mostly for petty offenses that resulted in a minor slap on the wrist, and yet another warning to walk the straight and narrow or be ready to suffer the consequences. He skated so often he began to see himself as invincible. Then, on a blistering July night, he was arrested and charged with robbery and aggravated assault against a police officer. Two felonies that had him facing serious jail time. But the judge and the district attorney, impressed by his innate intelligence, saw him as being a cut above the usual street thug. In an effort to salvage him and his future, they agreed to give Russell a choice: prison or the military. Two days later his mother signed the papers allowing her underage son to join the Army. This was more than two years ago. Fully aware of the opportunity he had been given, Russell proved to be an exemplary soldier.

Jackson swatted at another mosquito, cursing as he watched it fly away and disappear in the rain.

"Why you tryin' to kill mosquitoes?" Russell asked, seriously. "Me, I'm prayin' the one that bit Sarge bites my black ass. Get me out of this place."

Sarge was Staff Sergeant Kaleb Daniels. Two weeks ago, after contracting malaria, he had been shipped to a hospital in Honolulu.

"Malaria's a tough ticket home," Jackson said. "I damn sure don't want any part of it."

"What exactly is malaria, anyway?" Mullins said.

"What am I, a doctor?" Jackson answered. "It can kill you—that's all I know. And that's all you need to know."

"I don't think we have malaria in Nebraska," Mullins said. "Different kind of mosquitoes, I suppose."

Russell leaned forward, picked up his canteen and took a long drink. Screwing the cap back on, he said, "Where the hell is the captain? Thought he was only going to be gone for a couple of hours. He should've been back by now."

"He said wait until eleven-hundred hours," Jackson replied. "If he's not back by then, we go looking for him."

"Hell, we're supposed to be his security detail, yet he wanders off alone." Russell shook his head, sending water flying off his helmet. "Either he's nuts or this mission ain't all that dangerous."

"The captain isn't nuts," Jackson said, taking a drink from his canteen. "Sarge said the captain is the smartest guy he's ever been around."

"I'm just sayin', him wandering off to meet someone without us to protect him isn't all that wise."

Mullins's thoughts were still on the mosquitoes. "Man, I would hate to get malaria and die. Killed by a mosquito is not how I want to be remembered. I mean, if I'm going to die here in Vietnam, I want it to be in combat."

"We're not in Vietnam," Jackson pointed out.

"Where the hell are we?" Russell said.

"Laos."

"Laos? Why the hell are we in Laos?"

"I don't know. The captain never said why."

"I signed up to fight in Vietnam, not Laos," Russell protested. "We have no reason to be in Laos."

"We're soldiers—we follow orders. Our orders are to guard the captain, to make sure he's okay. That's what we'll do."

"And in the meantime, the man we're supposed to be guarding strolls off into the jungle all by his lonesome." Russell snickered. "How much sense does that make?"

"The captain knows what he's doing."

"What *is* he doing?" Russell said. "What *is* our mission? Explain that to me, will you?"

"Man, you're asking questions I can't answer. All I know is he had to meet a guy. Who or why . . . I don't know. It must be pretty serious, though, or we wouldn't be here. After all, the war is not in Laos."

"Yeah. And we shouldn't be here, either," Russell snapped.

Jackson shrugged. "Well, we are here. And we'll suck it up and do our job, like we always do."

Mullins said, "How much longer do we wait, Scholar? The captain has been gone a long time."

Jackson stretched his left arm out from beneath his poncho and checked his watch. "Okay, it's eleven-hundred-twenty hours. We've waited long enough. Let's gear up and move out."

"Where are we going?" Mullins said.

"Follow the same trail the captain took," Jackson said.

Russell stood, stretched his legs, picked up his M16 and slung it over his shoulder. "Laos? I left one shithole country only to end up in another shithole country. Fuckin' hilarious."

"Let's go find the captain," Jackson said, heading toward the jungle.

"Yeah," Russell said, flipping his poncho hood over his helmet. "So we can *protect* him."

CHAPTER ONE

Lexington, Kentucky, Present Day

Detective Jack Dantzler dropped into a catcher's squat, and with his right hand swept dead leaves and grass from two grave markers. When the debris had been brushed away, he carefully placed a single rose on each marker, whispered a soft "I love you and miss you" and stood.

```
John David Dantzler    Sarah Elizabeth Dantzler
     1942–1970               1941–1978
```

Dantzler was six when his father died in Vietnam. Even now, he could remember with perfect clarity that cool Saturday afternoon in September when the two uniformed officers came to the house to deliver the grim news that Staff Sergeant John Dantzler had been killed when his squad was ambushed by Viet Cong snipers. The rest of what the officers said came out as one long run-on sentence: bullet to the chest . . . died instantly . . . died a hero in the service of his country . . . burial with full military honors . . . you have our condolences.

The men spoke in whispers, as if by keeping a six-year-old boy from hearing the bad news, then the dreadful event somehow had not actually occurred. But he had heard. And it had happened. His father was gone. Forever.

Dantzler could still see the dazed, disbelieving look in his mother's eyes. He had thought at the time that this was how a boxer looked after being hit by one of Muhammad Ali's lightning-fast jabs. Dazed and disbelieving. At that moment, he wanted to run and hide, to make it all disappear like a horrible nightmare. But there was nowhere to run, no place to hide. This was a nightmare that would never end.

For what seemed like an eternity he felt a depth of sadness and hurt he doubted could ever be rivaled. No one experiences this level of pain more than once in a lifetime. It wasn't possible. God would never allow it. But he had been wrong. He would feel it again, and the second time would cause more pain and hurt and sorrow than he could possibly have imagined.

Eight years later, when his beloved mother was murdered.

He had often been told that God never gives us more than we can handle.

Well, he wasn't buying it. It was bullshit. A bogus platitude. God gives us plenty that we can't handle, and anyone who believes otherwise is blind to what's happening around them. As a cop, Dantzler understood this better than most. He had come face to face with too much suffering caused by evil men and women to ever believe any platitude could hide the plain truth—that God not only gives us more than we can handle, he also turns a blind eye to what is happening.

Sarah Dantzler murdered. Her killer never apprehended. What platitude covers that?

*****

Leaving the cemetery, Dantzler gave some thought to dropping by the tennis center and playing a couple of sets. But with night rapidly closing in, he chose to pass on visiting the tennis center. Beating another hapless opponent held no appeal for him.

Instead, he grabbed a hamburger and fries from franchise row and headed home, arriving at a little past nine. Dantzler lived on Lakeshore Drive in a small ranch-style house he purchased in the mid-1990s. Nice and cozy. Nothing special. Three bedrooms, two full baths, den, living room, kitchen, basement and screened-in back porch. The backyard, though relatively small, bumped up against a large lake. The lake had been the selling point for him. Dantzler loved the water, and although the lake was a long way from the ocean, it would do just fine until the day he could retire and move to the beach.

Finished with his meal, he went into the kitchen and fixed his favorite drink—Pernod and orange juice. After taking a sip, he strolled into the den and flipped on the TV. Within minutes, he was faced with an impossible choice. Which movie to watch? John Garfield in *Body and Soul* or Montgomery Clift in *From Here to Eternity*? Two of his favorite actors in two of his all-time favorite flicks. Most nights he was lucky to find a single good movie on the tube; tonight there were two classics competing for his attention. Solomon would have a hard time making this decision. Fortunately for Dantzler, his dilemma was averted. A knock on the front door saved him from having to split the baby and choose between Garfield and Clift.

Like all cops, Dantzler was wary of unexpected late-night visitors. And he had reason to be. Many of the scumbags he helped put away promised to extract revenge somewhere down the road. He viewed such outbursts as little more than angry rants from men about to be put behind bars for many, many years. False, loud threats, not to be taken seriously. But . . . there was always the chance that one of those scumbags was here to deliver on his promise. Given that possibility a wise cop never takes things for granted. He looked at his Glock lying on the desk, considered taking it, then decided he would take his chances.

Dantzler clicked off the TV, turned on the porch light and cracked the door maybe six inches. Standing outside was a man he didn't recognize. The man was probably in his mid-fifties, but looked much older. He was thin to the point of appearing emaciated, with long hair pulled back into a ponytail. Dark circles ringed his hollow eyes, his cheeks were sunken, and the color of his skin was an unhealthy yellow. Dantzler wondered if the man's color was caused by the overhead light or by an illness. Either way, the man did not look well.

"Are you Detective Jack Dantzler?" the man asked

"Yes. And who are you?"

"Roger Walters."

"What can I do for you, Mr. Walters?" Dantzler said, pushing the door open a few more inches while keeping his eyes on the man's hands.

"I need a few minutes of your time."

"A little late for a chat, isn't it? Can't this wait until Monday?"

"I won't be in town Monday," Walters said, shaking his head. "And I think you'll want to hear what I have to say."

"If this is police business there are proper channels you need to follow."

"This isn't police business. It's . . . well, it's personal. Not for me. For you."

"What's this about?"

"Your father. Captain Johnny Dantzler."

Dantzler eyed the man skeptically. "I'm afraid you are way off base here, Mr. Walters. My father was a staff sergeant, not a captain."

"No. Your father was a captain."

"I think maybe you've got the wrong Dantzler."

"Believe me, I wish that were true," Walters said, adding, "I regret having to tell you any of this, but you deserve to know the truth. And the truth is, there is much about your father that you don't know."

"I'm sure that's true. I was only six when he was killed."

"Where do you think your father was killed?"

"Vietnam. Outside of Pleiku."

"How were you told that he died?"

"Killed by a sniper while on patrol."

"Your father died in Laos, not Vietnam. And he wasn't killed by the Vietnamese or the Laotians."

"Who killed him?"

"The CIA."

Dantzler shook his head. "Mr. Walters, I don't know where you obtained your information, but you are dead wrong. My father was . . ."

"Your father, *Captain* Johnny Dantzler, was in Special Forces. He was working for the CIA as part of a highly covert special op aimed at uncovering rogue elements within the CIA who were heavily into drug production, sales and distribution. They used the dirty money from their operation to bring drugs back to the United States, and to fund what amounted to a private war in Laos and Cambodia. Your father died because he was a threat to the drug dealers. More important, he was a threat to those within the CIA who were running the operation. Based on what happened to him, it's safe to assume he was getting close to uncovering the names of those men. They weren't about to let that happen. Therefore, he had to be eliminated. That's who your father was, that's what his mission was, and that is why he was murdered."

Walters waited several seconds, and then said, "Could we talk about this inside? I need to sit down and take a load off."

Dantzler led the man into the den and motioned for him to sit on the sofa. Dantzler sat in a leather chair across from him.

Dantzler said, "My mother received dozens of letters from my father. He was awarded medals. He was given a military funeral. There is a photo of him in his uniform, and he has staff sergeant stripes. There's no mention anywhere of him being a captain."

"That staff sergeant stuff was bullshit, part of his cover. Your father operated in a world of shadows, lies, secrets and deceit. His task, his mission, was dark and dangerous. The only thing you know about your father that is true is he died in Southeast Asia. Everything else is as fictional as a Lee Child novel."

"How do you know this?"

"Because I served with your father."

Dantzler leaned forward. "You were with him when he died?"

"No," Walters said, shaking he head. "I was in the hospital in Hawaii, recovering from malaria. None of the other three guys in the squad were with him either. But they were the ones who found his body."

Dantzler leaned back, confusion written on his face. "I'll need to check on you, Mr. Walters, before I can believe any of this."

"That would be a waste of time. If you check on Roger Walters, you'll learn that he died in Hawaii in nineteen-seventy from severe wounds received in Nam."

"You're not really Roger Walters?"

"My name is Kaleb Daniels. If you check on me, you'll learn that I was reported MIA in nineteen-seventy. Two years later, I was reclassified as KIA. But as you can see, I am alive. For the past forty years I have lived in Amsterdam."

"Why the subterfuge?"

"Several days after your father was killed I received a phone call from Terry Jackson, one of the guys in our squad. He told me about finding your father's body. Terry was mystified and scared. All he kept telling me was 'some serious shit' was going down, and he had no idea what it was. Within ten days, Terry and the other two men in the squad were dead. Naturally, it was reported that they died in combat in Nam. Of course, that was another falsehood, more of the cover up. Who knows where they really died, or who actually killed them?

"I was a staff sergeant, so I knew more about the mission than the other three guys did," Daniels continued. "I didn't know it all, but I did have some idea what your father was into. He shared some things with me that he hadn't shared with the others. Anyway, when I heard about Terry, Damon and Kenton, I figured I was next on the hit list, and that it was in my best interest to disappear. I knew Roger Walters had just died—he had been in the hospital room next to mine—so I swiped his driver's license and a couple of other pieces of ID. I left the hospital early and caught a flight to New York. I put my photo on his DL, bought a ticket to Amsterdam and left the country. I only came back three days ago."

"You're not worried about your safety anymore?"

"I was recently diagnosed with inoperable cancer. I have less than three months to live. If there is anyone out there who still wants to kill me, they would be doing me a huge favor. It would certainly be a lot easier than what I am about to go through. My parents are dead, but I do have a younger sister I want to see before I die. She thinks I've been dead for forty years, so I'm sure she'll be more than a little shocked to see me."

Daniels looked down for several seconds. Tears welled in his eyes. "There is another reason why I came to see you today. It has to do with your mother."

"What about my mother?"

"I'm the reason she is dead."

Dantzler's entire body tensed, his hands balled into fists. "You killed her?"

"No. But I may be responsible."

"How?"

"I sent your mother a long letter detailing what I have just told you. I'm sure she was as confused and disbelieving as you are. At some point, in an effort to uncover the truth, she must have made some phone calls. That's only natural—anyone in her position would have done the same thing. Obviously, she contacted someone who knew the truth and didn't want it to come out. She had to be silenced. I should have warned her not to mention to anyone what I revealed to her. Not doing so was a fatal mistake on my part."

"Any idea who she might have contacted?"

"No."

"Do you know who killed my mother?" Dantzler asked.

"No, I don't."

"How can I find out who did?"

Daniels shook his head. "I don't know."

"Do you know David Langley?"

"No. Who is he?"

Dantzler shrugged. "His name is mentioned in my mother's murder book."

"Never heard of him. Sorry?"

"What about Lucas White?"

"I knew *of* him," Daniels said. "Big-time four-star general. How do you know about him?"

"His name is also in the murder book."

"That's strange."

"Was Lucas White involved with the CIA?"

"Not that I'm aware of."

"How do I contact Lucas White?" Dantzler said, looking around for paper and pen.

"You can't. He's dead. Committed suicide last year." Daniels thought for a second. "There is one man who might be able to help you. If you could locate him."

"Who?"

"Cain.

"Cain? Who is he? How can he help me?"

"He was something of a legend in Nam. An assassin. Spent almost five years in those jungles, doing God knows what. Tales of his exploits are almost beyond belief."

"What is Cain's first name? And where does he live?"

"Cain is only his code name. You know, like the biblical Cain, the first assassin. His real name is Michael Collins. Mickey. Until recently, he taught literature at a college in North Carolina. But it's my understanding he quit and kind of dropped off the radar."

"How do you know about Cain?"

"Everyone who was in Nam knows about him. Like I said, he's a legend."

"Where did he teach?"

"I don't know. But you might try contacting a guy named Andy Waltz. His code name was Houdini. He did the scrounging for Cain's squad. He's now a reporter for the *New York Times*. He and Cain were close. He might be able to give you some help."

"Could Cain have killed my mother?"

"Could have, but he didn't. That's not his style. Now, the same can't be said of Seneca."

"Who the hell is Seneca?" Dantzler said, scribbling the name on an envelope.

"A full-blooded Cherokee named Dwight David Rainwater. He was part of Cain's squad. He had a reputation for being extremely ruthless. Killing your mother would have been just another job for him."

"Where can I find Seneca?"

"I don't know." Daniels's eyes again filled with tears. "I'm truly sorry about your mother, for what happened to her. I ask your forgiveness if my actions played any part in her death."

"If you didn't kill her you have no need to apologize."

Daniels stood. "Johnny Dantzler was a great man, a terrific soldier, a true patriot. He talked about you all the time, about what a great kid you were, how much he loved you and missed you. Said he called you 'Doc' because of how you would imitate Bugs Bunny and say, 'What's up, Doc?' He said you sounded exactly like Bugs. Any kid who loses a parent at a young age misses out on a lot. You missed out on plenty and that's sad. Johnny Dantzler was the real deal."

Stepping out onto the porch, Daniels turned, said, "Find Cain. If you seek answers to your questions, he's your best bet for finding them. However . . . the smart play, the *safe* play, would be to let the ghosts from the past rest in peace."

"I want the truth about my father and justice for my mother," Dantzler said. "I need to know what happened."

"You already know *what* happened, Detective Dantzler. I just told you. The two people you loved most were murdered. What you're looking for is *who* and *why*. Finding the answers will not be easy. If you're lucky, the ones who did it are dead and buried. But if you're not lucky and they're still alive, they will be more dangerous than a thousand rattlesnakes."

"I've faced danger before," Dantzler said. "I know how to handle myself."

Daniels smiled. "The kind of danger you've faced is far different from the kind of danger I'm talking about. Something like this is a spider's web that branches out in all directions. Who knows where it goes, or how high up it goes? But know this: Wherever it goes, it will be guarded by men with too much to lose to let a lone homicide detective crash the party. That's why you'll need Cain. He'll at least even the odds, maybe give you a fighting chance."

Mind racing, more mystified than confused, Dantzler watched Daniels drive off into the night. What to make of the man's tale? he wondered. How much was truth, how much was fiction? Was *any* of it true? Dantzler's detective instincts said the man was telling the truth. A dying man has no reason to lie. However, his instincts as a son whispered something different. How was it possible that so much of his father's past didn't fit with what he had been told all his life? A captain, not a sergeant? Special Forces? Died in Laos, not Vietnam? Worked for the CIA? Was any of this possible? Could so many secrets be buried for so long? Did his mother know or suspect any of this? If so, did it play a role in her death?

Only one way to find out for sure—start digging.

Closing the door, he went back into the house, grabbed his cell phone and placed a call to the *New York Times*. He had to speak with Andy Waltz. He needed Houdini to perform some magic.

CHAPTER TWO

Four days later and still no word from Houdini.

Sitting at his desk, having completed a week's worth of paperwork in one afternoon, Dantzler wondered if his message had been given to Houdini, or if it had found its way into a wastebasket. He had spoken with a female reporter from the *Times*, who informed him that Andy Waltz was retired but still worked part-time, primarily as one of the Op Ed page editors. She took Dantzler's cell phone number and promised to give it to Waltz the next time she saw him. Maybe she did, maybe she didn't. After four days of silence Dantzler had his doubts. Either his message was lost, or the reporter forgot to pass it along to Waltz. Or perhaps Waltz simply did not want to speak with him.

Dantzler decided he wouldn't wait any longer. The time had come to act, to take control of the situation. Flipping through the Rolodex on his desk, he quickly found the number for Bobby Brennan and dialed it. Brennan, a New York City detective who worked with Dantzler during the Victor Sammael case, answered on the second ring.

"Detective Bobby Brennan. How can I help you?"

"Well, for starters, you can sound more civil when answering an important phone call."

"Ah, hell, Dantzler, I'm a New Yorker. An Irishman to boot. We're brash, rude, unruly and not overly friendly. Civility isn't in our DNA. You got a problem with that, call some schmuck in South Carolina or Mississippi, or one of those other genteel Southern states where folks drink iced tea, have picnics, recite Bible passages and pen sappy poems to their Southern belles. Scarlett O'Hara doesn't live in Manhattan."

"O'Hara? Think maybe she was an Irish lass?"

"Come to think of it, she might've been. She was something of a hard-headed smart aleck."

"Sounds like a woman only you could love," Dantzler said. "But she was way too beautiful for you."

Brennan laughed. "No doubt about that. So . . . how is life in the Bluegrass state? You still putting the bad guys behind bars?"

"They don't stand a chance."

"You always were a cocky bastard. That's what I admire about you the most."

"Being admired by a prince like you is my life's goal."

"Yeah, right. Okay, enough bullshit. If you're calling, you need something. What can I do for you?"

"Do you know Andy Waltz?"

"The *New York Times'* Andy Waltz?"

"Yeah."

"Sure I know Andy," Brennan said. "Known him for years. He's a good guy. Why are you asking about him?"

"I need to contact him."

"What business could you possibly have with Andy Waltz?"

"It's a long story. Can you get me his number?"

"Hell, I have it right here." Brennan was silent for several seconds, and then said, "Office or cell?"

"Cell."

Brennan rattled off the number. "You get that?"

"Got it. And listen, Bobby. I really appreciate you helping me out with this."

"No problem, my friend. All I ask in return is that someday in the future you tell me why you need to speak with Andy Waltz. That's a mystery I can't even begin to figure out."

"It involves a mystery I shouldn't even begin looking into."

"Well, if that's the case, watch your ass. Those usually turn out to be the dangerous kind."

After hanging up with Brennan, Dantzler dialed Andy Waltz's cell number. The call went straight to voice mail.

"This message is for Andy Waltz. Andy, I'm a homicide detective in Lexington, Kentucky. I need to get in touch with Cain, and I was told you might be able to help me. If you would, please call me at this number as soon as you can. Or have Cain call me. Call day or night. This is an urgent matter. Thanks."

As Dantzler closed his cell phone, it dawned on him that he had not given his name to Waltz. He thought about making a second call, but decided not to. Waltz had his phone number. That was enough. Either he would return the call or he wouldn't. Dantzler could only hope that he would.

*****

"You're here later than usual," Captain Richard Bird said, opening the door to Dantzler's office. "Anything going on I need to know about?"

Dantzler shook his head. "Just catching up on some paperwork that could sue me for neglect."

"Speaking of paperwork, I got your request for some time off." Bird took a seat across from Dantzler's desk. "Almost had a coronary when I read it. I can't remember the last time you actually put in for a vacation."

"I'm not sure I've ever taken a real vacation."

"Where are you planning on going?"

"Not sure yet."

"You didn't request a specific number of days," Bird noted. "Any idea how long you'll be gone?"

"Put me down for two weeks. But I could be gone longer than that."

"What's going on here, Jack? What are you not telling me?"

"Nothing's going on. I need some time away from the job, that's all. My batteries are running low. They need to be recharged."

"I don't believe you for one minute, but God knows you've got enough time built up to take off six months if you wanted to. When are you planning on leaving?"

"Couple of days."

"Make sure everything is squared away with the other detectives before you leave."

"Will do, Boss."

"Don't be a smart ass." Bird stood. "And try to have some fun while you're away. That's what vacations are for."

CHAPTER THREE

For the next two days Dantzler cleaned up loose ends at work while waiting for Waltz to return his call. He also researched Waltz via the Internet. What he learned was intriguing. Waltz was the son of a wealthy New York senator and his socialite wife. After graduating from Columbia University, he joined the Army, where he remained for eight years, eventually rising to the rank of captain. He worked in Military Intelligence, and was rumored to have been involved with the CIA. Upon leaving the military, he went to work for the *New York Times* as an investigative reporter. In a thirty-year career that was nothing short of dazzling, Waltz captured virtually every journalism award possible, including the Pulitzer Prize on two occasions.

As Dantzler dug into Waltz's background, what grabbed his attention was the time Waltz spent in Vietnam. From 1969 until late 1972. A time frame that included the year Johnny Dantzler was in Vietnam. The year he died.

Or was murdered.

Could it be Kaleb Daniels was telling the truth? That everything Dantzler knew about his father was a lie? That his mother's death was linked to his father's death? That *both* parents were murdered?

Questions followed by more questions.

Dammit, Houdini, pick up the phone and make the call.

*****

At six-thirty, after taking care of another handful of long-neglected tasks, Dantzler left the office and went in search of something to eat. Steak was his first and only choice, so he went to the Chop House. New York strip, baked potato, salad and a Diet Pepsi . . . his standard fare at any steakhouse. He had often been accused of being a boring eater, but he preferred to stick with what he knew and enjoyed. An expensive restaurant was not the place to be adventurous. No sense risking hard-earned money on something that could turn out to be a disaster.

It was almost nine when he pulled his Outback into the garage. He went into the kitchen, fixed a drink, walked out onto the deck and stared at the lake for almost two minutes. Flicking on the light, he was surprised to find he was not alone. A man was sitting in a chair, looking calm and relaxed enough to convince Dantzler that he wasn't a thief or murderer. His demeanor was that of a family member or close friend with easy and complete access to the house. But he wasn't a family member or a friend. He was a total stranger, yet Dantzler knew who his intruder was.

The man was ruggedly handsome, lean, muscular, about six-three, the same height as Dantzler. His brown hair was long, his eyes a cold bluish-gray. He wore faded Levis, a black T-shirt, brown sport coat and sneakers. Looked like a writer or a college professor. But it wasn't the man's attire or his calm demeanor that grabbed and held Dantzler's attention. It was his hands. Big, powerful hands. Lethal hands.

"I assume you are at least vaguely familiar with the legal definition of breaking and entering," Dantzler said.

"Yeah, I've heard it mentioned a few times," the man said. "Never paid much attention to it, if you want to know the truth."

"A man can be arrested for B and E. Do serious prison time."

"Not this man."

"Why? Are you exempt from the rules?"

"Depends on the rules."

"That's a rather arrogant attitude."

The man remained silent.

"Are you Cain?" Dantzler asked.

"Mickey Collins."

"I don't need a literature teacher. I need Cain."

"People don't always get what they want. Sometimes they have to take what they can get."

"Are you Cain?"

"Who do you think I am?"

"I'll stick with Cain."

"How did you find out about Cain?"

"I'd prefer not to reveal my source."

"Your source? You a cop or a newspaper reporter?"

"A cop who prefers to protect the identity of his source."

"If I were so inclined, I could make you reveal it."

Dantzler's right hand eased down and touched his Glock.

"I would advise against making that move," the man warned. "You'll be dead before you unsnap the holster."

"You're that good?"

"I'm that good."

"I take it that was Cain speaking."

Cain smiled. "What do you want, Detective?"

"Your help in digging up the truth."

"There is no shortage of truth buried out there. Which truth are you looking to uncover?"

"My father's death in nineteen-seventy, and my mother's death eight years later."

"Are their deaths connected?"

"I have reason to believe they are."

"Where did your father die?"

"Vietnam or Laos—I'm not certain. His name was Johnny Dantzler. Captain Dantzler. Did you know him?"

"No."

"Did you know a Staff Sergeant Dantzler?"

"I knew no one named Dantzler."

"What about General Lucas White? Did you know him?"

"He was my commanding officer for almost seven years," Cain said. "Why do you ask about Lucas?"

"It's a name I came across in my mother's murder book. What about David Langley? Know him?"

"No."

Dantzler was silent for several seconds, and then said, "How did you find me?"

"Wasn't hard."

"When I left a message with Houdini, I failed to give him my name. So . . . how did you find me?"

"Two plus two equals four, Detective."

"What the hell does that mean?"

"It means Houdini gave me your phone number. The rest was easy." Cain waited several beats, and then said, "Tell me about your mother? Where did she die?"

"Here, in Lexington."

"What were the circumstances?"

"She was murdered. Strangled and left in a Dumpster behind a school."

"On the surface it would seem highly unlikely that a death in Vietnam or Laos, and a murder in Kentucky eight years later would be connected."

"Not many answers are found on the surface."

"Sometimes answers aren't found anywhere," Cain said. "Some truths are best left buried."

"Did you kill her?"

"No."

"Would you submit to a polygraph?"

"No."

"Why not?"

"Because I don't have time to waste on silly nonsense."

"There is nothing about my mother's murder that I consider silly nonsense."

"I'm sure that's true. And I meant no disrespect. But questioning me about it would be a waste of time. I'm not your man."

"Did Seneca kill her?"

Cain grinned. "You're a well-spring of information, aren't you, Detective? I'm impressed."

"I have no interest in impressing you. I only want answers."

"The answer is, no, Seneca didn't kill her."

"How can you be so sure?"

"You said she was strangled. Was she also raped?"

"No."

"Seneca would have killed her with a knife. But not before he sexually assaulted her and tortured her."

"Where can I find Seneca?"

"You can't."

"Why not?"

"Seneca has departed this earthly realm."

"You know that for a fact?"

Cain held up both hands. "Seneca is *dead*. Take my word on it."

The message to Dantzler was clear: Cain killed Seneca.

"Will you help me?" Dantzler asked.

"Help you with what, exactly?"

"Finding out who killed my mother."

"You're a detective. You don't need my help."

"Your world is not my world, and I can't navigate in your world without you. I would be a lost pilgrim in need of a Virgil to guide me."

"Well said, Detective." Cain stood and walked to the door. "Probably not many cops reference Dante when asking for help. I like that."

"So . . ." Dantzler said. "What's your answer?"

"I'll think about it."

Dantzler took a step forward. "Think all you want, but I'm going to do this . . . with or without you."

"Then you'll be a dead pilgrim."

*****

Cain's cell phone rang seconds after he drove away from Dantzler's house. The call was from Houdini.

"Did you meet with the detective?" Houdini asked.

"I did."

"And?"

"He wants me to help him uncover the truth about the death of his parents, which in this case would mean looking into some dark corners."

"What's your take on this guy?"

"He's sharp, like his old man."

"Who is his old man?" Houdini said.

"Dantzler."

"Oh, shit."

"Yep, Johnny's kid."

CHAPTER FOUR

Sonia Ivanovna loathed Las Vegas. It was her least favorite city in the world, a garish, gaudy Mecca for foolish idiots willing to cast their fate on the next roll of the dice, turn of the card, or spin of the wheel, all while keeping fingers crossed that their lives will be changed forever. Only in this country, Sonia thought, where so many with so much greedily grab for that much more. Instant wealth—The Great American Dream. How pathetic. Someone needs to remind these spoiled Americans that their sacred Declaration of Independence guarantees only the pursuit of happiness, not that their much-dreamt-of happiness will ever become a reality. And even if by some stroke of magic happiness does come their way, it certainly won't be found in Las Vegas.

Sonia was sitting in a small restaurant one block off the main strip. She had been in this Sodom in the desert for almost a week, and now that her latest job was finished she couldn't wait to leave. And she would. First plane out, tomorrow morning. Las Vegas to New York, then to Paris, and on to Nice, where she owned a luxury apartment. Good-bye to the stifling heat, the phony glitz and glitter, and the endless parade of fools who substitute luck for hard work and honest endeavor. The sooner she was out of here, the better.

Pushing away a cold cup of coffee, she picked up the letter and read it for the third time. Then she placed it back on the table and shook her head for the third time. She simply could not believe Dimitrios Sotirios, a man she respected, could have made such an outrageous claim. How could he? After all she had done for him, and for others, for more than two decades, how could he possibly make such a ludicrous assertion?

Sonia's blood raged through her arteries and veins like a fiery river. She couldn't remember the last time she had been this angry. This upset. This disappointed. Yes, she was Russian, and Russians tend to see darkness where others see light. It was in the Russian soul to expect the worse, to find the negative, to see disaster lurking around the next corner. Russians tend not to be happy people. Sonia understood this better than most.

But . . . this. This was genuine cause for anger.

Perhaps, she thought, I am overreacting. Making too much of it. Yes, this must be the reason for such sudden outrage. She picked up the letter and read it a fourth time. Put it down and shook her head a fourth time. No, she whispered to herself, I have every right to be angry. What Dimitrios has written is such bullshit.

In fairness to him, some of what he said was okay. Sonia judged the first three paragraphs to be acceptable, accurate and on point. In them, the Greek had said all the right things, pointed out all the positives, offered the proper amount of praise. He thanked her for the work she had done for him in the past, and told her he would not hesitate to utilize her great talents in the future. So far, so good.

It was in the fourth paragraph that Dimitrios's words turned to crap. That his credibility went down the toilet. Here, he had written the words that caused her blood to boil. In this brief paragraph, consisting of a single sentence, he rated her as the third best assassin in the world. *Third*? She simply could not believe what she was reading. How could he possibly be so misguided? So ignorant? He *had* to know better than this. There was no way Dimitrios Sotirios truly believed what he was saying. This had to be a big mistake. Maybe a misprint. An oversight. And yet, there it was in black and white.

Okay, Sonia thought, what's his reasoning? Why did he rate me third, when, in truth, I should have been second? Why would he make such a claim? Dimitrios is not ignorant. He's been in this business for decades, had dealings with virtually every top assassin in the world at one time or another. He knows talent when he sees it.

Why, then, did he rank me third? There can only be a single answer, Sonia concluded. Because, like most men worldwide, at the core of his being he's a sexist pig. This is the only explanation that makes any sense. The way he sees it, a man's size and strength advantage automatically makes him a better assassin than a woman. Naturally, he would think such thoughts. He is a man, after all. Of course, Sonia would quickly point out, his assessment is simply not true. Certainly not in her case. In fact, she had always felt that being a woman gave her a distinct advantage over most of her male rivals. Her beauty, her sex appeal, her willingness to flirt or act coy when necessary—those were tools that could be more deadly than a gun or a knife. Why? Because most male targets tend to let down their guard, to not regard her as potential danger. They see a beautiful woman, not a serious threat. In which case, they became easy prey. When a man thinks with his dick, he's never much of a challenge.

Sonia stared at the name of the man ranked number two on Dimitrios's list—Ramon Garcia. This was especially galling to her. To be ranked behind Ramon in anything except grossness was nothing less than a slap in the face. Dimitrios must have been hitting the Ouzo harder than usual when he made this assessment.

She met Ramon once, five years ago, when their paths crossed in the Mexico City airport. She was heading home from a vacation in Costa Rica, he was en route to Bogota to eliminate a top drug thug. On a rainy afternoon, she spent two of the most miserable hours of her life sitting at a table in the bar, listening to Ramon talk endlessly about his favorite subject—himself.

Rarely stopping to breathe, he extolled the virtues of his own greatness, celebrating himself with every word, every sentence. An incessant braggart, he was quick to mention the names of those he had killed, as though that somehow increased his greatness. He told her how one of his favorite jobs had gone down easy, while another had been slightly more difficult. He bragged about the hundreds of women he had made love to over the years, all of whom left the encounter longing for more. And, naturally, he spoke about money, telling her he was now commanding—and getting—half-a-million per hit, a figure she knew to be greatly inflated.

Ramon Garcia was in every way a repulsive man. No taller than five-five, weighing in excess of two-hundred pounds, he resembled a bowling ball supported by two sawed-off tree stumps. He was almost completely bald, which he tried to hide with that hideous comb-over, had a thick mustache, perspired profusely, and had such bad breath that Sonia spent the entire two hours facing away from him with her hand over her mouth and nose. He was a buffoon, one of the least-impressive humans she had ever encountered.

Sonia picked up the letter, stared at it for several seconds, then shook her head once again. Ramon Garcia? In what universe could he possibly be a better assassin than me? she asked herself. A better *anything* than me? None, was her silent answer.

What could Dimitrios have been thinking?

The same could not be said of the man rated at the very top of the list. With this assessment she had no issues. No problems. There would be no argument from her. And, she suspected, not from anyone else in the assassination business. Dimitrios got this one right.

Cain. The American ghost. The lone wolf. The most shadowy of all assassins. And, without question, the most legendary. No, Sonia had no problem being ranked behind him. He stood alone at the top, unrivaled by even the most serious challenger. He was the one they most aspired to emulate. And for good reason—the sheer number of his victims. If only a third of his exploits were accurate, it would still be more than enough to rate him number one.

Cain.

Sonia was still in her teens when she first heard his name mentioned by her KGB instructors. Even now, all these years later, she recalled how they seemed to whisper his name rather than speak it out loud. They said it with reverence, awe. And, she felt, a hint of fear. This she found surprising. After all, these men, her teachers, were not easily scared. They were hard, cold, brutal and ruthless. They could kill without blinking an eye, and they had done so on many occasions. And yet . . . this lone individual, the American known as Cain, caused them such obvious unease.

The more she learned about Cain the more intrigued she became. She discovered that his legend was born in the jungles of Vietnam, where the numbers he was reputed to have killed were staggering. It was said he rarely killed with any weapon other than his hands, and that what became known as a "Cain kill" was so swift, so precise, it was almost humane. After the war he became a college professor and taught literature. On the surface, it would seem the greatest assassin of them all had simply walked away from the business. That would, of course, be a false assumption, which was exactly what he and his handlers wanted the world to believe. No one knew for sure how many more kills could be attributed to him over the past three decades. But this much was known for certain: A handful of high-level targets around the globe were quietly and efficiently eliminated, and that, in all likelihood, he was the only assassin capable of successfully carrying out those jobs.

Sonia also knew for a fact that at least four countries, including her own, had openly placed a bounty on Cain. Five million dead, ten million alive. There had not been a single taker.

That was respect.

There was something else about Cain that Sonia found to be both intriguing and puzzling—he never took money for a kill. Unlike her and her colleagues, Cain was not a paid assassin. At least, not in the same way they were. He killed only in the line of duty, mostly taking jobs assigned by the U.S. military, the CIA, British MI6 or Mossad. He was not a rogue killer who worked on a contract basis.

Okay, Sonia thought, so he kills for principle, not monetary gain. Noble, maybe, but not the way she wanted to do business. Nobility was overrated, she had long ago concluded. Besides, principle couldn't begin to pay for the lifestyle she enjoyed. It takes hard, cold cash to afford a penthouse apartment in Nice. Therefore, she accepted the paychecks with no qualms whatsoever. If Cain wanted no money for his labor, then he should've been a communist.

Sonia was aware that until very recently there had been a second American on the list of top assassins—Seneca. The Native American Cherokee Indian with the dark, brooding good looks and a reputation for extreme savagery. Sonia knew Seneca well, having worked with him in Afghanistan and Chechnya. She judged him to be highly competent, but not nearly as talented or skilled as he liked to believe. According to the international grapevine, Seneca went after Cain in New York's Central Park. With a knife, no less. Why he elected to make such an insane move against a killer like Cain was a question no one could answer. But he did. And the outcome of that tussle was never in question. The Indian was good, but he was no match for Cain. Seneca's death was as inevitable as the sun rising in the east tomorrow morning.

Sonia remembered seeing several photos of Cain in his KGB file. One, in particular, stayed with her. It was in color, a close-up of Cain's face. On several occasions she had stared long and hard at the photo, trying to determine if his eyes were blue or gray. She never could decide.

She had heard that Cain once famously told a colleague that at the moment of the kill, which he called blood time, every assassin's eyes are gray. Sonia wondered if this were true in her own case.

Sonia looked out the window and watched the steady stream of dreamers pass by like drugged sheep heading to slaughter. Night was closing in, although you'd be hard pressed to know it in Las Vegas. With so many bright lights, darkness never really made an appearance in this desert Sodom. Here, it was noon twenty-four hours a day.

She laid twenty dollars on the table, folded Dimitrios's letter, put it in her coat pocket and stood. The anger she felt earlier was gone now, replaced by self-confidence and a feeling of inner peace. She knew how good she was, regardless of what Dimitrios or anyone else said. She didn't need the opinion of others to validate her own self-esteem. Her record was beyond petty criticism. If Dimitrios wanted to rate her behind Ramon Garcia, that was fine with her. In the end it meant nothing.

As she stepped out of the restaurant and joined the crowd of dreamers heading toward the big casinos, Sonia made a promise to seek out the great Cain. She wanted to meet him, to shake his hand, to tell him how much she admired and respected him. She wanted to see for herself if his eyes were blue or gray.

She wanted to pay homage to the greatest assassin of them all.

And then she would kill him.

CHAPTER FIVE

Every legend has its own story, its own genesis. Whether the tale is fact or fiction hardly matters. To the person hearing the story, interest rather than veracity is all important. Disbelief is acceptable, boredom is not. But the normal guidelines don't apply when hearing Cain's story. Also, there should be no doubt or skepticism. No disbelief. Every word is true.

In the beginning . . .

Like a snake shedding its skin, Michael James Collins shed his persona in the jungles of Vietnam and became Cain. It was in the steaming heat in that faraway land that his legend was born. He went there as an inexperienced eighteen-year-old, and emerged nearly five years later as a skilled and accomplished assassin.

And no one, not his family or his few close friends, could have predicted that his life would follow this particular path.

Five generations of Collins men had been career soldiers, and Mickey was expected to follow in their footsteps. A rebellious kid with anti-establishment leanings and a near-genius IQ, Mickey had no desire to toe the family line. He much preferred to engage in intellectual warfare against the likes of Socrates and Kierkegaard than to put on a uniform and carry a rifle and bayonet. Enlisting in the military, with its strict discipline and rigid rules, was simply out of the question.

Military brats traditionally end up in one of two camps. Either they follow in their father's footsteps, or they rebel completely and go in a totally different direction. Also, they tend to be loners. To a child who might have to move at a moment's notice, friendships were heartbreaks waiting to happen. After enough sudden good-byes, a child learned to isolate himself, to back away from making friends. To avoid disappointment, they built walls for protection.

For Mickey Collins the isolation was total. Condemned to the life of a nomad by his father's frequent transfers, he found friends not in the various military outposts, but in the books he read. He didn't need or want contact with other human beings, so he used his books and music to lock them out of his world. Indeed, such behavior was a common defense mechanism for military brats. But few took isolation to such an extreme level.

Then one day after his eighteenth birthday he enlisted in the Army. In the infantry, the most dangerous choice he could have made. General Richard Collins's pride in his son's decision was surpassed by his shock and disbelief. The son who detested all things military was now in the military.

One week after being commissioned a second lieutenant, Mickey Collins was in Vietnam. In less than three months, thanks to his leadership skills and the death of several fellow officers, he was promoted to the rank of captain. He was then, and remains so today, the youngest captain in Army history.

His first confirmed kill came on a scalding afternoon in a small village near Pleiku. The village, inhabited by fewer than two-hundred people, was a suspected Viet Cong stronghold. Collins had been ordered to infiltrate, look for signs of Viet Cong activity or sympathizers, kill the sympathizers and torch the village if positive evidence was found.

When they entered the village an emaciated old man came out of his hut, approached rapidly on spindly legs, and in broken English told Collins that no Viet Cong sympathizers lived here. He cursed Ho Chi Minh, praised the United States, railed against the war, saying in a voice choked with emotion that the fighting had cost him two sons, a daughter and a grandson.

Collins suspected the old man was lying, and his suspicions were confirmed when one of his men emerged from a small building, holding a large burlap sack in each hand. Inside the sacks, Collins found weapons, Army rations, clothes and more than three grand in cash.

As Collins aimed his M16 at the old man's head, several shots rang out from his left. Within seconds, two of his men were down, one seriously wounded, the other already dead. Kneeling and looking to his left, Collins saw the shooter darting between huts, running low, rifle in hand.

The next few seconds seemed to happen in slow motion. Images moved in a halting, almost poetic way, voices and noises sounded as though they might be coming from a phonograph record played at the wrong speed. His own movements, slow and precise, were more dream-like than real.

Scrambling to his feet, Collins raced to his right, intent on intercepting the sniper before he could disappear into the jungle or the network of tunnels that ran underground. If that happened, the shooter would be lost, and with it any chance of killing him.

When Collins came around the last hut, he saw the man running toward him, not more than thirty feet away, struggling to insert a banana-shaped clip into his AK47.

The sniper stopped dead in his tracks. Collins raised his M16, sighted and squeezed off a single round. The sniper's head exploded, coming apart faster than a water balloon dropped from a tall building. The bullet entered just below the man's nose, blowing out the back of his head, opening a gaping hole the size of a grapefruit. Most of his teeth were splintered by the bullet's impact, and his left eye, blown free from its socket, dangled on his cheek. Although he died instantly, his right leg continued to twitch for several seconds after he hit the ground.

Looking down at the man's body, Collins felt a strange calm inside—a sense of detachment, like he was standing outside the scene looking in. There was no voice inside his head pleading for compassion, for empathy. Those were signs of weakness, and in this moment, in the searing heat and dust of some shitty gook village, he understood with clear certainty that weakness did not reside within him.

He understood something else as well—he possessed the stone cold heart of a killer.

Cain had been born at that moment, although it didn't become apparent until many months later. That first tour of duty in Nam only fertilized the egg; birth wouldn't occur until well into his second tour. It was then that his ability to kill manifested itself in ways no one could have anticipated.

Cain quickly became a legend, a myth, more feared than any predator in those jungles. Stories of his kills wove their way from the DMZ to the Delta. Much of his legend was fueled by the "midnight missions," those solitary excursions into the jungle darkness, where, using only his bare hands, he sometimes killed a dozen or more of the enemy before returning to base camp at sunrise.

The first of those midnight mission occurred on a blistering August evening. On this night the ultimate assassin made his debut. The night predator was unleashed. In the deep jungle darkness, the genesis of Cain's legend was born.

He knew, even at this moment, that he was entering into a different realm. That from this night onward his life would be changed forever. That once he began the killing there was no turning back.

Cain would be more assassin than soldier. A ghost. A shadow among shadows.

General Lucas White approached him with the idea, arguing that certain types of "nocturnal killings" were more valuable and would carry more weight. They would, he contended, make a "more emphatic" statement to the enemy, play on the "enemy's psyche" like a nightmare come true.

"I will find you targets," Lucas said. "Get you locations. You, with those marvelous skills of yours, will do the rest."

Cain's first two targets were a North Vietnamese captain and the mayor of Da Lat, a small village west of Cam Ranh Bay. The mayor, a distant cousin of Vietnam's flamboyant vice president Nguyen Cao Key, was a CIA asset who had been supplying the North with valuable U.S. military intelligence for almost a year. The two men had a three a.m. meeting scheduled in the back room of a small bar just off the main street.

After darkening his face and hands with black shoe polish, Cain left Cam

Ranh Bay by chopper, and was dropped off in a clearing three kilometers from Da Lat. He worked his way through the jungle, eventually reaching the edge of the village an hour before sunset. There, leaning against a big tree, he waited until darkness fell. Until he was just one more shadow in the night.

His two targets weren't alone—a third man, armed with a machine gun, stood watch outside the back entrance. Cain was not surprised at seeing an extra body at the site; his faith in the accuracy of Army Intel had long ago given way to doubt and skepticism. This led to one of his key rules for surviving: Never put your fate in the hands of others.

The sentry leaned his weapon against the building, took out a pack of cigarettes, extracted one and held it up to his lips. As he reached into his shirt pocket to take out a box of matches, Cain closed in quickly from behind. He delivered a sharp blow to the man's throat, then a second blow to the neck. The man grunted, stumbled, and dropped to one knee. He was dead by the time his second knee touched the ground, his neck broken by a savage snap of the head.

Cain rolled the man's body behind a large barrel, laid the machine gun in a flower bed, and then slowly opened a screen door. As he moved down the narrow hallway, he could hear the sound of laughter coming from a small room to his left. He eased forward until he could see the two men. They were sitting at a table, each with a large paper cup in hand. An almost-empty bottle of whiskey rested on the table between them.

Perhaps it was the shock of seeing a black-face intruder coming at them like a crazed panther, or maybe it was the alcohol fog that denied movement, but neither man rose from his chair when Cain entered the room. The man dressed in military clothing fumbled his cup while reaching for his pistol. Cain went for him first, hitting him across the bridge of his nose with a judo chop. Blood spurted from the damaged nose, spraying the table and the whiskey bottle. Cain moved behind the captain and snapped his head violently to the right, instantly ending his life.

The mayor sat frozen, immobilized by fear, eyes wide. He seemed incapable of moving, even as Cain reached out and grabbed him by the throat. The mayor's mouth moved but no sounds came out.

Cain's large right hand increased the pressure on the mayor's throat, cutting off his air passage. Next, Cain pinched the mayor's nostrils, eliminated the breathing process entirely. The panicked mayor began to violently thrash his lower body, kicking the table and knocking over the bottle of whiskey.

Cain asked the mayor a single question.

Ten seconds later, Cain had the information he sought, and the mayor lay dead on the floor.

*****

Among the Viet Cong, Cain's legend took on a powerful, even sinister force. They saw him as a demon spirit, indestructible, immune to death. He was the shadow that awaited them in the night. He was their nightmare come to life.

General Lucas White was the first to recognize the change from ordinary soldier to walking nightmare, later noting that he saw it more in Cain's eyes rather than in his actions. At certain moments, Lucas said, those blue eyes turned gray, revealing something dark, hidden, empty. They were, Lucas sensed, the eyes of a jungle predator—cold and keen, brutal, cunning, savage.

In early 1968, Lucas needed those predator eyes, those killing skills. He had been ordered back to Washington, where he was to put into place and oversee a new operation, one that would eventually replace the infamous Phoenix Project. It would be highly covert, and even more secretive than its predecessor.

The Phoenix Project, also known as Operation Phoenix, was born deep within the belly of the CIA in the mid-1960s. From its inception Operation Phoenix was nothing less than an assassination program. Its mission was to cripple the Viet Cong by killing influential local village and hamlet leaders like mayors, teachers and doctors. Guerrillas from the North, or any leader suspected of aiding the South's parallel government, were also deemed legitimate targets for assassination.

Heading up the program were legendary spymaster Ted Shackley, the CIA Saigon station chief, and Shackley's long-time friend, General Lucas White.

Operation Phoenix was a natural successor to an earlier CIA black op—Project Pale Horse. Named for a passage from the Book of Revelation, Project Pale Horse ran for six years, operating primarily in the northeastern provinces of Laos.

Pale Horse eventually ran its course, giving way to Operation Phoenix, which proved to be both efficient and highly controversial. Before Operation Phoenix was turned over to the South Vietnamese and spiraled out of control, it was estimated that the death toll exceeded forty thousand.

With Phoenix flaming out, the need for a new operation became a high priority matter for the generals running the war. Thus, the plan for a new assassination operation went into effect. It was to be known as Project Armageddon. Lucas, because of his close association with both Pale Horse and Phoenix, was the natural choice to head the operation.

It was a project Lucas believed in wholeheartedly, and was only too willing to oversee. And in Cain he had the perfect instructor. Who better to teach the art of killing than a man with a doctorate in death?

Together, they opened what became known as "the Shop" at Aberdeen Proving Ground in Maryland. They spent many weeks carefully screening more than one hundred potential candidates. Of that initial group, only six survived the cut and returned to Vietnam with Cain.

For the next three years, Cain's team killed hundreds of enemy soldiers on both sides of the DMZ. No Viet Cong or ARVN soldier was safe, and they knew it. To them, Cain and his team had become monsters to be feared.

But of all their many highly praised missions, it was Operation Nightcrawlers that sealed their legend. On this mission, they traveled to a village less than an hour from Hanoi in North Vietnam, where they killed nine high-level ARVN leaders and two Russian generals who were suspected of planning another Tet-like offensive. Eleven men were eliminated in less than five minutes, and not a sound made.

It couldn't have been done more efficiently.

After the last victim was eliminated, Cain walked to the corner of the room, picked up a decapitated head, and placed it at the center of the table. He then reached in his pocket, took out a playing card, the ace of spades, and propped it up in front of the dead man's face.

Mission accomplished.

Legend confirmed.

CHAPTER SIX

Nick Marlow wasn't the cocktail party type. Never had been, never would be. It was simply not the kind of affair where he wanted to spend his time. Not one hour, one minute. Wearing a suit and tie was bad enough; having to get dressed up in a tux put him way out of his element. Out of his comfort zone. Give him combat fatigues and boots anytime rather than this damn monkey suit, with its asinine cummerbund and polished-to-a-sheen shiny black shoes.

He hated everything about a scene like this.

Yet, here he was, in a Manhattan penthouse apartment on the Upper West Side, decked out like George Clooney, mingling with phony, arrogant socialites who had exactly as much in common with him as he had with them. Which, of course, was nothing.

Well, that wasn't totally accurate. They all did have one thing in common —Lee Bartlett. He was the common denominator, the reason why they were here. They had come to co-mingle with the grand old man himself. To spend precious time in his presence. Men like Lee Bartlett never lack for company.

This was Lee place, one of maybe a half-dozen houses or apartments or estates he owned in various locations around the world, none of which was valued at less than ten-million dollars. He was one of the richest, most-powerful, most-influential men in this country, the last remaining descendant of a proud New England family that could be traced back to Josiah Bartlett, one of the signers of the Declaration of Independence. As a consequence, all he had to do was snap his fingers and people came running. Senators, congressmen, Supreme Court justices, military powerhouses, Hollywood heavyweights, media moguls, business tycoons—they all sought out and courted Lee Bartlett for his patronage, support and, most of all, his money. They wanted—*needed*—him in their corner. Conversely, what they dreaded most—and hoped to avoid at all cost—was landing on Lee's enemies' list. That would have been disastrous. Every individual in this room, regardless of status or financial wherewithal, was fully cognizant of the reality that the snap of the finger that helped take them to the top could just as easily send them crashing to the bottom.

Or worse.

Get them killed.

Now, killing was something Nick Marlow understood. *That* was his world. *That* was where he was most comfortable. Not here, not with these people. He much preferred standing shoulder to shoulder with men of great courage, those brave warriors like himself who were unafraid to stare death in the eyes and say, "screw you, pal, you ain't gettin' me today" even as bullets and mortar shells rained down on them like vengeance from heaven.

Nick looked around the room, carefully taking it all in. With the trained eye of a soldier on guard he surveyed these weak people, this posse of self-professed elites, all of whom were absolutely convinced the world would stop spinning if they ceased to exist. Old men bent and stooped like withered fence posts, victims of the march of time and the cruel ravages of gravity. Blue-haired women draped with expensive jewelry, their faces pumped full of Botox and collagen. If he had the money these old birds spent on plastic surgery he'd be a millionaire three times over. Watching these posers made him choke with hate and disgust. How many of them had ever been tested? Put their life on the line? Faced real danger? Was there a single man in this room who would run straight into enemy fire to save a wounded comrade? Did any of them know the true meaning of courage? He seriously doubted it.

They were sycophants. Accolytes. All willing to serve the master—Lee Bartlett. Well, Nick thought, at least they're not stupid. He had to give them credit for that. They recognized real power when they saw it, and power, even more than money, draws people like bees to honey. And God knows Lee Bartlett had power.

But money and power meant nothing to Nick, even though he had considerably more of both than the people in this room would have suspected. No, he wasn't here because of Lee's money or power. He was here because he loved the old man with his heart and soul. More than loved him, really. He revered Lee, and had since he was barely a teen-ager, when Lee took him under his wing. From the beginning, Lee had been Nick's friend, mentor, benefactor. He had been the closest thing to a real father Nick had ever known. Everything Nick had, he owed to Lee Bartlett. Which is why he would do anything for Lee.

And there was little he hadn't done.

Nick smiled as he watched Lee work the room. Eighty-two, yet he still had a spring in his step and a twinkle in his eyes. Smiling, shaking hands with the men, hugging the ladies. Making each one feel special, as though he or she was the only person in the room. The only person in the world. Coming across as everyone's lovable grandfather, or favorite uncle. Kind, witty Prince Charming. Oh, if these bozos only knew. If they had even the slightest inkling of what Lee was capable of doing. What he *had* done. If they did know, Nick wondered, would they still worship at his altar with such enthusiasm? Probably so. The weak always bow to the strong.

Nick needed fresh air so he headed toward the balcony overlooking

Central Park. He kept his head down, hoping to avoid conversation with one of these ancient clowns. Not that that was likely to happen. None of these folks had any interest in speaking with a commoner like him. That would have been beneath them. People of a certain class instinctively recognize those of a lesser status. Those, like Nick, who lack proper breeding. He was an alien, a misfit, in this crowd. And he wouldn't have wanted it any other way.

Outside, alone on the balcony, he stretched and breathed in the cool, fresh night air. Rain had been in the forecast but as of now it had not materialized. Above him, stars dotted the dark sky like diamonds on black velvet. Damn near a perfect night, he thought.

His cell phone chirped. He snapped it open, put it to his ear and listened. Female voice, sexy, familiar.

"Is Alexander Pushkin available?" she asked.

"I'm sorry. You have the wrong number," Nick replied, closing his phone and dropping it into his shirt pocket.

Nick went back into the apartment, carefully weaving his way through the crowd, this time keeping his head up. He was looking for Lee, who was standing near the bar, speaking with one of the Supreme Court justices and his wife. Nick moved behind the old man, leaned down and whispered in his ear.

"The dice came up seven," he said.

Lee smiled and nodded, never interrupting his chat with his two guests. Message delivered, Nick eased out from behind the old man, put his head down and worked his way toward the balcony. He had to get away from these leeches, these phonies, these pretenders.

Standing on the balcony, he turned and studied the crowd. He watched them come and go, talking, chuckling, glad-handing. They were smug, confident, fully aware of their own superiority. Feeling superior was as vital to these people as their heartbeat. Oh, well, he thought, if that's what it takes for them to get through the day, so be it.

After awhile, his gaze settled on Lee. Standing in the middle of the room, Lee was now surrounded by more than a dozen people, each one hanging on his every word as if he were Jesus Christ delivering the Sermon on the Mount. Or Richard Burton reciting one of Hamlet's soliloquies.

A spellbound audience dazzled by the master.

Nick smiled.

Oh, if they only knew.

CHAPTER SEVEN

Over the years, Dantzler had studied the murder book for the Sarah Elizabeth Dantzler case at least fifty times. With each reading he had dug into the details, taken them apart piece by piece, looked at them from every conceivable angle, yet he had not found a single clue that would help solve the case. Although he was positive a fifty-first reading wouldn't offer anything new, he spent nearly two hours studying the work put together by the original detectives—Lee Hutchinson and Sam Harper. Again, he found nothing new or enlightening. Despite their best efforts, the two men, both superb detectives, were never able to zero in on a single legitimate suspect, much less bring the killer to justice.

Sarah Dantzler's murderer had evaded capture.

What Dantzler concentrated on with this reading was finding out where or how Hutchinson and Harper came up with the two names scribbled at the top of the very last page—David Langley and Lucas White. Where had those names come from, and why? What, if any, role did they play in the investigation? Who, exactly, were they? By what path had those two names found their way into the murder book? Neither man was contacted or interviewed. No address or phone number was listed. None of those who were interviewed mentioned them. There was simply nothing about either man anywhere in the murder book. They were a mystery within a mystery.

Closing the murder book, Dantzler reached into the cardboard box on the floor and brought out a handful of old photos his father sent from Vietnam. Most were of Johnny Dantzler alone, while a few others showed him with some of his fellow soldiers. The men all looked young and thin and tired. There were no names on any of the photos, so Dantzler had no clue who his father's buddies were. Maybe one of them was David Langley or Lucas White. Dantzler wondered if he would ever know.

Putting the photos aside, he went back into the box and scooped up three stacks of letters his father sent to his mother. Each stack, which consisted of approximately twenty-five letters, was bound by a blue ribbon. Dantzler carefully read each letter, and felt very uncomfortable doing so. These letters were deeply personal and meant for one set of eyes only—Sarah Dantzler's. Reading them made Dantzler feel cheap, dirty, like he was invading the privacy of others. Of course, that's precisely what he was doing. But he had no choice.

He had to read them. Study them. He could only hope that maybe his father had mentioned the names of David Langley or Lucas White in one of the letters. This was, he felt, the only way he was going to uncover who these men were. If he could do that, then maybe he could take it one step further and tie them into the case.

But Dantzler's father never mentioned either man.

Dantzler stood and stretched, then went to the fridge, pulled out a package of turkey, some mustard and a Diet Pepsi. After slapping together a sandwich, he opened a bag of chips, sat and ate. And let his mind wander. What *did* he know? Well, he knew Lucas White was dead. Cain had told him that. But what about David Langley? Was he alive or dead? Dantzler suddenly realized that for whatever reason he had assumed Langley was also dead. What if he wasn't? After all, there was a fifty-fifty chance he was still alive. If he was, then maybe he could be tracked down.

Time to let Google do some work.

Dantzler thought about typing in Lucas White's name but decided it would be a waste of time. The man was dead; he had no tale to tell. And, Dantzler knew, if he needed information about Lucas White, he could get it from Cain or Houdini.

Instead, Dantzler typed in **David Langley** and came up with several pages of hits. It didn't take him long to find the David Langley he was looking for. Halfway down the first page was **David Langley - Military Analyst.** Dantzler instinctively knew he had found his man.

David Allen Langley was born in Boston in 1944. He earned undergraduate degrees from Boston University before obtaining his doctorate in military affairs from the Army War College. He was a military analyst from 1970 to 1975. In 1976, he became Director of Apollo Enterprises, Inc., which was, according to the article, the first private security firm in the United States.

Next, Dantzler typed in **Apollo Enterprises, Inc.** Again, there were plenty of hits, including one with the official website. He opened the page, scanned it briefly, and clicked on the Staff icon. David Langley's name was at the top, along with his designation as Director of Operations. There was no photo of him or any of the other staff members listed. Then Dantzler clicked on the Contact Us icon. Grabbing a pen and some paper, he wrote down the address and phone number.

His cell phone was buried beneath the letters and photos, so it took him a few seconds to locate it. Once he did, he opened it and punched in the numbers, fully expecting to hear an automated voice rattling off a series of numbers for different departments. He was wrong. A man answered on the second ring.

"Apollo Enterprise, how may I direct your call?"

"My name is Jack Dantzler, and I would like to speak with David Langley, if he's available."

"He's not available," the man said, sounding hurried. "David is currently out of town."

"Any idea when he'll be returning?"

"I'm not privy to David's itinerary. So, I have no clue when he'll be back."

"Do you have his cell phone number?"

"Yeah, but I'm not giving it to you," the man answered, now adding sarcastic and irritated to hurried.

"Mind if I leave a message with you, then?"

"Mind my asking what business you have with him?"

Dantzler started to tell the guy it was none of his business, but refrained from doing so. He didn't want to piss the guy off. At least not before he got the information he needed. "I'm a homicide detective in Lexington, Kentucky. I need to speak to him about—"

"Homicide?" the man asked, his interest now suddenly piqued. "What? David murder somebody?"

"Not that I'm aware of. I simply need to ask him about a certain matter."

"Sure, I'll let him know you called. Would you give me your name again?"

Dantzler repeated his name twice, finally having to spell out his last name after the man mangled the spelling several times. Once he was certain the guy got it right, he gave him his cell phone number, and told him to let David Langley know he could call anytime, day or night. The man promised to pass along the message, but Dantzler had his doubts about whether or not that promise would be fulfilled.

Glancing at the clock above the stove, he saw that it was a little past noon. He'd been at it since seven-thirty, so he decided it was time for a break. He opened a new can of Diet Pepsi, shuffled into the den and switched on the TV. Found CNN and upped the volume several notches. In less than twenty minutes, he learned there was unrest in Syria, four Pennsylvania high school students had been shot to death by a fellow classmate, two oil companies had recorded record profits (again) for the latest quarter, and one of Hollywood's most famous couples was splitting up.

The stories stay the same, he thought. Only the names and places seem to change.

He went back into the kitchen, sat and pondered his next move. It didn't take him long to realize the obvious. He wanted to know more about Cain. Opening the laptop, he started to type Cain. He didn't; that would have been a waste. The name Cain would elicit a million hits, the vast majority of which would relate to Adam and Eve's homicidal first-born son. What he needed was something more specific. So he typed in Cain + Vietnam. Nothing. Next, he tried Cain + Assassin and Cain + U.S. Army. Again, he came up empty.

He recalled Kaleb Daniels telling him that Cain's real name was Mickey Collins, so he tried that. Lots of hits, none relating to Cain. Finally, he tried **Michael Collins + College Professor** and found the man he was looking for. But to his great surprise and disappointment, there were only two hits, virtually identical in content, neither one longer than three paragraphs.

Michael James Collins, the son of a decorated Army general, spent eight years in the Army, served in Vietnam, and left the military with the rank of major. After leaving the Army he earned a doctorate in literature from Columbia University, and then spent fourteen years as a full professor at Duke University.

That was it. Bare bones information and nothing more. Certainly not much for a man considered to be a legend. Heavily redacted, Dantzler suspected. And for obvious reasons. The kind of deeds Cain performed weren't meant for the public's eyes. They were meant to be buried along with his many victims. Certain "activities" need not be made known to American citizens who might not appreciate or understand them. And, therefore, not condone them.

"Find anything interesting?"

Dantzler spun, his hand going to his side in search of a weapon that wasn't there.

"Easy," Cain said. "Don't want to wrench your back. It might hurt your tennis game."

"Damn, man. You keep sneaking up on me like that, I will shoot you someday."

"I'm not too worried about it."

Cain moved closer to the table. He opened the murder book and thumbed through it, eventually stopping at the page with a black and white photograph of Sarah Dantzler on it. In the photo she was lying in a Dumpster, eyes open, her nude body partially covered by a fresh blanket of snow. He studied the picture for several seconds, then closed the book.

"Sorry about your mother."

"Thanks."

"What else you been looking at?" Cain said.

Before Dantzler could answer, Cain raised his hand in a silencing gesture. Moving toward the TV, he said, "Turn that up a notch, will you?"

Dantzler picked up the remote and upped the volume. Both he and Cain inched closer to the TV. On screen, one of the CNN correspondents was reporting from outside the Bellagio Casino in Las Vegas. In the upper right corner was the picture of a man in full military dress. Three stars on his collar, a name beneath the picture: Lieutenant General Raymond C. Dunlap.

". . . was found dead in his room in the Bellagio early this morning. He was found by one of the casino's housekeeping staff. Investigators have issued no details concerning cause of death, but a CNN source tells us that General

Dunlap died from a single gunshot wound to the head. This much is known about General Dunlap. A veteran of several wars, he worked at the Pentagon, serving under the Deputy Secretary of Defense. General Dunlap is survived by his wife, two children and five grandchildren."

Cain muted the TV, took out his cell phone and punched in a number. After a single ring, Houdini answered.

"You hear the news? Yeah, this is bad shit. Sure, it's them. Has to be. It's time to scrounge again, Houdini."

"What do you need?"

"Find out who is heading the investigation. Every agency out there is going to try to get involved, but I want to know who the top dog is. Yeah, I'm going to Vegas. I'll catch the first flight out. You do your thing. Then let me know what you find out."

Cain punched off, closed his phone and went back into the kitchen. Standing by the table, he picked up the yellow legal pad. His attention immediately zeroed in on the information Dantzler had written concerning Apollo Enterprises, Inc.

"You didn't call this number, did you?" Cain asked, fingers tapping the paper.

"Yes, I did. David Langley is the Director."

"You speak with him?"

Dantzler shook his head. "He wasn't in, so I left a message for him to call me."

"Bad move, Detective."

"Why is it a bad move?"

"Look, Detective. I have no doubt that you are a superb investigator. And I don't question your resolve or your courage. If I were in your shoes I'd want answers as much as you do. And I would do just about anything to get those answers. But you can't let desire make you stupid. You have to be smart about how you find those answers you're seeking. That means thinking like a cop, not like an aggrieved son. You said you wanted my help. Well, here I am. But we do things my way, okay? Otherwise, I'm out the door."

"I made a simple phone call, that's all," Dantzler said, anger rising in his voice.

"Yeah, you did. And let me tell you something about that simple phone call."

"What?"

"It very well may get you killed."

"Why? Do you know David Langley?"

Cain was silent.

"You know what this is all about, don't you?" Dantzler said.

"What I know is this. If you want me to help you find the man who murdered your mother, then no more cowboy stunts. You do only what I tell you to do, when I tell you to do it. If you don't, you'll be the next Dantzler they bury."

"Look, Cain, I'm not much better at taking orders than you are. So I think we need to set some firm ground rules. I'll do—"

"Pack a bag, Detective," Cain interrupted. "We're going to Vegas. Bring your laptop, but don't bother packing your weapon. That will only cause more hassle at the airport than I care to deal with."

"But what if I need a weapon?"

"You already have one—me."

"I can only hope you're as good as you say you are."

"I am."

*****

After Dantzer went to his room to pack, Cain sat at the kitchen table, his thoughts on Ray Dunlap. A good guy, an exemplary soldier. A smile creased Cain's face when he recalled their first mission together. It involved a notorious Cambodian war lord who demanded that everyone call him Hank. A loathsome creature, Hank had been on the CIA's payroll for nearly a decade. What Hank didn't know was that his usefulness to the CIA and the U.S. military had run its course. Therefore, it was deemed necessary to remove him from the world stage, which is exactly what Cain and Dunlap had done. But they hadn't acted alone. For this mission they elicited the help of a couple of friends. On a scalding afternoon, Cain and Dunlap tossed Hank from a bridge into a small pond. Unfortunately for Hank, the pond was home to Samson and Hercules, two full-grown alligators. In a matter of minutes, Hank was long gone and the gators were resting on the bank, enjoying the sun.

Cain began sifting through the photos, pausing when he found one that showed Johnny Dantzler standing next to another man. They were shirtless, smiling, each man holding a can of beer. Cain flipped the picture over; no names on the back. It didn't matter. He knew their names.

Johnny Dantzler and Ray Dunlap.

He slipped the photo into his shirt pocket.

And thought about the men he was going to kill.

And the man who once saved his life.

Johnny Dantzler.

CHAPTER EIGHT

Vietnam, July, 1970

By the mid-60s, rogue elements within the CIA were well into conducting a secret war inside the borders of Laos, a desperate nation in the middle of bloody civil unrest. This operation, unauthorized by CIA officials, and far removed from any hint of military or Congressional oversight, was undertaken for the purpose of helping certain warlords fight against the North Vietnamese and the local communist. It was a fight the CIA believed in wholeheartedly.

This secret operation was funded by the opium poppy, thanks primarily to a financially successful crop planted by the CIA a decade earlier. Top CIA officials, going back to the days of Allen Dulles, had long dreamt of finding the means to finance covert operations without having to beg for Congressional funding and support. In Laos, Cambodia, and later in Vietnam, illegal drug production, distribution and sales provided the answer to this problem. The operation, now essentially privatized, paid for itself, thus eliminating the necessity of dealing with Washington red-tape bureaucracy.

Johnny Dantzler's mission was to learn the name of the top CIA official running the illegal operation.

Dantzler and Cain were sitting at a table near the back of the Mississippi Bar in Qui Nhon, a decent-size town that rested comfortably on the beautiful South China Sea. Qui Nhon, home to a huge U.S. supply depot, had been virtually free of combat action prior to the Tet Offensive in January, 1968, when, like virtually every city in South Vietnam, it had been attacked. Now Qui Nhon, like all cities south of the DMZ, was on high alert.

In the heart of Qui Nhon were two streets that ran parallel to one another, each one lined on both sides by bars, most of which were named for American states. The Mississippi Bar, one of the most popular with G.I.'s, was rumored to be owned by the U.S. government. Much of the bar's popularity stemmed from the fact that the whores working there were given weekly medical inspections by Army doctors, thus ensuring they were free of venereal disease. It was the only bar in town where G.I.'s could have their fun without need of a condom. Not surprisingly, the place did brisk business.

The second rumor concerning the Mississippi Bar was that it was jointly owned by the CIA and Santos Trafficante, the Mob boss often linked to the JFK assassination. It was no secret that Trafficante was in cahoots with rogue elements of the CIA involved in the drug business in Southeast Asia. It was also no secret—and was well-documented—that the CIA had long-standing connections to the Mafia, dating back to the days when certain Mob leaders were recruited to help eliminate Cuban dictator Fidel Castro.

Sometimes you have to dance with one devil in order to kill another devil.

"How well do you know this guy?" Cain asked. He and Dantzler were waiting to meet a CIA operative named Jeff Toland.

"Don't know him at all," Dantzler answered. "Only met him one time, very briefly. Why do you ask?"

"Lucas says we shouldn't trust him."

General Lucas White was Cain's boss.

Dantzler laughed. "Hell, I don't trust any of those guys. They all seem more than a little untrustworthy to me."

"One thing's for sure . . . the guy can't tell time," Cain said. "I have better things to do than sit on my ass waiting for some CIA desk jockey to show up."

"Yeah, patience isn't one of my strongest attributes, either."

Toland was already an hour late for the meeting, and for the fourth time in that hour a waitress asked Dantzler and Cain if they wanted some Saigon Tea. For the fourth time they declined. They did, however, order two Cokes.

Toland showed up thirty minutes later. He was in his mid- to late-twenties, on the plump side, with dark hair cut short, dark eyes and a wide nose. He was dressed head to toe in all white. He looked like a Southern plantation owner from a not-so-distant American past. Upon recognizing Dantzler, Toland moved quickly to their table, scooted back a chair and sat.

Cain knew from the bulge under Toland's shirt that he was armed. Pistol, most likely a .45. And based on the positioning of the weapon, Cain also knew Toland was left-handed.

"Captain Dantzler," Toland said. "Good to see you again."

"You're more than an hour late," Cain said. "What . . . you guys operate on a different clock than we do?"

Toland ignored Cain's barb and spoke directly to Dantzler. "Tomorrow we'll be going to Kontum. It's in . . . ."

"I know where Kontum is," Cain said. "I've been there. Killed guys there."

Again, Toland ignored Cain. "The Central Highlands. The guy we'll be meeting is named Nong Duc Chinh. Likes to be called 'Ducky'. He's a doctor. Our sources tell us he's probably not hands-on involved with the CIA in Laos, but he knows the names of those who are. But we don't want *names*; we want a *name*. We need to find out who's running the operation."

"You keep saying *we*," Dantzler said. "Are you going with us?"

"Of course."

Cain said, "Why? What do you bring to the table?"

"It's my mission," Toland said, looking at Cain for the first time.

"No, it's his mission," Cain said, nodding at Dantzler. "You're only a messenger boy."

"You appear to have very little respect for my position."

"Wrong. I have no respect for your position."

"What's with you, Cain?" Toland said. "Do you have a buzz up your ass about me, or what?"

"No. I just don't like you, that's all."

"Well, get the fuck over it," Toland snapped. "I'm going, and fuck you if you don't like it."

Cain leaned forward. "Be careful, Toland. I've killed men for a lot less than what you just said."

"When do we leave?" Dantzler interjected, hoping to defuse the situation and cool the rising heat. "And where do we meet this Doctor Ducky?"

"He works out of a small building on the western edge of Kontum," Toland answered. "He's usually there until late at night. Does quite a bit of drinking once he's finished with his last patient. When he's alone, you guys will go in and secure him. Then I'll come in. You do what needs to be done to get him to cough up the name of the CIA operative we're looking for. After he gives us a name, you're free to either let him go or kill him."

"Does he have any security?" Dantzler said.

"He's a doctor; why would he need security?"

"Just asking," Dantzler said. "I don't much care for surprises."

"No, no. It'll just be him and us." Toland stood and pushed his chair back. "We leave tomorrow at oh-eight-hundred."

After Toland was gone, Dantzler said, "What do you think?"

"I think I'd like to kill him," Cain said.

Dantzler laughed. "Other than that, what do you think?"

"I think Lucas was right . . . we shouldn't trust him."

"Affirmative on that."

*****

The next morning a helicopter dropped the three men off at an LZ near an Army base two kilometers outside of Kontum. The base was home to the 4th Infantry. Once on the base, Cain and Dantzler hung out in a rec room for much of the afternoon, shooting pool and playing cards. Toland disappeared an hour after they arrived, and they didn't see him again until sundown. Neither Cain nor Dantzler missed having him around.

After darkness fell, they commandeered a jeep, drove into the village, found Doctor Ducky's building, parked fifty feet away and waited. For the next two hours a steady stream of villagers came and went, ranging from mothers carrying infants, to ex-soldiers with missing limbs, to the very old walking with the aid of crutches. Clearly, Doctor Ducky was a popular guy.

By ten o'clock the steady stream had dwindled down to a slow dribble. By eleven, with no further traffic either coming or going, and with all but a single light having been turned off inside the building, it was obvious no more patients were with the doctor.

"Time to move," Toland announced.

"Not yet," Cain said. "We'll give it another fifteen minutes, just to be on the safe side."

"Why? We know he's alone."

"Are you sure of that? Just because no patients have come out doesn't mean there aren't others in there with him. Let's face it—your Intel leaves a lot to be desired."

"We can't wait," Toland protested. "What if he leaves?"

"We'll grab him outside," Cain said. "It doesn't matter where we collar him. I can make him talk anywhere."

"No. It needs to be inside the building," Toland argued. "We can't be seen beating up the local doctor." He turned to Dantzler. "What do you say?"

"I'm with Cain," Dantzler answered. "He knows more about this shit than we do."

Toland slumped, pouted like an angry child, but offered no further protest.

Fifteen minutes later, after no one entered or emerged from the building, Cain said, "Okay, let's pay the good doctor a late-night visit."

They climbed out of the jeep and sprinted toward the building. Dantzler was the only one with a weapon in hand, his M16. He also had a pistol, which he offered to Cain, who politely refused.

"Is there a back door?" Dantzler asked Toland when they reached the front entrance.

"No. There are two exam rooms on the right side, and two exam rooms and a bathroom on the left." Toland lifted his shirt, reached in and grabbed his .45. "Signal me when he's ready to talk."

Doctor Ducky was sitting behind a wooden desk near the back wall, scribbling notes in a journal when Cain and Dantzler came through the front door. An empty shot glass and a half-filled bottle of Jack Daniels rested on the table. Glancing up, the doctor smiled and placed the pen carefully on the table, closed the journal and stood.

Cain was struck by the fact that the man showed not a hint of fear or surprise. It was almost as if he had been expecting them. Cain wondered if doctors were immune to surprises.

Dantzler and Cain slowly walked straight toward the doctor, who remained standing, the smile frozen on his face.

"We're here to gather information," Dantzler said, pointing his rifle at the doctor, "and we're not leaving until we have it. So . . . this can go down easy, or it can go down hard. Your choice."

"Information? What are you talking about? I have no information for you."

"We'll see about that," Dantzler said.

"Who are you, anyway?" the doctor said, his English perfect.

"Your worst nightmare come true," Cain said.

"Have a seat, Doc," Dantzler ordered. "And keep your hands where we can see them."

As the doctor scooted his chair back and prepared to sit, Cain felt the old floor vibrate beneath his feet seconds before he heard the creaking door open behind him. Instinctively, he knew what was happening. *Ambush.* He pushed Dantzler to the floor, then spun away to his right, ducked down, turned quickly, looked up and saw a man coming at him with a machete. He breathed a sigh of relief—a man using a machete was not a serious threat once Cain had him located. Still in a semi-crouch, he drove his right foot into the attacker's left kidney, knocking him breathless and causing him to stumble. Cain stood, grabbed the man's right hand, the one holding the machete, straightened the man's arm, and then swung it hard, cutting the man's head off. The head hit the floor and rolled toward the doctor, who was still standing frozen, but no longer smiling.

At the same time two doors opened on the left side and a pair of attackers emerged, one holding a pistol, the other carrying a Russian-made AK47. They were young, wild-eyed, inexperienced. And judging by their haphazard shooting, obviously more scared than efficient. Definitely not trained soldiers. They fired wildly, spraying bullets everywhere, none of their shots coming close to hitting Dantzler or Cain. Most of their shots were high, punching holes in the old wooden wall and ceiling. Dantzler's shooting wasn't haphazard; he took them out, hitting each man twice in the chest while lying on his back.

The noise from all the shooting was so deafening Cain failed to hear the door creak behind him. Or sense that another attacker was about to emerge. Only at the last second, his survival instinct on high alert, did he realize he was in danger. He dove to his right, and as he did, Dantzler shot the attacker in his right eye, blowing the man's face away.

Cain stood and nodded at Dantzler, who said, "You know, Cain, it's not every day I get to save a legend's ass."

"There's your lead story for the grandkids," Cain said.

By now Doctor Ducky's smile had given way to the shakes. His entire body was trembling like he had just stepped out of an iceberg. Tears flowed down his face.

"You are Cain?" he said.

"I'm Cain."

"I've heard of you. The jungle ghost."

"Then you know what I'll do if you refuse to tell us what we want to know."

The doctor looked at Dantzler. "What information do you seek?"

"The name of the CIA operative who's running the show in Laos," Dantzler said.

"If I give you the name, will you let me live?" Ducky pleaded.

Dantzler turned to Cain, said, "What do you think, Cain? Should we let him live?"

"I don't know. He did try to have us killed."

Ducky raised both hands to protest. "No, no, I had nothing to do with this. I was as surprised as you when they showed up."

"Somehow, I doubt that," Dantzler said, raising his rifle and pointing it at Ducky. "Give me the name, or I'll let Cain get it from you. And my hunch is, that might be painful for you."

Ducky was silent for several seconds, stuck both hands into his pants pocket, and then said, "Okay, okay, I will give you the name."

At that moment a bullet smashed into Ducky's forehead, sending a mist of blood, bone and brain matter onto a map hanging on the wall behind the desk. Ducky slammed against the wall, slid down to the floor and slumped onto his right side.

Dantzler and Cain turned and saw Toland standing in the classic shooter's position, .45 in both hands, arms extended, knees bent slightly. Smoke drifted upward from the barrel of his weapon. The smell of cordite filled the room. Lowering the weapon, he walked toward Cain and Dantzler, a smug look on his face.

"What the fuck did you do that for?" Dantzler said, anger in his voice. "He was about to talk. You just silenced your informant."

"His hands went into his pockets," Toland said. "I wasn't taking any chances that he had a weapon."

"You stupid asshole," Cain said. "That man was about as much of a threat to me as you are. He could've pulled out a bazooka and I would have stopped him. He was no threat to us."

"You don't know that for sure."

"Here's what I do know for sure. You're a bonehead and an idiot and a worthless piece of shit. So, why don't you consider me a threat and raise that forty-five? Give me a reason to kill your sorry ass?"

Toland tucked his .45 away, looked at Cain, and said, "You know something, Cain. I have a hunch that you're a classic bully. Which means you aren't the bad ass everyone says you are. Personally, I don't think you're all that tough."

Having said his piece, and not inclined to hang around for Cain's response, Toland spun on his heels and quickly walked out of the building.

Grinning, Dantzler put a hand on Cain's shoulder, said, "Damn, what a disappointment to find out you aren't a bad ass."

"You know, sometime down the road, I just might have to kill that little bastard."

"Well, be careful. Remember, you aren't all that tough."

CHAPTER NINE

Sitting in Jack Dantzler's kitchen, Cain thought about that night in Kontum all those years ago. He had questioned then, just as he questioned now, how it all went down. He had always felt there was something off about the whole situation.

Especially the shooting of Doctor Ducky.

That had stink written all over it.

Righteous kill is a relatively recent term, one likely coined by law enforcement to indicate that the fatal shooting of a suspect was justified. It meant the cop felt his life, or the lives of others, was in imminent danger, and he had no other alternative but to use deadly force. If the shooting was deemed to be justified—righteous—then the cop was off the hook. He would face no sanctions or legal repercussions.

Was the shooting of Doctor Ducky a righteous kill? Cain had his doubts. In his mind, it was nothing more than an execution. Cold-blooded murder. Toland wanted Ducky dead, so he shot him. Simple as that. But why? Toland needed a name, and Ducky likely could have provided it. If not *the* name, then one that could take them one step up the ladder, closer to the top.

Ducky's death made no sense.

But, Cain wondered, was he casting doubt on Toland's actions out of his dislike for the man? Was he being unfair in his assessment? Maybe Toland really did sense danger. Maybe his actions were justified. To him, at least. After all, Ducky did put both hands in his pockets. Toland, not being a combat veteran, could easily have read that as a move meant to get a weapon. Maybe Toland genuinely felt Ducky was a threat. Maybe Toland deserved the benefit of doubt.

Righteous or not, it was a kill that had extended consequences. Especially for Johnny Dantzler. The name his superiors were seeking still had to be uncovered, and it was up to him to find it. Those were his orders, and that was what he would do. He would continue the quest, like any good investigator was expected to do. Keep searching, keep digging, keep turning over rocks until he accomplished his mission. He would travel as many roads as necessary in order to find the answer he was looking for. His investigation would eventually take him to a single road, one that led him out of Vietnam and into Laos.

And to his death.

CHAPTER TEN

Nick Marlow leaned down and surveyed his shot. The nine-ball was resting in the middle of the table, eight inches from the side pocket. To successfully execute the shot required Nick to cut the nine-ball enough to ease it to the right maybe two inches. Most players would consider it a somewhat tricky shot, but it posed no problem for Nick, who spent much of his youth mastering the game on this classic Brunswick pool table. For a player of his caliber it wasn't even a white-knuckler. He could make it with his eyes closed. It all came down to simple geometry, and the proper use of energy.

Speed of the cue ball was his lone concern. He had to be careful not to hit it with too much force, especially since he would be applying high left-hand English. Striking the cue ball too hard would send it into the far side rail, where it would then carom off two cushions and continue rolling toward the corner pocket on the opposite side of the table. He would scratch if he wasn't careful. And that would mean losing.

But did he really want to make the shot? Win the five-dollar bet? Notch yet another victory? Or should he miss on purpose, and in so doing leave the nine-ball hanging in the side pocket? Leave such an easy shot even a blind man could make it? Should he let Lee have the win? Give the old man reason to gloat? Those questions ran through his mind as he contemplated the shot.

He didn't wait long before making his decision. Maybe two seconds, at most. Nick Marlow wasn't a man who wasted time contemplating his next move. He applied chalk to the tip of his cue stick, bent over, lined up the shot and easily sank the nine-ball. Straightening up, he laid his cue stick on the green felt table and held out his right hand, palm open.

"That's five you owe me, old man," he said.

"Don't spend it all in one place," Lee Bartlett said, placing the crisp bill in Nick's hand. "For a moment there, I was certain you were going to miss on purpose."

"Thought about it, but you know me. I hate to lose."

"I have taught you well, Nick," Lee said. "Never show an opponent mercy. Never give him a second life. As someone once said, when your enemy is drowning, throw the bastard an anvil."

"I think it was James Carville who said that."

"Sounds like something that crazy Cajun would say." Lee pulled back one of the bar stools and sat. "Tell me again what David said."

Nick went behind the bar, opened a cooler and lifted out a Heineken. "Want one?" he asked, knowing what Lee's answer would be. Lee never drank beer, only the most expensive scotch or the finest wine. "I'll open it for you."

"No. But you can pour me some of the single malt. No ice."

Nick poured the scotch, handed the glass to Lee, and said, "A homicide detective from Lexington, Kentucky, phoned Apollo Enterprises and ask to speak with Langley. Left a message for Langley to call him as soon as possible."

"And?"

"Langley seemed pretty shook up about it."

Lee sipped his scotch, said, "Why on earth would David be concerned about some cop from Kentucky?"

Nick shook his head. "I have no idea why. All I can tell you is, Langley sounded worried."

"David has always been a worrier."

"Langley has always been weak, Lee. You know it; you just refuse to admit it." Nick took a long drink of beer. "Why you protect that man I'll never understand. But you have, ever since I've known you. Everyone knows if it weren't for you he'd be less than nothing. Probably, he'd be dead."

"David has his positives, which you refuse to acknowledge. He is loyal, and he is obedient. Those qualities make him useful." Lee sipped more scotch. "You have never cared for David, have you?"

"No."

"Why the animosity?"

"I detest weakness," Nick answered.

"I agree that weakness is a most despicable trait in a man," Lee said. "But the weak have their place in the world. The good Lord, in his infinite wisdom, put them here to serve those of us who are strong. And David has served me well for almost forty years. That's not something I take for granted. I also happen to believe he has more strength than you give him credit for."

"Where's your evidence? Your proof? You can't answer that, because the evidence and proof don't exist. He's never once been tested under fire. Never. The man would crap his pants if he found himself in a combat situation. Just like all the rest of those ass-kissers at the party last week."

"I suppose you would prefer that I ignore them?"

"I'd prefer that you line them up against the wall and let me shoot them."

"We really must work on your social skills, Nick." Lee swept an arm through the air. "Someday in the near future, I will be gone. When that happens, most of what I have will be yours. You will have power, and you will control a fortune. From your vantage point now, you have the luxury of distancing yourself from those people you detest. However, when you are sitting in my chair, you'll quickly learn that making a deal with the devil is oftentimes the best route to take. At times, the only route you can take. And trust me, Nick. You will shake the devil's hand more times than you can count. It's how certain things get done."

Nick chuckled. "Nice sermon, old man. But not good enough to persuade me. My opinion of Langley hasn't changed."

"Fair enough. All I'm asking is that you be more tolerant." Lee finished his scotch, poured more into his glass, and sipped. "Let's table our discussion of David for the moment and discuss matters of more importance."

"Las Vegas?"

Lee nodded.

"Not much to discuss. It went well."

"Excellent," Lee said, smiling. "Now we must address the second half of our problem."

"The senator?"

"Yes. And it needs to be done quickly."

"How quickly?"

"Within days. A week at the latest."

"Do you think that's wise?" Nick said. "Two high-profile murders so close together is bound to bring serious heat. Especially if they are linked, which they will be at some point."

"Let me worry about the heat. That's of no concern to me. Our main focus is making sure the investigation is shut down. With the general and the senator out of the way, it will be. For a time, at least. At some point the investigation will continue. That's inevitable. But by that time I will have made sure certain individuals sympathetic to our cause will have leading roles in the investigation. So, yes, Nick. The sooner, the better."

"Do you want to use the girl again?"

"I see no reason not to. She's very good."

"She may demand more money this time. Maybe as high as a million."

"Hell, give her what she wants. If she eliminates the senator, the million we pay her will only be a pittance of what we'll make down the road. The way I see it, a million is a bargain."

"I'll make the call to Dimitrios tonight."

"No," Lee said, shaking his head. "Leave the Greek out of it. You contact the girl."

"Dimitrios isn't going to like that. He'll demand his cut."

"If he makes too much noise we'll send the girl to Athens. Let her silence the greedy bastard. Then he'll never demand anything again."

"I'll call her."

Lee said, "Regarding the other matter. How concerned are you about David? The cop thing?"

"All I can say is, Langley seemed plenty worried."

"David is probably seeing demons where none exist. But just to err on the side of caution, have him give me a call. I need to find out why he's so worried."

CHAPTER ELEVEN

When Kayce Clark first heard the news that General Ray Dunlap had been murdered, she was equal parts horrified and angry. Horrified that a distinguished soldier's life had been snuffed out in such a senseless way, and angry because the source for a potentially huge story was no longer available to her. In the end, her anger ruled the day. This neither surprised nor disappointed her. Nor did it stir feelings of guilt. As a highly committed and extremely competitive person, it was only natural that she would feel this way. Any investigative journalist worth his or her salt would.

Losing an inside source as highly placed as a three-star general was a bitter pill to swallow. This was especially true when the general in question worked at the Pentagon. Kayce knew this first hand. Most of the folks who toil in the famous five-sided structure were more tight-lipped than a baseball player testifying before Congress about steroid use. Getting a Pentagon official to give more than name, rank and serial number was a major accomplishment. To lose a source like General Dunlap was like cutting the wings off an airplane. Without him, her story might not fly.

At thirty-one, Kayce Clark was considered the rising star among investigative journalist, successor to Bob Woodward, Carl Bernstein, Andy Waltz and the multitude of followers who voyaged in their wake. She was blessed with talent, brains and, most of all, tenacity. She had a miner's mentality: dig, dig, dig, until she struck gold. Then, once found, she protected her gold with the ferociousness of a pit bull on crack.

Kayce made her bones as an investigative journalist during only her third year at the *New York Times*. She spent six months working on the story, which involved shady dealings by a celebrated Wall Street investor. After Kayce's story ran, the man was arrested, his firm went belly up, and more than four-hundred investors filed lawsuits. It was estimated that he had bilked more than half-a-billion dollars from those investors, none of whom had any chance of recouping even a small fraction of their loss.

Kayce's story, which earned her the Pulitizer Prize, drew the interest of an editor at Random House. Nine months later, Kayce's book recounting the investigation was sitting at number three on the *New York Times* Top Ten list. It remained a best seller for fifteen weeks before going on to do equally well in paperback form. A movie studio optioned the book for a year, and although nothing was in the works at this point, Kayce had taken home a nice paycheck. With that one case—and the book—Kayce had not only made her bones, she also made more money than she ever dreamed she'd have.

Having turned the page on that adventure, Kayce began looking around for her next big story. There were several possibilities but none that truly excited her. Then, out of the blue, she received the call from General Dunlap. The call lasted three minutes, with the general doing most of the talking. Although he provided little in the way of solid details, Kayce instinctively knew this was something big.

There was, however, a huge barrier confronting her—the general's reluctance to speak of what he termed "extremely sensitive matters." He made it clear, saying he was still undecided about how best to proceed. Or if, indeed, he wanted to proceed at all. Leaking top-secret information could land him in hot water up to his ass, he said. And one final point: If he did opt to talk, was she the right person to hear his tale?

Kayce tried to pry details from the general, but he was far too cagey to let anything important slip out. But he did agree to meet with her, which Kayce saw as a positive first step. Naturally, she wanted to meet the next day, but he told her he would be unavailable for a week. They finally agreed to meet the following Monday in the Rose Reading Room at the New York City Public Library.

But now there would be no meeting—a murderer in Las Vegas made sure of that. Whatever information Dunlap had was going to the grave with him. Kayce couldn't help but believe Dunlap's death was connected to the story he was going to tell. But was that the case, or was she simply projecting? It could just as easily have been a random murder. Maybe Dunlap was killed by a jealous husband, or a loan shark he owed money to. Or maybe it was a straight-up robbery gone bad. Yeah, and maybe pigs really can fly.

No, Kayce concluded, General Ray Dunlap was murdered in order to silence him.

Kayce pulled out her cell phone, opened it and punched in Andy Waltz's number. Andy answered after four rings. Kayce knew from the background noise that Andy was in a bar, most likely the Minetta Tavern in the Village, his favorite watering hole.

"What's up, Kayce?" Waltz screamed. "Hang on for a second, will you? Let me go outside, where it's quieter." A minute later, he was back on the phone. "There, that's much better. So, back to my original question. What's up?"

"I need some advice, some guidance," Kayce said.

"All right. Shoot."

"You read about the general who was murdered in Vegas, didn't you? General Ray Dunlap?" Kayce asked. Waltz was silent for so long Kayce thought their connection had been broken. "You there, Andy?"

"Why are you inquiring about General Dunlap?" Waltz finally said.

"I was supposed to meet him on Monday."

"You were meeting with Ray Dunlap?"

"Yes. At the public library."

"Why?"

"He phoned me and—"

"Phoned you? When?"

"Three days before he was murdered. The call came straight out of the blue."

Waltz was quiet for several seconds, then said, "Did he say why he was calling?"

"Not really. Only that he had some important information he was thinking about giving me. He said it would make for a helluva story."

"But no details?" Waltz said. "Nothing specific?"

"No. But I sensed that whatever he wanted to tell me, it was big. And call me crazy, but I also have a feeling that his death is somehow connected to the information he was thinking about revealing. In other words, someone silenced him."

"You don't know that."

"I *feel* it, Andy," Kayce said. "I *believe* it. And I'm going to pursue it. That's why I came to you. If you were in my shoes, what would be your next move?"

"Drop it, and look elsewhere for a story. That's my advice."

"Bullshit. I know you better than that. I'm a baby bulldog compared to you. You would pursue a story into Hades if that's where the truth could be found. Andy Waltz didn't get to be the best by walking away."

"I've walked away plenty of times," Waltz said.

"What should I do, Andy? What would *you* do?"

"Like I said, I would walk away."

"Not gonna happen."

"No way I can persuade you to change your mind?"

"No."

After more extended silence, Waltz said, "Then I would contact Senator Carlin."

"John Carlin?"

"Yes."

"Why?"

"Call his office, tomorrow. Tell him—and *only* him—what you've told me. Maybe he'll talk to you, maybe he won't. That will be up to him. But that's what I would do."

Now it was Kayce who was silent for almost a minute. "What's the connection between Carlin and Dunlap," she asked. "And if there is a connection, how is it that you know about it?"

"You wanted my advice, Kayce. Well, there it is. Make the call, see what happens."

"Why do I get the feeling that you're already about ten steps ahead of me on this?"

"Here's one final piece of advice, Kayce. If the senator is willing to talk, and if you proceed with your investigation, you'll want to fly well below the radar at all times. Keep everything you learn close to the vest. And most of all . . . trust no one."

CHAPTER TWELVE

Dantzler and Cain left Lexington in Dantzler's car and drove to the airport in Louisville, where they caught the first available flight to Las Vegas. Southwest, with a one-hour stop in Dallas. During the layover, Cain phoned Andy Waltz and asked him to reserve a rental car from Avis, and book them a suite in Caesar's Palace. Waltz said it would all be taken care of by the time they arrived in Vegas.

The flight was smooth and uneventful, with neither man saying much. Cain's thoughts were on finding and eliminating those responsible for Ray Dunlap's death, while Dantzler wondered just what in the hell he'd gotten himself into. He also wondered if there was a role for him in what was clearly Cain's game all the way. On that question he had serious doubts. It was clear to Dantzler that Cain was the classic lone wolf, a solitary creature accustomed to taking orders from no one, comfortable living a private existence. How much of that privacy was Cain willing to give up? Dantzler wondered. A little or a lot? Maybe none at all. For guys like Cain, it all came down to trust. And, Dantzler knew, Cain didn't trust many people. In his line of work he couldn't afford to.

Arriving in Las Vegas was like stepping onto the sun. The desert heat was brutal, attaching itself to the skin like a blanket of fire. The blast of hot air smacked them in the face the moment they left the cool interior of McCarran International. The heat sucked the breath from their lungs. It was as though they had landed in a desert inferno.

Fifteen minutes later, the time it took to retrieve their rental and head toward the strip, both men were sweating profusely and totally miserable. The car's air conditioner was on full blast, doing all it could, but it was fighting a losing battle. There simply was no relief, and there wouldn't be until they were out of this heat.

It was a full hour later, after checking into Caesar's and going to their suite, before they began to cool down. Their first act was to crank the air conditioner up to the highest level. This one did the trick, sending out air so cold they could see their breath. But it wasn't until each man had taken a shower that their body temperature began to feel normal again.

"Who's picking up the tab for this little excursion?" Dantzler asked. "Or do I even want to know?"

"Not to worry, Detective. It's all taken care of."

"Does that include food?"

"Everything goes on a single tab. Why? You hungry?"

"Starved."

"Is room service okay with you? I want to hang around here until I hear from Houdini."

"Yeah, room service is fine," Dantzler said. "Want to look at this menu?"

"Order me a steak, medium, baked potato, salad and a soft drink."

"Dessert?"

"No."

As Dantzler was about to call room service, Cain's cell phone buzzed. Dantzler held off making his call, choosing instead to listen in on Cain's conversation. To his surprise, Cain put the call on speaker phone.

"Was the rental car and suite up to your high standards, Cain?" Waltz said. "Can I chalk up another successful mission for the master magician?"

"I hate a man who begs for compliments, Houdini," Cain replied. "Yes, as always, you done good."

"Okay, here's the rest of the story. The FBI agent in charge is Steven Pearce. He has twenty-two years on the job, spotless record, considered a top-notch investigator. Married to his high school sweetheart, three kids, a slew of grandkids. No chinks in his armor whatsoever. Whether or not he's the kind of guy who will share information with you, I can't say."

"I doubt he'll be very willing," Cain said. "What did you find out about the local guys?"

"Here's where we might be in luck. The Las Vegas Metropolitan Police Department is one of those joint city/county setups. The head guy is the sheriff of Clark County. His name is Mitch Greenwood. Been there forever. And here's the best part—he's a Vietnam vet. Was in-country in seventy and seventy-one. Army. Buck sergeant. Was awarded the Purple Heart, so he saw action. You and Greenwood have some things in common. Maybe that'll be enough to get him to open up about the Dunlap case."

"Terrific work, Houdini."

"There's something else I need to share with you. And I doubt you'll be happy to hear it."

"What?"

"An investigative reporter, a colleague of mine at the paper named Kayce Clark, phoned me two nights ago. Told me she had spoken with Dunlap, and was scheduled to meet him in New York on Monday."

"Why would she contact Ray Dunlap?" Cain asked.

"She didn't. He called her. Said he might have some information that would lead to a big story. He gave no details."

"And she called you, seeking advice? Right?"

"I told her to contact John Carlin," Houdini said. "I did so only because I know her. She's not the type to back off. She would have done her own digging, and who knows what she might have unearthed. Or whose names she might have stumbled upon. Sending her straight to the senator seemed like the best alternative. My hunch is, he won't speak with her. If he does, he won't give away much. He can't afford to."

"Kayce Clark? Didn't I meet her once? In your office?"

"Come to think of it, you did. About a year ago."

"Monitor her, Houdini. Anything she learns, I want to know about it. And tell her to be careful. She's heading toward a nest of vipers."

"Will do. What's your next step?"

"Track down Steven Pearce. Listen to him tell me to get lost."

"Ah, hell, Cain, with your charm, you'll have him spilling his guts in a matter of seconds."

"See you, Houdini." Cain closed his phone and looked up at Dantzler. "Where's the beef, Detective?"

"I'll order it now."

"About time."

Dantzler picked up the phone, started to dial, then immediately placed the phone back on the receiver, and said, "I'm going with you when you meet with Steven Pearce."

"No, you're not."

Dantzler frowned. "Look, Cain, I'm not gonna sit here like a tree stump while you do your thing. I'm here. I want to help."

"I have every intention of you helping."

"How? By being executive in charge of room service?"

"You're going to talk with Mitch Greenwood. See what he'll tell you about the Dunlap case."

"What makes you think he'll talk to me about the case? I have no authority to inquire about General Dunlap's murder. He'll tell me to mind my own business. To get lost. And he'll have every right to tell me that. I would, if I were him."

"Okay, so don't tell him you're there to talk about the case. Tell him you're trying to learn more about your father. Let him know you were just a kid when your dad died, and you're thirsty for information about him. Greenwood was in Nam the same time your dad was, so he'll be thrilled to have the chance to tell you what it was like back in those days. Then, once you've got him talking, once he's on your side, ease him into the Dunlap case. Ask him about being bumped to the sidelines by the Feds. That's sure to crank his engine."

"And once I've met with him? What then?"

"We meet back here and compare notes. Does that meet with your approval, Detective?"

"Yeah."

"Good. Now order the food before we die of starvation."

CHAPTER THIRTEEN

Cain found Steven Pearce sitting alone in a booth in a small hamburger joint two blocks off the main strip. Pearce had federal agent written all over him. Blue suit, white shirt, red tie, shiny shoes. Hair buzzed close on the sides, slightly longer on top. Sunglasses folded and tucked safely inside his shirt pocket. Deadly serious look on his face. He could easily have been the model used in the FBI's recruitment brochure.

Dantzler slipped into the seat across from Pearce, who had his head down, studying the bill.

"Do I know you?" Pearce asked, looking up.

"No. But we need to talk."

Pearce reached into his shirt pocket, took out a business card and carefully placed it on the table. "That's my office number," he snapped. "Call me. Maybe I can work you in."

The tough-guy posturing didn't impress Cain. It never had and never would. Why? Because it was pure bullshit, that's why. And absolutely meaningless. What assholes like Pearce didn't understand was that genuine tough guys don't posture. They don't have to.

Sliding the card back toward Pearce, Cain said, "I need some information regarding the Dunlap case."

"Yeah. And I need a bigger pecker."

"I'm sure your wife would agree with you on that."

"A comedian, huh? There's a comedy club around the corner. Check it out. Maybe you can land a gig there."

"What can you tell me about the Dunlap case?"

"That's an on-going investigation," Pearce said. "I'm not currently at liberty to . . ."

"Save the canned speech for your next press conference, Agent Pearce. I don't have time to deal with bullshit."

"Who the hell are you, anyway?"

"Cain."

"Well, Cain, here's the deal. You want information, then make it a point to show up at the next press conference. Because that's the only way you'll hear anything from me."

"Was Dunlap . . .?"

"Are you fuckin' deaf? I'm not telling you anything. Got it?"

Cain was silent.

"Who are you with, Cain?" Pearce said, staring hard at Cain. "You work in radio or print journalism? Has to be one of those two, 'cause you're too old and too ugly for TV. Unless you're a TV producer. Now, that I could see. Most of those guys are pushy and belligerent. But where you work, or who you work for, makes no difference to me. I'm not talking to you. You'll have to find another source for your next big scoop."

"Do I look like the media type to you?"

"No. You look like an arrogant jerk who bullies people into giving you what you want. Well, I have a flash for you, hotshot. That won't work with me. I'm not easily intimidated."

Cain smiled while contemplating how he wanted to deal with this situation. He had two obvious choices. He could acquiesce and go all meek and mild, thus allowing this asshole to see himself as the alpha male. Or he could reach across the table, grab the guy by the throat and choke him until he either gave up the information or died. Cain chose neither option. Instead, he opted to enlighten the man.

"Have it your way, Agent Pearce," Cain said. "But . . ."

"I usually do."

Cain nodded. "Riddle me this, Batman. Was the weapon that killed Dunlap a SigArms P239 or a Beretta-Cheetah?"

Pearce's face flushed red, his jaw clenched. A nerve in his neck began to twitch wildly. He looked like a man who had just been told he was dying from some horrible disease.

"A P239," Pearce said. "How did you know that? That information hasn't been released to the media or the public."

"The Bellagio must have hundreds of cameras. Did you get the shooter on tape?"

"Only when he entered and exited Dunlap's floor. After that, surveillance cameras lose him."

"Describe the shooter," Cain said.

"Who the hell are you?"

"The shooter? Give me a description."

"Male, dark complexion, medium height. I'd estimate him to be between five-six and five-nine."

"How was the shooter dressed?"

"Sneakers, jeans, sweater, black windbreaker, baseball cap. He wore dark shades, kept his head down and away from the camera. He had a mustache, looked to be of Middle Eastern or Latin American descent. That's our best guess, anyway."

Cain slid out of the booth and stood. "Well, Agent Pearce, hate to tell you this, but you're dead wrong on all counts. The shooter is female, not male. And she's not Middle Eastern or Latin American. She's Russian."

Cain turned and walked away before the stunned agent had time to open his mouth and ask the first of his many questions.

CHAPTER FOURTEEN

Mitch Greenwood was a big, barrel-chested, beefy man with a hearty laugh and eyes so green you felt like you were staring at two large emeralds. He had a 50's style crew-cut, an old scar that ran along his right cheekbone, and a bulbous heavily veined nose. A drinker's nose. Dantzler judged him to be a straight bourbon drinker. For guys like him, mixed drinks were for sissies.

Dantzler also judged him to be a man who was easily—and unwisely—underestimated, probably to the detriment of those foolish enough to make snap judgments about another man's abilities. In this instance, they would be wrong. Dantzler recognized a good cop when he saw one, and he had no doubt that Greenwood was a pro's pro.

"So your old man was KIA in Nam, huh?" Greenwood said, leaning back in his chair. Dantzler sat across from Greenwood, having been invited into the Chief's office without hesitation. "Sorry to hear that. Lots of fine, young Americans never came home from that damn place. Hell, it's a miracle I made it back. Almost didn't."

"How were you wounded?" Dantzler said.

"Mortar round. Ripped up my right side pretty good, too." His finger traced the scar along his cheekbone. "Damn near ruined this pretty face of mine. I always felt I could've made it in Hollywood if it weren't for this damn scar. Been right up there on the big movie screen with Warren Beatty and Clint Eastwood."

His bellowing laugh rattled the office walls. "Seriously, though, what was your father's name?"

"Johnny Dantzler."

"When did he die?"

"September, nineteen-seventy."

"I got over there in June of that year. Where was he when he bought it? I mean, where was he when he died?"

Dantzler said, "I'm not real sure. Initially, we were told he was killed while on patrol near Pleiku. However, I was recently told that he may have died in Laos."

"Why in hell would he have been in Laos?"

"Good question."

"Was he in the Army?" Greenwood said.

"Yes."

"Laos? That's strange. We had no mission there. At least, none that were on the books."

Eager to change the subject, Dantzler stood and asked if he could look at the numerous photographs, plaques and letters of commendation covering most of three walls. Greenwood was only too happy to grant permission. What Dantzler saw was impressive evidence of an outstanding career in law enforcement. Underestimated or not, Mitch Greenwood had been a superb police officer. Everything on these walls bore witness to that fact.

"How long have you been a cop?" Dantzler asked.

"I joined the force two months after I was discharged from the service. It's the only job I've ever had."

"Looks like you've been a good one."

"Partner, I can honestly say I did the best I could with what little talent and brains God gave me. I never took a bribe, never mistreated a suspect and never phoned it in. I always gave it a one-hundred-percent effort. And I made it a point to be honest to a fault. Sadly, not everyone in our line of work plays it that way. Some guys go off the reservation, give up their integrity. When you go down that road, there's no turning back. You can never be one of the good guys ever again. Once you have dirt on your hands, they can never be washed clean. You're a detective, so you know what the temptations are. It takes a man of strong character to resist."

"What's the most high-profile case you ever worked?" Dantzler said.

"Ted Binion, Tupac Shakur . . . those come to mind most quickly. But there have been a bunch of them over the years."

"It's my understanding you have one on your hands now. The Ray Dunlap case."

"*Had* it," Greenwood corrected. "The FBI yanked it away from us before you could say J. Edgar Hoover. Pretty much told us to take a hike."

"I've gone toe to toe with those guys before," Dantzler said. "They have a way of getting under your skin rather quickly."

"Well, I don't much care for someone else coming in and doing my job for me. That's especially true when I'm positive I can do the job as well as or better than they can. But I can't deny that they have more money, more resources and better equipment than I have. They've got some fantastic, state-of-the-art toys at their disposal. My biggest beef with them is they don't share information like they should. We need to know what's going on."

"From what you know, do think it was a random killing?"

"No. It was an execution, pure and simple."

"Why are you so certain that it was an execution?" Dantzler asked.

"Because of how it went down."

"How did it go down?"

"The shooter was either invited into the room, or he used his gun to force Dunlap to step back when the door was open. Once inside, he ordered Dunlap to turn around. Then he shot him point blank in the back of the head."

"And no one heard the shot?"

"The shooter used a silencer."

"Any idea what caliber weapon was used?"

Greenwood shook his head. "No clue. The Feds ushered us out of there before we even got started. They promised to keep us in the loop, but that was bullshit. We've not seen crime scene photos, the autopsy results or the ballistics report. For all I know, Dunlap's killer may have used a BB gun."

"You figure the shooter used a twenty-two? That's what most pros use."

"Wasn't a twenty-two."

"How can you be so sure?"

"I saw the body before the Feds ran us off. Much more damage to Dunlap's head than a twenty-two causes."

"Any leads or possible suspects?"

"If there are, the Feds haven't told me about it. When it comes to the Dunlap case, I'm like a caveman living in the dark."

"Chief, it's been a pleasure and an honor," Dantzler said, extending his hand to Greenwood. "I can only hope I conduct myself the way you have. You're one of the good guys."

"Any chance I could get you to drop by the house later tonight and tell that to my wife? I doubt she'd believe you, but it might be worth a try."

"I think I'd better take a pass on that. Thanks, anyway."

"Don't blame you a bit, partner."

"One more thing," Dantzler said, opening the office door. "When you were in Vietnam, did you ever hear of someone called Cain?"

"You bet," Greenwood said, nodding.

"What did you hear?"

"That he was the greatest one-man killing machine since Achilles."

*****

Cain was lying on the bed watching a rerun of *NCIS* when Dantzler walked into the suite. "You talk with the Chief?" Cain asked, sitting up and muting the TV.

"Yeah. For about an hour."

"And?"

"He's a good man, a terrific cop. But he has no information regarding the case. Shut out from the start by the Feds."

"That's typical."

"He's heard about you, though."

Cain shrugged.

Dantzler sat on his bed. "Did you meet with the FBI guy?"

"Yeah. For about five minutes."

"Learn anything?"

"Only that I already know more about the case than he does."

"Why am I not surprised?" Dantzler said.

"You hungry?"

Dantzler shook his head. "Nah, I'm good."

"Something on your mind, Detective?" Cain said.

"Not particularly. Why do you ask?"

"You seem a little . . . pensive."

Dantzler shrugged. "I don't know. It's just that I find it strange how people's lives intersect in the most peculiar ways."

"We travel a lot of roads during the course of a lifetime. You never know whose path might cross with yours."

"True . . . but. Here I am with you, a guy who was in Vietnam the same time my father was there. I just spent an hour with Mitch Greenwood, another guy who was in Vietnam the same time as my father. I would hit a real trifecta if I somehow found out Ray Dunlap was also over there at the same time."

Cain came off the bed, picked up his duffel bag, unzipped it and took out the photo of the two soldiers he had taken from Dantzler's kitchen table. He handed the photo to Dantzler.

"The man with your father, that's Ray Dunlap," Cain said.

Dantzler studied the photo for several seconds, then looked up at Cain. "You knew my father, didn't you?"

"Yes."

"How well?"

"Well enough."

"Do you ever tell the truth?"

Cain smiled. "I only tell the truth. I'm just very careful who I tell it to."

CHAPTER FIFTEEN

With his propensity for back-slapping and glad-handing, Dimitrios Sotirios could have been a successful American politician. Certainly, the owners and regular customers at Antonio's Bar would agree. Antonio's was one of the oldest bars in Athens, and Dimitrios, a regular for more than thirty-five years, was beloved by those who knew him best. To them, he was a friendly man, a loyal patron and a more-than-generous tipper. He loved mingling with strangers, and was famous for sending an expensive bottle of wine to young couples who appeared to be in love. Dimitrios was the best ambassador Antonio's could ever hope to have.

Everyone associated with Antonio's treated Dimitrios Sotirios like he was Zeus.

In particular, Dimitrios loved Americans and all things American. Like the majority of individuals who had never been to the United States, most of what Dimitrios knew about the U.S. came from the movies. He loved American movies, and had ever since he was a young boy. Those screen images he watched transported him to locales he could barely imagine, while introducing him to memorable characters portrayed by the grandest actors. Movies did, in fact, play a central role in his early education. It was his desire to understand what the actors were saying that led him to learn English at a young age. He did not want to rely on subtitles, and he steadfastly refused to watch any movie where the actor's voice was dubbed. When Butch Cassidy and the Sundance Kid spoke, he wanted to hear Paul Newman and Robert Redford, not two Greek actors giving second-rate impersonations.

Although Dimitrios had been a regular at Antonio's for more than four decades, those who owned the bar and worked there knew surprisingly little about him. Given his generosity and the freedom of his lifestyle, they all assumed he was very wealthy. But how he came about his wealth was a question none of them could answer. He didn't seem to have a regular job, or any job for that matter. His parents, both deceased, had been working class people, so it's doubtful he inherited his fortune. He had never been married, which ruled out his getting money from a spouse, or from a spouse's wealthy family. Of course, none of this really mattered to them. What did matter was that Dimitrios came to the bar virtually every night, stayed several hours and always spent a considerable amount of money.

Those who worked at the bar also didn't know the reason for Dimitrios's slight limp when he walked. It was less than a limp, really, and more like he dragged his right leg with each step. They assumed his limp resulted from either a birth defect or an accident. Out of respect for Dimitrios, and not wanting to possibly embarrass him, they never inquired about the cause of his impairment.

What they didn't know, and never would, was that neither an injury nor a birth defect caused Dimitrios to drag his right leg. The real reason was far simpler—a holstered .38 snub-nose pistol was strapped to his ankle. Locating the pistol there rather than utilizing the more traditional shoulder holster was a little something he picked up from watching American movies. He not only thought it was cool, he also deemed it to be a strategically sound location for a weapon. It was out of view, yet it was convenient in case he needed it.

A cool evening breeze kicked up as Dimitrios started the short journey home. His house, which he had grown up in, was barely four blocks away from Antonio's, located in the old historical neighborhood of Plaka. To get home required him to trudge up a small incline, turn right at the top of the hill, walk twenty paces and then cut through an alley that ended at the street in front of his house. It was a journey he had made more times than he could count.

Walking these ancient streets filled Dimitrios with a sense of pride and a feeling that he was part of history. Greece was the true cradle of civilization, and Athens had been the very heart and soul of Greece's greatness. Giants had once walked these narrow stone streets, some of the most celebrated humans who ever existed. He imagined Plato and Aristotle walking several feet in front of him, involved in a deep philosophical discussion. Or perhaps it might be Euripides and Sophocles talking about drama, and how best to present their plays. Maybe the gods occasionally came down from Mount Olympus to walk on these same stones and mingle with the people. During these short walks home, Dimitrios felt as though he was being accompanied by the immortals.

But tonight's trip was more difficult than usual. His step was uncertain, his legs unsteady, and it had nothing to do with the pistol strapped to his ankle. His unsteadiness resulted from drinking too much Ouzo on an empty stomach. No one should drink Ouzo, Greece's most-famous alcoholic beverage, without having first consumed some food. Dimitrios knew this better than most. Most nights he had a snack known as mezedes while drinking. Yet, tonight he drank on an empty stomach. With no food to keep the effects of the alcohol from overwhelming him, Dimitrios was completely drunk. Twice, while in the alley, he had to stop and lean against the wall in order to remain upright.

Never again, he mumbled. It was a promise he had made countless times in the past, and one he would no doubt break countless times in the future. That last thought caused him to giggle out loud.

Arriving at his house, he sat on the steps for almost thirty minutes, letting the cool night air clear his head. Looking up at the sky, he wondered if those were the same stars Socrates gazed upon all those centuries ago. He decided they were. The great Greek teacher had surely reveled in their beauty and mystery then, just as Dimitrios did tonight. Times change but the heavens don't.

Dimitrios felt better now. The dizziness and nausea had passed, his legs had regained their steadiness. Standing, he thought about tonight's agenda. Get some food on his stomach, have some more Ouzo, and watch a movie. Last year he purchased a 50-inch Plasma TV, a DVD player with Blu-ray capabilities, and nearly one-hundred movies. Tonight, he planned to watch one of the classics, maybe *The Searchers*, the John Ford-directed Western starring John Wayne. Or perhaps he would choose Stanley Kubrick's darkly brilliant *Dr. Strangelove*. In the end, Dimitrios decided, he would watch both movies before going to bed.

Opening the door to his house, he walked inside, flipped on a hall light, went into the living room, turned and . . . felt the blood drain from his face. He went white as a ghost. Feeling faint, he braced himself against the wall to keep from tumbling over. Standing in the shadows was a man he had never before laid eyes on, and yet Dimitrios recognized him instantly from photos he had seen. Dimitrios blinked several times, praying the man wasn't real, that this was nothing more than an alcohol-induced hallucination. Unfortunately, it wasn't. The man was very real indeed.

Cain.

"You know who I am," Cain said, more statement than question.

Dimitrios tried to answer but couldn't locate his voice. Fear prevented it. Never in his life could he ever remember being this scared. Never had he experienced such raw panic. His entire body was trembling like a man who had just been pulled from an icy river. At this moment he knew what absolute terror felt like. This had to be what an opponent felt when staring into the eyes of Achilles.

Despite the fear, his mind was racing a thousand miles a second, trying to piece together an out, a way to survive. A way to stay alive.

"You know who I am," Cain repeated.

Dimitrios nodded.

"Good. Then you also know why I'm here."

"No, I don't," Dimitrios finally managed to say.

"I'll give you one guess."

"To kill me."

"And they told me you aren't very intelligent."

Dimitrios tried to steady his nerves. He had to regain control of his emotions, to stay as calm as possible, to put together a plan. To overcome the panic that engulfed him. *Think*. What did he have in his favor? What was his

The List

advantage? *The gun.* That was his salvation. Cain's only weapon was his hands. Wasn't that part of the man's legend? That he only killed with his hands? Well, a gun beats hands every time. If Dimitrios could somehow manage to get the gun, he might survive this. He could kill the greatest assassin of them all. He would stay alive.

"Why do you want to kill me?" Dimitrios said, taking a step backward. "I have done nothing to you."

"Ray Dunlap. You have to answer for his death."

"But I didn't kill Ray Dunlap. Hell, I've never killed anyone in my life."

"You sent the killer," Cain said. "You took money. Dunlap's blood is on your hands. Therefore, you have to die."

Dimitrios realized he had no chance of getting the gun while standing. Maybe, he thought, the Americans weren't so smart after all, strapping a weapon to the ankle. Great in the movies, but not so great in the real world. Too difficult to reach. To have any chance at all, he needed to be seated. Taking another step back, he dropped into the leather chair against the wall, letting his right arm dangle to the side. He also shifted his body slightly to the right, thus preventing Cain from seeing the gun hand. Dimitrios stretched his fingers until he could feel the .38's handle. Simply touching the gun helped steady his nerves.

"I have money," Dimitrios said. "Let me live and I can make you a very rich man."

"No deal. I don't take blood money."

"I can give you the names of Dunlap's killers."

"I know their names," Cain said, taking a step forward.

"You can't possibly know them all."

"Then I've got some work to do, don't I?"

"Please, Cain. Show me some mercy."

"You get the same mercy Ray Dunlap got."

Dimitrios knew the moment of truth had arrived. Waiting and talking were no longer viable options. Nothing was going to change Cain's mind. He had to act . . . now. And it all had to be done in a single, unified motion. Unsnap the holster, secure the pistol, lift it steady in his hand, aim and fire. Do it all in three seconds, tops. Two, if possible.

His fingers found the snap on the holster.

"If you plan on using that weapon, you'd better go for it now," Cain said.

Simultaneously, Dimitrios unsnapped the holster, grabbed the gun and wet his pants.

The gun never cleared the holster.

In less than a second Cain was close enough to Dimitrios to deliver a vicious judo chop to the Greek's neck. The force of the blow drove Dimitrios out of the chair and onto the floor. His survival instincts told him to scramble, but his damaged brain was in no shape to relay the message to his body. Unable to move, he simply laid there, a crippled animal, helpless, waiting for the predator to finish the job.

Cain rolled Dimitrios onto his stomach and kicked him hard in the face, shattering his nose and knocking out several teeth. Then he put a knee in the Greek's back, cupped his chin with both hands, and gave a savage backward pull. The sound of breaking bones echoed off the walls.

Cain had no use for men like Dimitrios Sotirios. He saw them for what they were, scavengers who live on the periphery, never dirtying their own hands, getting rich and fat while letting others do the actual bloody work. He had known many men like Dimitrios, men who believed in war so long as others did the fighting. Combat isn't scary for the man sitting behind an office desk.

Later that evening, as he walked down dark Athens streets, Cain thought about those names Dimitrios wanted to use as a bargaining chip for his life. Mentally, he ran through the list, cataloging them according to priority. First to last, least important to most important. In the end, order didn't matter. They would all be dead within a matter of days. He would see to that.

Ray Dunlap's killers were out there laughing and smiling, living their lives, feeling safe, unaware of the violent storm that was approaching.

A storm that would obliterate them all.

And he was that storm.

CHAPTER SIXTEEN

"I need your help with this, Andy," Kayce Clark said. She was in her New York apartment, sitting at the kitchen table. "Do this for me and I'll owe you big-time."

"You already owe me big-time, Kiddo," Waltz replied, adding, "although if I do help, I'm not sure I'd be doing you any favors."

"Well, help me on this and I'll be your love slave for the next five years."

"The senator won't meet with you, huh?" Waltz said.

"How do I know? I never came close to speaking with him. One of his aides, a Nazi general who calls herself Maggie, told me in no uncertain terms to get lost. According to her, the senator simply cannot take time out from his busy schedule to grant an interview. That's bullshit. If he wanted something he'd call me in a New York minute."

"You didn't tell Maggie the real reason why you wanted the interview, did you?"

"No. I gave her a solid, legitimate reason. Said I wanted to ask Senator Carlin how, as a moderate, progressive Republican, he felt about constantly coming under fire from the far right contingent and the Tea Party bunch. In other words, his being viewed as the enemy within his own party."

"And this Maggie person said no dice?"

"She told me she would pass along my request to the senator. But she won't. He'll never know I called."

"Even if she does, there's no guarantee he'll grant an interview," Waltz said. "Those folks are busy."

"That's why I need your help, Andy."

"What makes you think I would have better luck than you had?"

"Because you're Andy Waltz. Busy people suddenly become unbusy when you call."

"You're giving me too much credit, Kayce."

"No, I'm not."

"Then you're laying on the bullshit a little too thick."

"Will you help me?"

"I'd prefer to talk you out of it."

"We've ridden down that road before," Kayce said. "And my stance on the matter hasn't changed. I'm not going to walk away from this."

Following several seconds of silence, Waltz said, "Let me make a couple of calls, see what apples I can shake from the tree."

"Thanks, Andy. You're the best."

"Just don't get your hopes too high, Kayce. I may run into the same brick wall you came up against."

"Give it your best shot. Okay?"

Exactly twenty-three minutes later Kayce's cell phone rang. She opened it and put it against her ear, fully expecting it to be Andy calling to inform her that he also ran slam-bang into the brick wall known as Maggie. Or perhaps it was Maggie herself, calling to gleefully deliver the news that the senator was still off-limits. But she was wrong. The caller was a man, and he began speaking without introduction or preamble.

"I understand you wish to speak with me, Miss Clark. But I'm afraid that is not possible."

Senator Carlin.

Kayce was so stunned to hear his voice she could not find her own. She was silent as a stone. Never in all her years as a journalist, whether meeting with the famous or non-famous, was she more flabbergasted and speechless than she was at this moment. All she could do was think, *Damn, Andy. How do you do it?*

Finally, after several seconds, which felt like an hour to her, she managed to locate her voice. "Thank you for calling, Senator. Yes, I would like to speak to you about . . ."

"I know what you want to talk about, Miss Clark," the senator interrupted. "Andy Waltz informed me. But like I just said, that is not going to happen."

Damn you, Andy. "But . . ."

"Nothing you say is going to make me change my mind, Miss Clark. Ray Dunlap is dead, and it's very likely my life is in danger. If I speak with you, I could be putting you in harm's way as well. I do not want your death on my conscience."

"I'm not worried about being killed, Senator."

"Then you are a naïve fool, Miss Clark. If a three-star general and a United States senator aren't considered off-limits to these people, how much thought do you think they would give to killing a journalist?"

"What people?"

"Do not pursue this any further, Miss Clark. No story is worth your life."

"I'm not . . ."

"Good day, Miss Clark," Carlin said before hanging up.

Kayce stood there for almost a minute, letting her mind process the information given to her by Senator Carlin. He said a lot, yet told her virtually nothing. Every politician she knew was a master at non-communication, and that included John Carlin. But he had said more than enough to trigger a handful of questions that needed to be answered. Did he truly feel that his life was in danger, or was that mere hyperbole? Was it his way of getting her to walk away from pursuing the story? What was his connection to Ray Dunlap? And who are 'these people' willing to murder a general and a senator? Do they really exist?

What in the hell is going on here?

Kayce was certain Andy could answer many of her questions. But he wouldn't, and she wasn't going to ask him to. No way. Right now, she was pissed at him for ratting her out to the senator. That was a traitorous act on his part. Okay, so she would proceed without his help. She simply had to figure a way to get close to the senator. And there was always a way.

Think, dammit.

All politicians surround themselves with a phalanx of advisers, followers, gofers and a variety of others who fill various roles, some important, some not so important. Primarily, their main function is to protect the politician, either from outside danger or ill-advised acts on his or her part. When danger threatens, they naturally close ranks. It's like a series of concentric circles, with each circle getting smaller in number the closer it is to the person in the center. His inner circle, those he trusts most, would have the fewest number of people. The second ring would be a larger group, the third even larger. Maggie, the iron maiden who nixed the interview, would likely be in the third circle, possibly the second, definitely not the inner circle.

Okay, Kayce thought, in order to reach the person in the middle—Senator Carlin—I have to find a way to crash through his protective barrier. And it can be done. Every wall, no matter how well constructed, has its weak points. A hole, a crack, a leak. There is always one deficiency that allows a way in.

Now all she had to do was find a way to breach the wall of protection surrounding Senator Carlin.

If anyone could show her the way, it was Elena Sanchez. Elena covered politics for *The Washington Post*, and was known to have a close relationship with many in the senate. She was among the few journalists they trusted enough to speak with on the record. Kayce opened her phone, scrolled down the list of contacts until she found Elena's name. She dialed Elena's number and waited. Elena answered after two rings.

"What a surprise," Elena said, laughing. "Didn't expect a call from Miss Pulitzer herself."

"Sometimes even the high and mighty need the assistance of lowly peons like you."

"Still a smart ass, I see. Good to know winning the big prize and making the big bucks didn't change you in the least. So . . . how are you doing, good buddy?"

"I'm hanging in," Kayce said. "But I wasn't kidding when I said I needed your assistance."

"What do you need, and how can I help?"

"I need to interview John Carlin."

"Good luck with that," Elena said.

"What's going on with him? Why is he suddenly so difficult to reach?"

"You tell me," Elena said. "All I know is that in the past two weeks he's gone from being one of the most accessible men on the Hill to one of the least accessible. I'm not sure what's going on, but something certainly is. He's become about as unreachable as the president. That's sad, because he's intelligent, honest and articulate. And that's not something I can say about very many politicians."

"I spoke to someone in his office named Maggie. She shut me down quick."

"Maggie O'Hearn. She's known as the Siegfried Line. Very protective of the senator."

Kayce said, "There has to be one person in Senator Carlin's entourage who has loose lips. Every politician has someone like that, someone who wants to make it known that he or she is in the inner circle. Someone willing to speak off the record. Who, in Carlin's group, would fit the bill?"

"His son. Jason."

"Why would his son be willing to break ranks and inform on his father?"

"Resentment, of course," Elena answered. "Jason is twenty-eight, highly educated and very bright. Despite all that, he lives in his father's shadow. And he knows if he ever achieves any meaningful goals, everyone will say he did so only with his father's help, or because of the family name. He feels trapped. Giving away insider stuff would be his way of letting you know he's in the inner circle, which, of course, he really isn't. But he is the senator's son, so he's probably heard things that are not for public consumption."

"Will I have trouble getting to him?" Kayce said.

"Are you kidding? With your looks, he'll say yes in five seconds, and be trying to get into your pants ten minutes later. Jason fancies himself a real Don Juan. And he is, by any set of standards, a damn good-looking hunk."

"I'll do my best to restrain my sexual urges," Kayce said. "Do you have his phone number?"

"Yeah. Give me a second to look it up."

Kayce wrote down Jason's number, thanked Elena and closed her phone. She smiled.

Didn't need your help, after all, Andy.

CHAPTER SEVENTEEN

David Langley always felt butterflies in his stomach any time he was summoned to meet Lee Bartlett. Although he had known Lee for forty years, and had worked for him thirty-five of those years, he never quite knew what to expect when the old man called. It could be something simple—maybe to have a drink and play gin rummy—or it could be more serious. Langley was aware of several instances when someone summoned to meet with Lee did not leave the room alive.

Langley had no reason to fear Lee. Or none that he could think of. While he no longer held the same power he once did—yes, he was still listed as Director of Operations at Apollo Enterprises, but it was common knowledge that Lee's fair-haired boy, Nick Marlow, actually ran the day-to-day business—he still considered himself to be among the handful of people Lee trusted completely. There was nothing he wouldn't do for Lee Bartlett, and Lee was well aware of that loyalty.

Still . . . those damn butterflies wouldn't go away.

Langley was alone in Lee's huge den, sitting in a leather chair next to the fireplace, slowly sipping the scotch and soda he made moments after arriving. When his glass was empty, he stood, went to the bar and fixed another drink. He had just returned to his chair when Lee and Nick came into the room.

Neither man was smiling. Langley took this as a bad omen.

"So, David, tell me about this phone call that has you so upset," Lee said, while Nick was closing the door. "Is it something real, or something imagined?"

"Real," Langley said, adding almost apologetically, "Unfortunately."

"Details, please," Lee said, sitting in the chair across from to Langley's. Nick stood behind the bar, a sullen look on his face. "Why unfortunately?"

"Because the caller's name is Dantzler. From Lexington, Kentucky."

Lee looked at Nick, then turned back toward Langley and shrugged. "What does any of this have to do with me? With us?"

"Come on, Lee. Johnny Dantzler. You remember him, don't you?"

"Laos? Early seventies?"

"Yes."

"He was a bug that had to be exterminated. So what? That was ages ago. There is no way his death can be traced back to us."

"His wife, Lee. His wife."

"What the fuck are you talking about, Langley?" Nick asked.

Langley ignored Nick's question and spoke directly to Lee. "Dantzler's wife found out some things. How is anybody's guess. But she did. She made inquiries. Called and spoke to me. Hit me with a series of questions, which I shrugged off. Apparently, my non-answers didn't appease her. She threatened to contact people in high places. Could've caused big problems for us. So, I went to Lexington and took care of it."

"How exactly did you take care of it?" Lee asked.

"My first concern was to find out if she had actually contacted anyone. She hadn't. Then I asked her what information she had, and where she obtained this information. She told me what she had, but not who her source was. Once I ascertained that we were in the clear, that she was the only one who could hurt us, I did what needed to be done to ensure that what she did know remained only with her."

"I'm eagerly awaiting the denouement for this tale of yours," Lee said.

"I eliminated her."

"Eliminated her? How?"

"How do you think?"

Nick barked a laugh. "You killed her?"

Langley nodded.

"How?"

"I strangled her. Then I stripped off her clothes and left her body in a Dumpster."

"No way," Nick said, shaking his head. "This is a bullshit story. You haven't got the *cojones* to kill someone. You may have ordered the kill, but you did not do it yourself."

"You would be wrong, Nick."

Lee held up his hand to silence further debate. "Why are you so worried? We're talking thirty-five years ago. If the cops knew anything, or had incriminating evidence, don't you think they would have been knocking on your door before now? I certainly do."

"I agree," Langley said. "But ask yourself this: Why now? Why, after all these years? And doesn't it bother you that it's Dantzler's kid who's doing the investigating?"

"How do you know he's investigating anything having to do with either of his parents? Did he specifically indicate that he wanted to question you?"

"No. All he said was he wanted to speak with me. He didn't say what he wanted to talk about."

"Then it could be about anything. Right?"

"I don't think so."

"So, agree to meet with him. Hear what he has to say. Feel him out. If we determine that he could be a problem, we'll take care of it. Like we did with his father."

"You can *eliminate* him, Langley," Nick said. "Just like you *eliminated* his mother."

Nick's cell phone rang. He opened it, listened intently for less than a minute, then closed the phone, a puzzled look on his face.

"I know that expression, Nick." Lee said. "Usually means bad news."

"Dimitrios Sotirios was found dead in his house early this morning," Nick said. "No clue who might have killed him."

"Think maybe our Russian lady friend took him out?" Lee said.

"He wasn't shot," Nick answered.

"What was the cause of his demise?"

"His neck was broken."

"Interesting," Lee said. He thought about the new information for almost a minute before speaking. "As to the other matter. David, do exactly as I told you. Contact this detective who has you so concerned and see what he wants. Once you've done so, get back to me. We'll proceed from there."

CHAPTER EIGHTEEN

Dantzler had been back in Lexington three days and hadn't heard a peep from Cain. Not that he expected to. Cain was a man of secrets, and sharing an itinerary was not something he would be inclined to do. For men like Cain, keeping information close to the vest was tantamount to staying alive. Being a cop, Dantzler understood this better than most.

Cain left Vegas first, saying only that he had a job he needed to take care of. Dantzler nodded and said nothing. He didn't inquire what the job entailed. Nor did he ask where the job was located, or how long Cain expected to be gone. Dantzler didn't ask those questions for two simple reasons: Cain likely wouldn't have answered, and if he had, the odds were great that he wouldn't tell the truth.

Dantzler spent much of the past two days thinking about Cain. He had to admit that he liked the man, though he and Cain were essentially strangers. Certainly, he respected Cain. It was almost impossible not to. But why? Why did he feel this instant connection to a man he barely knew? Perhaps it was because Cain knew Johnny Dantzler and genuinely seemed to hold him in high regard. That meant a lot to Dantzler, knowing his father was a skilled soldier who could function successfully in the presence of a man Kaleb Daniels called a legend. If Johnny Dantzler hadn't been competent and highly skilled, he would not have operated in the same world as a man like Cain. A man in Cain's position would never associate with anyone who had second-rate talent.

But more than anything else, Dantzler was intrigued by Cain. By where he had been, and by the things he had done. By his aloneness. Dantzler had never met a man more alone than Cain. Whether this was due to his natural disposition or to his occupation, Dantzler couldn't say. Maybe Cain simply chose to be alone.

Given his profession, who could blame him?

Dantzler was so intrigued by Cain that he phoned Houdini and pleaded for details. Initially, Houdini was reluctant to speak about his friend and comrade. But he relented, saying he was only doing so because he also knew and respected Johnny Dantzler. Therefore, he felt no qualms about sharing Cain's story with Johnny's kid.

Cain lived a strange, almost invisible existence, Houdini said. He resided in shadows, in the crease that runs between the normal world we all inhabit, and a darker, dangerous underworld most Americans are unaware of. For almost five decades, beginning before his twentieth birthday, he had been deployed by his government—and others—to perform what could only be termed "off-the-book" deeds. Wet ops. In short, he eliminated people. The man might look like a college professor, Houdini said, but he was more deadly than a heart attack.

The greatest one-man killing machine since Achilles was how Mitch Greenwood, the Vegas cop, described Cain. And Dantzler had no reason to doubt Greenwood's assessment.

How many men had Cain killed? Dantzler wondered. One-hundred? Two-hundred? More? If those numbers were even close to accurate, then that leads to a host of inevitable follow-up questions: How can a man take so many human lives and still retain any measure of sanity? How can you have that much blood on your hands and not go crazy? How do you sleep without continually seeing the faces and hearing the voices of those you have killed? Was a dreamless sleep even possible?

Dantzler had killed three men in the line of duty. Each kill was necessary and justified. He had not lost a night's sleep over any of the three incidents. He was alive, they were dead, and in the end, that's really all that matters. Still, the taking of another human life, regardless of the circumstances, was not something easily shrugged off or forgotten. It stayed buried somewhere inside your brain, a potentially volcanic memory always in danger of erupting and making its way to the surface. How did Cain keep all those memories from rising up and overtaking him? How did he fend off a nightmarish horde of slain insurgents seeking revenge against their assassin? And when Cain looked in the mirror, what did he see staring back at him?

Who did he see staring back at him?

Dantzler's phone chirped. He snapped it open, said, "Jack Dantzler."

"Detective Dantzler, this is David Langley. You left a message asking that I give you a call. Sorry it took so long, but I was out of the country until this morning."

"Not a problem. I'm sure you are very busy. Thanks for working me into your schedule."

"If I'm not mistaken, your message indicated that you have some questions for me. Questions regarding what, exactly?"

"My mother's murder in nineteen seventy-eight."

"Your mother's murder? Why would you want to question me about that?"

"Because your name is in the murder book compiled by the detectives who worked the case. I was wondering if you could explain that."

"First off, let me say how sorry I am about your mother," Langley said. "That's horrible, a real tragedy."

"Thanks for your concern."

"I'm guessing by this phone call that her killer remains at large."

"That's correct."

"Tell me again where you are calling from, Detective."

"I live in Lexington, Kentucky."

"Is that where your mother was murdered?"

"Yes."

"Well, then, you obviously have the wrong David Langley. I've never once set foot in Lexington."

"You weren't here on February the fifth, nineteen seventy-eight?"

"Not then, not ever."

"You're positive?"

"Absolutely."

"Were you ever contacted by Lee Hutchinson or Sam Harper?"

"Those names don't ring a bell. Who are they?"

"The detectives who investigated my mother's murder."

"No. I never spoke with either of those men."

Dantzler said, "Do you know General Lucas White?"

Langley went silent for several seconds. It was a telling silence, one Dantzler had encountered during dozens of interviews with suspects. A silence louder than a blast of thunder. Dantzler knew Langley was thinking how best to answer the question. He could almost hear the man's mind churning.

Langley was having that age-old internal debate all guilty suspects invariably have: continue with the lie or tell the truth. He had come to a fork in the road, and was now deciding which path to take.

"Do you know General Lucas White?" Dantzler repeated.

"I wouldn't say I knew him," Langley finally replied. "But I did meet him on a couple of occasions. Why do you ask about him?"

"His name is also mentioned in the murder book."

"Huh."

"Right next to yours."

"I have no explanation for that," Langley said. "He and I were nodding acquaintances at best. As for the David Langley name in the murder book, well, that simply cannot be me. Like I told you, I've never been to Lexington, Kentucky. Has to be another David Langley."

"Possible, I suppose."

"Detective Dantzler, if there is nothing else, I really need to get going. I'm extremely busy."

Of course you are. "Thanks for getting back in touch with me. It's been a very enlightening conversation."

"Good evening, Detective. Sorry I couldn't be more helpful. And I sincerely hope you catch your mother's killer."

I just did, you lying bastard.

CHAPTER NINETEEN

Jet.

That was the only way anyone referred to the man. Never a proper name, first or last. No mister, no sir, no title. Nothing else. Simply Jet.

Man of mystery.

Nick Marlow had always wondered if this was the man's given name. He had his doubts, but how was one to know for sure? Maybe it was a nickname. Could be he was a former athlete with exceptional speed. A guy who flew like a jet around the bases, or toward the goal line, or up and down the basketball court. Hence, the moniker. That made sense. Athletes get nicknames for all sorts of reasons. Harold Reese became "Pee Wee" because he was a marbles champions when he was a kid; Lawrence Peter Berra became "Yogi" because he looked like a Hindu holy man. Earvin Johnson became "Magic" because of all the tricks he could perform with a basketball. Maybe this guy became "Jet" because he possessed blazing speed.

Possibly, it was an acronym. Short for some long-winded name his parents laid on him at birth. Something as outrageous as Jedidiah Elijah Turnipseed or Josephus Ellsworth Titwiler. With a name like that, Jet sounded pretty good.

But how was Nick to know? In all his years with Lee Bartlett, Nick had never once laid eyes on this mystery man known as Jet. Never heard his voice, never seen a photo. For all Nick knew, the man was a figment of someone's wild imagination. Perhaps he was a phantom. After all, anything was possible in Lee Bartlett's kingdom, including phantoms.

What Nick did know for certain was this: Jet was the only man on this planet that Lee Bartlett considered an equal. Such lofty status belonged to no other human being. And given Lee's enormous sense of self, along with the infinite power he wielded, that was saying a lot. Whoever this Jet was, Nick knew, he had to be someone special for Lee to hold in such high esteem.

Then there were the stories about Jet. So many stories, branching out in all directions, yet they invariably followed the same narrative. Stories Lee told a million times, always with energy and enthusiasm. They were seared into Nick's memory like they had been branded with a hot iron. He could recite them verbatim. Jet is a true visionary, Lee would say, an absolute genius who saw the future. Who predicted the shifting winds of change and made us a fortune. Who read the tea leaves well enough to understand the mood of most Americans. Jet prophesied that after this country's long and disastrous involvement in Vietnam, the military draft was doomed. No more letters from Uncle Sam ordering America's mothers to send their precious baby sons into battle. Now you had to join if you wanted to be killed or maimed or psychologically damaged during combat. An all-volunteer military. This was the future, and Jet saw it before anyone else. And an all-volunteer military translated into fewer boots on the ground during America's next war. And, Jet accurately pointed out, there would always be a next war, somewhere, in some faraway country Americans could neither pronounce nor pinpoint on a map. To successfully wage those wars, America would need mercenaries—independent contractors—to make up for the military manpower shortage. Otherwise, victory could not be achieved.

Jet pointed out another truism, as well. The American people tend to believe they live in a God-fearing, peace-loving country, but the evidence clearly refutes that notion. America is always at war, preparing for a war, or aiding and abetting those who are at war. War is built into this country's economy. With no war America would suffer a drastic financial cataclysm. And Jet was always quick to add that America is by far the biggest arms dealer on the planet. You want military hardware? Come see us. Our store never closes.

If, then, America was going to continue fighting wars with fewer combat personnel, that meant help had to come from the private sector. Jet saw a glimpse of this in Vietnam and Southeast Asia, when elements of the CIA found ways—specifically regarding the production and sale of drugs—to privatize many of their off-the-books activities. Jet saw this as the way of the future. It was Jet who persuaded Lee Bartlett to cough up the cash that led to the forming of Apollo Enterprises, the first private security firm. And that had turned into a gold mine, thanks to Lee's many friends on the Hill who strongly believed in spending whatever it takes to keep America safe from foreign and domestic threats. By providing personnel and weapons to countries around the globe, some friendly with the U.S., some not so friendly, Apollo Enterprises had become a multi-billion-dollar organization.

All thanks to the visionary known as Jet.

Over the years Nick had often asked Lee when he would meet the mysterious Jet. Lee never answered, only smiled enigmatically, and changed the subject. However, when Nick asked the question three days ago, Lee said, "How do you know you haven't met him?"

"Well, have I?" Nick said. "Yes or no?"

"Your guess is as good as mine."

"What the hell does that mean?"

"It means maybe you have, maybe you haven't."

Nick had one more question he wanted to ask Lee but never had. Did the man really exist at all?

For two obvious reasons Nick had his doubts. First, he simply didn't think it feasible that he could have been so close to Lee for three decades and never once had met a man of such importance. The old man practically raised Nick. As a teen-ager, Nick lived with Lee for the better part of five years. Traveled with him everywhere, here and abroad. For him to have never once crossed paths with Jet was inconceivable to Nick.

Second, for all intents and purposes, Nick ran Apollo Enterprises. David Langley was boss in name only. Everyone knew this, even Langley. Nick was listed as Director of Security, but in truth he was the man in charge. Nothing happened unless Nick gave the okay. If Jet had been as involved with Apollo Enterprises as Lee claimed, then Nick would have dealt with the man at some point along the way. Yet, that had never happened.

Therefore, Nick wasn't convinced Jet was a real person. He wondered if perhaps Jet was Lee's alter ego. Like James Bond was Ian Fleming's alter ego. Or perhaps Jet was an amalgam of several different individuals, Nick included. Maybe Lee made up all the stories, then wove them together to fashion his own narrative. This made as much sense to Nick as anything else.

But . . .

Writing off anything Lee Bartlett says as pure fantasy wasn't the wisest thing to do. Only a fool would do so. And that fool likely would be dead within a matter of minutes. Better to believe Lee than doubt him. Sort of a Pascal's Wager kind of deal. Believe him and be wrong, you lose nothing; disbelieve and be wrong, you end up a corpse.

Nick had seen that happen. In fact, he had made it happen on numerous occasions.

CHAPTER TWENTY

While Nick Marlow was pondering the very existence of Jet, the man himself was in London, being escorted by two armed guards into a penthouse suite high atop one of the city's newest and most-luxurious hotels. Jet was slightly familiar with his two guards, both of whom were employees of Apollo Enterprises. He was also familiar with the man who occupied the suite, Sheikh Abdul-Aziz, youngest son of one of Saudi Arabia's wealthiest families.

One of the guards knocked on the door. Two seconds later the door was opened by one of the inside guards, whom Jet was unfamiliar with. The man was maybe five-nine, dark-complected, had a heavy beard and the wary eyes necessary for anyone protecting another individual. He was dressed in what Jet judged to be a moderately priced suit, and he had a pistol strapped to his belt. Most likely a member of Abdul-Aziz's family, Jet concluded. Or a lifelong friend. Definitely someone Abdul-Aziz trusted with his life, unlike the two American guards outside. Trust in foreigners only went so far, no matter how well they were paid, or who was cutting the paychecks.

Although Jet had never met Sheikh Abdul-Aziz, he was familiar with the man's background. Or more precisely, his reputation. Abdul-Aziz had studied in America and England, then like a dutiful son, after completing his studies he went to work in the family business, one of the leading oil producing companies in the world. But Abdul-Aziz's interests were broader than simply selling much-needed oil to thirsty foreign governments. His interests were more political. And as the West's continued presence in the Middle East became more prominent, his ideas became more radicalized. He began to give money to jihadist causes and organizations, including al-Qaeda and the Taliban. The money was laundered, of course, making it virtually impossible to trace back to Abdul-Aziz. There was even one rumor that he was bin Laden's cousin, although that relationship had never been firmly established by U.S. authorities.

Abdul-Aziz was seated at a table, drinking tea from expensive china. He watched as the guard who had opened the door patted Jet down, the third time this had happened since Jet entered the hotel. The guard finished, nodded at Abdul-Aziz as if to say *he's clean*, and then stepped back toward the door. Abdul-Aziz motioned for Jet to take the chair across from him.

"Nasty weather," he said, looking out the window. "I am not a big fan of the rain. Certainly not this much rain."

"Not much we can do about the weather," Jet replied.

"No, I suppose not." Abdul-Aziz held up his cup. "Would you care for something to drink? Tea? Coffee? Orange juice?"

"No, I'm good."

"Then I will get straight to the point," Abdul-Aziz said, gently setting the cup down. "I'm sure you are wondering why I requested this meeting."

"You could say that."

"I am prepared to pay you fifty-million dollars for a particular job."

"I'm listening."

"I will pay the money if you acquire a list of names and addresses for me."

"Names and addresses?"

"Yes."

"Must be some very important names."

"Are you interested?" Abdul-Aziz asked.

Jet had been in on plenty of big deals before, some involving far more than fifty-million dollars, so he wasn't shocked or overwhelmed by the amount. But he was curious. He couldn't begin to imagine what names Sheikh Abdul-Aziz would be willing to pay that much money to obtain.

"I'm still here," Jet answered.

"Excellent."

"What names? What addresses?"

Abdul-Aziz answered Jet's question in less than ten seconds. It was not an answer Jet expected.

"That won't be easy," Jet said, looking out the window as the rain began to give way to a thick wall of fog. Turning back toward Abdul-Aziz, he said, "Fact is, it might be impossible."

"Nothing worthwhile is ever easy," Abdul-Aziz countered. "However, I strongly believe very few tasks are actually impossible to complete. Some are more difficult than others, yes. But in the end, with a little ingenuity, virtually any goal can be achieved."

"Why have you come to me with this offer?"

"Simple. Lee Bartlett."

"Makes sense," Jet said, nodding. "If anyone can do it, Lee's the guy."

"Then the only question is, will he climb on board?"

"Let me give him a call," Jet said, standing.

"Use the bedroom, if you prefer privacy."

"Thanks."

Seven minutes later, conversation completed, Jet walked out of the bedroom and stood next to Abdul-Aziz, who was at the window, looking down at the wet London streets through a telescope. Jet wondered what the man could possibly see through the fog. Several seconds passed in silence. Finally, Abdul-

Aziz pulled away from the telescope and turned to face Jet.

"What was Lee's response?" he said.

"Same as mine—it won't be easy."

"But . . ."

"He's in."

"Excellent," Abdul-Aziz said, clapping his hands.

"What's your time frame?" Jet said.

"Sooner is always preferable to later. But I am a patient man. Let's shoot for no later than a month from today. Is that reasonable?"

"If it can be done at all, then surely it can be done within a month's time."

"It can be done," Abdul-Aziz said, adding, "It *will* be done."

CHAPTER TWENTY-ONE

The Cellar, a hip bar on Dupont Circle, was not Kayce Clark's kind of place. Like many D.C.-area bars, it was too modern, too upscale for her. Too full of self-absorbed Gen X/Yuppie types. She preferred Irish pubs or darkly lit taverns, where the patrons, mostly men and women who had long ago given up chasing impossible and youthful dreams, freely discussed and debated subjects ranging from world affairs to politics to sports to sex. They told off-color jokes, drank hard liquor straight, smoked and made no apologies for indulging in any of these vices.

Kayce had never been to The Cellar but she had heard about it from friends and colleagues, some of whom were regulars. Standing outside the front entrance, having been given the scouting report by those familiar with the place, she knew exactly what was awaiting her once she stepped inside. Men and women in their late twenties and early thirties, most of whom were attorneys or low-level government employees, all of whom were filled with a burning desire to climb the corporate ladder. The men would be dressed in expensive suits, ties loosened, their hair gelled and slicked back. Kayce was convinced they all aspired to look like either Al Pacino in *The Godfather 2* or Michael Douglas in *Wall Street*. Most of the women would be in nice, conservative dresses, either all black or all white, that reached to mid-knee. Others, the more aggressive ones, would be in pants suits. Perfect hair, perfect teeth, trim figures. They would wear minimal jewelry, very little make-up, and their smiles would come quick and easy. They would laugh and act deferential when the men spoke, but deep down inside they felt superior to their male counterparts. And more often than not they would be right. These were not weak sisters. Even though they dressed like June Cleaver, their attitude was strictly Jane Fonda.

And all of them, male and female, would be buff and tan. To these folks, image was everything. Appearance counts plenty when trying to climb corporate and social ladders.

Not Kayce's scene at all.

What The Cellar needed, Kayce decided, was a touch of the sluttish. And the place was about to get it.

She wore a low-cut sleeveless red dress that ended four inches above her knees. Hoop earrings, and red glitter five-inch heels rounded out the risqué ensemble. Bright red lipstick and plenty of mascara brought her face to life. If she had to describe her appearance, she would say high-priced New York City call girl. This look, she knew, would garner attention from every straight guy and gay woman in the place. It was her *hey, folks, the Queen has arrived* look.

In truth, she didn't care what any of them thought. Except Jason Carlin. She was here to see him, and if he was half the horn dog Elena Sanchez said he was, he would be drawn to her like paparazzi to Brad and Angelina. Given the way she was dressed, Jason would have to be gay to not be interested.

Kayce's goal was to be the hottest broad in the joint, and judging by the number of heads swiveling to check her out, she had succeeded. Before she was halfway to the bar, four men and two women offered to buy her a drink. She politely refused their offers with a smile and shake of the head. If anyone was going to buy her a drink, it would be Jason Carlin.

Jason was at the far end of the bar, talking to two women. He was a hunk, like Elena said, but not *the* hunk. Tall, broad shouldered, he looked like a second-string linebacker, or the lead actor's best friend in a romantic movie. Not quite Ryan Gosling, but close enough to set female hearts fluttering. Kayce knew it was usually a mistake to make a flash judgment of an individual, but, like most humans, she did so anyway. Her instant assessment of Jason was that he was friendly, intelligent in a limited way, not much given to introspection or self-reflection, and adept at using false bravado to mask deep insecurities.

Typical, she figured, for the child of a famous parent.

When Jason saw Kayce coming toward him, he set his empty glass on the bar, excused himself from his two disappointed companions and worked his way forward.

Pointing his finger at Kayce, he said, "So, I finally get to meet the hotshot writer who won some big award?"

"That would be me," Kayce said, adding, "Award-winning hotshot writer in the flesh."

"Haven't seen you here before."

"First time."

Jason spread both arms like an orchestra conductor, said, "It's a great place, as anyone who has ever been here will tell you. The bartender, Spider, makes the best mixed drinks in the D.C. area. He never cheats you on the alcohol."

"That's good to know."

"I was surprised to get your e-mail. Surprised and delighted, I might add. It's not every day a famous and beautiful lady contacts me from out of the blue."

"Well, it was important that I meet with you."

"I like the sound of that," Jason said.

Easy, boy. I'm only here to use you. "Think we could find a place a little quieter?" Kayce said. "I can barely hear what you're saying."

"Sure. We can get a table in the back. Would you like a drink?"

"What are you having?"

"Glenlivet and soda."

"Make it two."

Jason ordered the drinks, pulled out a twenty and made a big show of telling Spider to keep the change. After getting their drinks, he led Kayce to a table near the back wall. When they were seated, a waitress placed their drinks on a napkin and told them to let her know when it was time for a refill.

"Okay, tell me. Why did you want to see me?" Jason said.

"I'm thinking of writing a story and I need your help."

"How can I help you?"

"Because it involves your father and—"

"That's exactly what I figured," Jason snapped. "You only want to use me in order to get to my father. I should have known."

"No, that's not why I wanted to meet with you. If you'll let me continue, I will explain."

Jason finished his drink in a single gulp, caught the waitresses' eye, lifted his glass and ordered two more. "Okay, so explain away."

"Everyone writes stories about the person in power . . . that's been done to death. What I want to do is a little off the beaten path. Approach it from a different angle. I want to do a story on the individual behind the person in power. In this case, the one person your father trusts the most. I'm talking about the person who has the senator's back, who knows all the secrets, who would give up his life to protect the boss. That's who I want to write about. And I was thinking you could tell me who that person might be."

"Sure, that's an easy one."

"Who would you recommend?"

"Me."

Thank you, Jason. You're even easier than I thought you would be. "Come on, Jason, I'm being serious here."

"So am I." Jason waited until their drinks arrived before continuing. "Come on, think about it. I'm the senator's *son*, for christsakes. Who could possibly be closer to him than his own flesh and blood?"

"You may be his son, but you aren't in his inner circle."

"So what? That's no big deal. Besides, that inner circle shit is way overrated."

"Yes, it is a big deal. It has to be someone your father confides in on a daily basis."

"Who do you have in mind?" Jason asked.

"I was thinking either Ted Dalton or Anne Rossman."

Jason took a drink, said, "I know everything they know and then some.

Plenty more than they know. Dad shares information with me when we are home alone. Information neither Ted nor Anne know."

Okay, Jason, I've got you hooked. Time to reel you in. "Put yourself in my shoes, Jason. If I go to my editor and try to sell this idea to him, he'll laugh me out of the office. He will insist that I use either Ted or Anne as the centerpiece of my story. That's the reality."

"Then your editor is an idiot."

"No. My editor wants to get it right."

"Well, there's a simple way to prove I'm the one you're looking for."

"And how would you propose to do that?" Kayce asked.

"Ask me a question relating to my father. Ask about anything. If I answer, you'll know I'm right."

Yes. The fish has been caught. Kayce leaned back, took a sip of scotch and furrowed her brow like she was deep in concentration. After a few seconds, she said, "Your father and General Ray Dunlap were working on something. What was it?"

Jason's smile disappeared and his expression turned deadly serious. Leaning forward, he said, "Ask me another question."

"So, you *don't* know everything your father is into, right?" Kayce said.

"Ask another question. I won't answer that one."

"Won't or can't?"

Jason shrugged, took another drink and looked away.

Kayce stood. "Let me give you a friendly piece of advice, Jason. Exaggerating your importance in the world may make you feel better, but it's also a very risky thing to do. It's risky because you're always one step away from being exposed as a fraud. And when that happens, like right now, it's not very becoming."

Kayce pointed at her glass. "Thanks for the drink, Jason. And sorry things didn't work out."

As Kayce started to walk away, Jason grabbed her arm. "Please, sit," he said, "I'll answer your question, but only on the condition that you will not use it in your story. You have to give me your word on that. This information cannot find its way into print. Can you give me that assurance?"

"Jason, this story is about an individual's role in the senator's life, not about any particular policy. It's a profile, not an expose. So, yes, I can give you that assurance."

Jason took another drink, this time draining his glass. "Are you familiar with Apollo Enterprises?"

"Vaguely. It's a private security firm, isn't it? Kind of like Blackwater."

"It's a helluva lot bigger than Blackwater ever was. They do all kinds of shit, all around the globe."

"Okay. So what?"

"My father was in the process of beginning an investigation into Apollo Enterprises. The investigation was based on information provided by General Dunlap."

So that's what General Dunlap wanted to talk to me about. "Was in the process?"

"Yeah, the investigation is on hold for the time being."

"What was the basis for the investigation?" Kayce said.

"That, I don't know. I don't think anyone other than my father and the general could answer that question for you."

"Well, it's for sure I won't get the answer from General Dunlap," Kayce said. "Think his murder was related to the investigation?"

"My father certainly thinks so," Jason said. "He now has twenty-four-hour security."

"So that's why he's suddenly become unreachable."

Jason nodded his head.

"Are you okay, Jason?"

"Yeah, but I am worried about him."

"I'm sure you are. But, if he has round-the-clock protection, I'd say he'll be all right."

"I sure hope so."

Kayce said, "Thanks for the information, Jason. You more than redeemed yourself."

"You'll do the story, then?"

"I'll run it by my editor, see what he says. If he gives the green light, then I'll contact you and we'll get started on it."

"And you won't use what I just told you, right?"

"You have my word, Jason. It will not be in the profile I do on you."

CHAPTER TWENTY-TWO

Lee Bartlett chuckled as he watched Nick Marlow make short work of a steak that only a few minutes ago was the size of a hubcap. "I take it your steak was satisfactory," he said.

"Excellent," Nick answered.

Lee pushed his plate away, raised his arm and snapped his fingers. A waiter was at their table before the sound died away. Even waiters knew better than to tarry when Lee Bartlett summoned them.

The waiter, a tall, thin man who looked like he could have been the town's undertaker in an old cowboy movie, noticed that Lee had barely touched his food. Picking up the plate, he said, "Was the salad not up to your standards, sir?"

"No, the salad was perfectly fine, Phillip," Lee said. "I'm not hungry, that's all. You see, old age has robbed me of many things, and appetite is, I'm sorry to say, one of them. So in lieu of healthy food, just bring me another scotch. How about you Nick? Would you care for something to wash down that cow you just inhaled?"

"Heineken," Nick answered, looking at his watch.

"Time seems to be of utmost importance to you, Nick. That's the fourth time you've consulted your watch. Got some place you have to be?"

"Yeah, I do."

"And how is the lovely Candace doing these days?"

"Great."

"That's nice. Send her my warmest regards when you see her. I've always thought very highly of Candace."

"I will."

Lee waited until Phillip brought their drinks, and then said, "Do you love her, Nick?"

"I wouldn't go that far."

"She loves you, you know. But, then, how is a man to know for sure when the lady in question is a prostitute?"

Nick shrugged. "Come on, old man. You didn't bring me to the most expensive steak house in Manhattan to discuss my love life. What's on your mind?"

"Such impatience. Haven't I warned you a million times that you need to take it down a few notches or you're going to have a coronary? You need not go full throttle every minute of every day. But . . . you are a young man, and you have a beautiful lady awaiting your arrival, so I can forgive your lack of patience. Believe it or not, Nick, but I too was once a young man."

"Okay, so out with it. Why am I here?"

"I brought you here because I have two pieces of information I want to share with you. I also have a task for you to perform."

"I'm all ears."

"For the time being, our plan regarding the senator has been put on hold. You'll need to contact our Russian friend and tell her to stand down."

"Why? I thought removing him from the scene was essential. What changed?"

"My source tells me the good senator has postponed the investigation indefinitely. For now, at least, it seems we are in the clear. Until I hear otherwise, there is no need to take risky and unnecessary action."

"You trust your source?"

"Absolutely." Lee sipped his scotch. "I can only deduce from this that the general had not provided enough details for the senator to proceed with his investigation. Of course, I am fully aware that the senator will continue digging, and that at some point in the future he might once again become a threat. When that happens he will be dealt with accordingly."

"The Russian will be disappointed."

"Yes, she does seem to thoroughly enjoy her work," Lee said. "But that comes as no surprise. In my experience, I have found Russians to be genuinely ruthless people. I cannot claim to know why this is so. But in the case of our lady friend, I can tell you that she comes by her ruthlessness naturally. Her aunt, Nastasia, was more cold-blooded than any reptile you might happen upon. But Nastasia had class, which is not something you find in many Russians. They are generally a dour and negative people. Not many would recognize joy or happiness if it slapped them in the face. Nastasia wasn't like that at all."

"Okay, enough with psychoanalyzing the Russian people. I'm not interested. What's your second piece of information?"

"Ah, yes, I forgot. You are in a hurry. The lovely Candace is eagerly anticipating the arrival of her Prince Charming."

"Speak, please, before I die of old age."

"A certain individual has offered to pay us a substantial sum of money if we deliver a list of names and addresses. I have given him my assurance that we will get him what he requests."

"How substantial a sum of money?" Nick asked.

"Fifty million."

"Whose names and addresses could possibly be worth fifty-million dollars?"

Lee told him.

"And who is paying?" Nick said.

"Abdul-Aziz."

Nick shook his head and frowned. "Bad idea, Lee."

"Why is it a bad idea?"

"For starters, Abdul-Aziz is a maniac. Everybody knows that. He can't be trusted."

"I don't want his trust, only his money," Lee said.

"You have more money than most countries, old man. How much money do you need?"

"In the long run, it's not about the money, Nick. It never has been. That's what you don't seem to understand. It's about the challenge, the thrill."

"You need to take a pass on this one. Those guys on the list, they are heroes. What they did was right, and it was justified. It would be wrong to help take them out."

"Why, Nick. I never figured you for a moralist."

"I'm not, and you know it. But this is simply wrong. It's treason."

"Half of what we do is treasonous, Nick. That's never troubled you before."

"This is different."

"How is it different?"

"Too many innocent people would die."

"Innocent people die every day, Nick. That's a sad fact of life."

"Say no to this one, Lee. It's not worth it."

"Too late. Jet has already informed Abdul-Aziz that I'm in."

"How do you plan on getting the list?" Nick asked.

"From Benjamin Parker."

"He won't give up the names. No way."

"Oh, he'll give them up, Nick. I'll make sure of that."

"I don't like it."

"Duly noted."

"Is that it?" Nick said. "I need to get going."

"The task I mentioned earlier? I want you to check with David on his status concerning this detective from Kentucky. The more I think about it, the more troubled I become. Find out if David has communicated with the detective. If he has, get him to tell you how their discussion went. Once you do that, get back with me and we'll evaluate the situation."

Nick stood. "Anything else?"

"No, that's it for now." Lee put his hand on Nick's arm. "I'm sorry you disagree with me on the list project. But you're a grown man and you have every right to dissent. I respect that. However, I expect you to be ready to perform any tasks that I might require, no matter how repugnant you judge them to be."

"I have never failed you in the past, old man. And I will never fail you in the future. You may not realize it, hell, you may not even want to acknowledge it, but I'm the only person in the entire world you can fully trust. The *only* one."

Lee smiled, nodded and gave Nick's arm a gentle squeeze. "Say hello to Candace for me," he said.

CHAPTER TWENTY-THREE

Killing Ray Dunlap was one of the easiest jobs Sonia Ivanovna ever had. So simple, in fact, that she rated it no better than boring. There was no challenge, and without a challenge there was no thrill. No sense of genuine achievement. No grand feeling of accomplishment. If all her jobs were this unfulfilling, she may as well work in a toll booth, or be a dull American housewife.

Yet, despite the ease in which her task unfolded, she had done the standard due diligence. Just like she always did. Never, ever take anything for granted. Prepare for all contingencies and expect the unexpected. Success depends on preparation. And preparation keeps you alive and out of jail. This was the first rule for any assassin.

She spent three days following and observing her prey. Studied and memorized his habits. Rode up on an elevator with him—disguised, of course —to learn what suite he was in. Trailed him when went to eat, or to take a stroll down the main strip. Ascertained that he was traveling alone, which only made her job that much simpler.

When the time came to eliminate him she walked up the stairwell, to one floor above his suite, and went into a maintenance room she knew to be empty. There, she put on jeans, a sweater, black windbreaker and a baseball cap. She replaced her flat shoes with sneakers. After putting on the mustache and dark shades, she went down the stairwell, checked to make sure the hallway was clear, then moved quickly to the general's suite. She knocked three times, and when the general opened the door she shouldered her way inside, pointed her P239 with silencer at him and ordered him to turn around. Then she shot him once in the head at the base of the skull. Just the way she had been taught by her KGB teachers. After checking to make sure he was dead, she moved quickly up the stairwell and into the maintenance room. There, she stripped off her outer layer of clothing, leaving only the beautiful sleeveless dress she had on underneath. Next, she took off the sunglasses and peeled off the mustache. After removing her sneakers and replacing them with her regular shoes, she stuffed the old clothes into a suitcase, extended the handles and walked to the elevator. Five minutes later she was one of maybe two dozen people leaving the Bellagio, just another happy customer in search of a taxi.

The easiest half-million she ever earned.

But . . .

Killing Senator John Carlin was not going to be quite so easy.

In fact, based on what she had seen during five days' surveillance, this might prove to be one of her more challenging assignments. Of course, killing someone—anyone—wasn't difficult at all. Every assassin and every politician was aware of that. John Kennedy once said something to the effect that if they want to kill you bad enough, they can do it. He couldn't have been more prophetic. The difficult part was getting away with it. Just ask Lee Harvey Oswald.

Sonia was parked on a quiet tree-lined street in a ritzy section of Georgetown. She was approximately twenty yards away from the senator's townhouse, and on the opposite side of the street. It was late afternoon, with maybe another hour of daylight remaining in what had been a magnificently beautiful day. She had only been in this spot for the past thirty minutes. To avoid suspicion, she parked in a different place every two hours. And each day she drove a different rented vehicle, and wore a different disguise. It was her firm belief that you can never be too careful.

The senator's routine had not varied once during the time she had been watching him. He left his townhouse at precisely seven a.m. and returned home at precisely seven p.m. He never left his office during the day, nor did he leave his house at night. The lights inside stayed on until around midnight, then the place went dark.

According to a recent newspaper article, his wife, Cynthia, was at their house in Indianapolis. Sonia doubted this. More than likely, she surmised, this was nothing more than misinformation. Probably, Cynthia was hidden safely away at some place on Martha's Vineyard, or up in the Hamptons.

From her research, Sonia knew that the senator's daughter, Vicki, was studying law at Harvard, and his son, Jason, lived in the D.C. area and worked for his father. Neither son nor daughter visited the senator during the time Sonia had been observing him. Nor had anyone else for that matter. The senator was living a hermit-like existence.

Well, this was only half true. On the inside, he was a solitary figure. On the outside, however, he was never alone.

The senator had round-the-clock protection, no doubt brought on by the death of General Ray Dunlap. A black sedan sat parked in front of the senator's townhouse. Inside were two agents. Sonia didn't know if they were federal, state, local or private. However, based on the way they operated, and how coordinated their movements were, she would put her money on federal, with either the FBI or the Secret Service being the most likely suspects.

At precisely seven o'clock each morning, a second black sedan would pull up behind the one that had been there all night. It would also have two agents inside. All four men would then exit their vehicles, walk up the steps to the townhouse, and then one of them would knock on the door. The senator would emerge and immediately be surrounded by the four men. They would walk him to the lead car and see him safely into the back seat. Once the car drove away, the second car would move up a few feet, and those two agents would spend the next twelve hours guarding an empty residence. The departing car would drive the senator to his office building, where he would be escorted inside. Twelve hours later the same routine would occur. A second sedan would show up, the four men would get out, surround the senator, and walk him briskly up the steps and into his townhouse. Then the agents who had been on the job all day would take off for home.

Sonia was also aware that an alley ran directly behind the senator's house, and that a black sedan was parked there around the clock. Presumably, the agents inside worked twelve-hour shifts just like their counterparts out front.

Sonia had no way of knowing how long such intense security measures had been in place, or how long they would last. Having this information would certainly make her prospects for a successful kill that much better. She could simply wait until security was relaxed, and then pop the senator with little or no problem. If that were the case, she would have a wide range of options for getting the job done. With the current setup, however, her options were severely limited.

Using a rifle was the obvious choice. There were no shortage of locations from where she could fire the weapon, and more important, there were plenty of excellent escape routes. She was an exceptionally skilled marksman, and had in fact successfully used a rifle on several previous jobs. But would she be able to get a clear shot at the senator? That was the big question. The four agents who escorted him to and from his house and car were all taller than the senator. When they surrounded him he was barely visible. Therefore, a clear shot would only be available if something unforeseen happened, like one of the agents tripping or dropping something, then bending down to pick it up. But what were the odds of that happening? Thousand to one at best. That would be a lucky break, and Sonia didn't believe in relying on luck for anything. No assassin ever did.

What about attacking from the rear? From the alley? She could wait until the middle of the night, when one or both of the agents were asleep, and take them out. No problem. But eliminating the agents wouldn't solve what would be the bigger problem—how to get into the senator's house. Every entrance would be locked tighter than a Fort Knox vault filled with gold, and there would undoubtedly be a very sophisticated alarm system in place. Maybe even a back-up in case the main system failed or was breached. Sonia's expertise was killing, not disarming security systems. So that plan was *kaput*.

Sonia ran through a list of different possibilities, quickly eliminating each one. Poison, car bomb, grenade . . . nothing fit. She also thought about getting to the senator through his children, and in particular, his son, who lived in the D.C. area. But she quickly dismissed that plan as well. Too complicated, too many unknown factors, too little chance of success.

How, then? She didn't know just yet. This one she would have to ponder.

Just as Sonia was about to start the car and drive back to the hotel, she saw a man turn the corner and begin walking down the sidewalk that ran in front of the senator's townhouse. He was dressed casually and seemed to be in no hurry. Probably someone from the neighborhood out for a quiet evening stroll, Sonia thought. She kept her eyes trained on him as he continued moving forward. She wasn't sure why, but she could not take her eyes off him. There was something about the man that seemed oddly familiar to Sonia. She had that feeling you sometimes get when you think maybe you know a person but can't quite place him.

When the man came within twenty feet of the senator's house, the two agents exited the sedan and moved quickly toward him, hands on their weapons. From the opposite end of the street a man and a woman hurried toward the two agents and the stranger. Sonia recognized them immediately. She had seen them sitting on a bench in the park located at the end of the street, and had judged them to be lovers sharing a quiet sunset together. She silently admonished herself for not having recognized them as agents.

Sonia picked up her binoculars and tried to get a closer look at the stranger. She couldn't; the four agents had him surrounded, and the one directly in front of the man was blocking her view. The agents were tense and alert, exactly what you would expect from consummate professionals. The lead agent spoke for a few seconds, most likely demanding that the stranger identify himself and explain his reason for being on this street, as if he really needed to. The man, a citizen of this country, had every right to be here, but the agents charged with protecting a United States senator wanted to make sure everything was kosher. They weren't about to let him pass without first being questioned and cleared. The man's rights be damned; keeping the senator safe trumped such trivial things like civil liberties.

Then something strange happened. The four agents' body language and demeanor changed completely. They instantly went from tense to relaxed, from stone-faced to smiling. It was almost as if the agents realized they were in the presence of a movie star or a famous athlete. Two of the agents shook his hand. Another, the female, patted him on the shoulder. Four tough, professionally trained agents were suddenly behaving like star-struck teen-agers.

Who the hell is this man, Sonia wondered.

Whoever he was, the man had serious clout. The agents led him down the sidewalk and up the steps to the senator's front door. The lead agent knocked, then stepped back as the senator opened the door. The stranger spoke briefly, the senator nodded, opened the door wider and invited him in. The lead agent tried to follow, but the senator motioned for him to remain outside. The agent's displeasure with being dismissed showed in his body language and the disappointed look on his face. But like any good public servant, he accepted his orders and did as he was told. He and his partner returned to the black sedan. Their two counterparts went back to the park.

For the next half-hour Sonia sat in the car and waited. Darkness was beginning to descend. The threat of rain hung heavy in the air. *Who is that man,* she asked herself over and over. *I know I have seen him before. But where? When?*

While Sonia was silently trying to answer her many questions the senator's door opened. The stranger, his back to Sonia, said a few parting words to the senator, shook his hand, turned and headed down the steps. The two agents in the sedan got out and spoke to him. As he was acknowledging them, Sonia trained her binoculars on his face.

And almost without realizing it, she suddenly began to tremble. She felt as if an electric shock had rocked her insides, blistering her with heat, yet she felt icy sweat covering her body. Her breathing was quick and shallow, her heart was racing. *This is not happening to me,* she silently whispered. *This is how a coward reacts, and I am no coward. Fear is the ultimate enemy. I cannot allow fear to overwhelm me.* Yet, even as she admonished herself, she remembered how her KGB teachers had displayed fear when speaking of this man.

There is no shame in being fearful when in the presence of a lion.

Summoning every ounce of inner strength, she willed herself to calm down, to slow her breathing, to stop her hands from shaking. She had to regain control of her emotions. Not easy to do, not under these circumstances.

Her hands steady, she looked through the binoculars once again. She had to know. She had to be sure. And she was.

It was *him.*

Cain.

The legend in the flesh, standing not more than a few yards away. *Here, right in front of my eyes,* she thought. Seldom had she experienced such a feeling of excitement. This was a thrilling moment. This was what she had been hoping for. Cain was in the same city she was in. The quarry had come to her. How fortuitous. How convenient.

How . . . perfect.

She had dreamt of this moment, and the gods had delivered.

Cain was now in her sights, and when Sonia had a target in sight, she never missed.

And she wouldn't miss this time.

The greatest assassin of them all would be dead within a matter of days.

*****

As Sonia was driving away, her cell phone buzzed. She snapped it open and checked the name on the caller ID. Nick Marlow.

"Yes," she said.

"Stand down," Nick said.

"For how long?"

"Indefinitely."

"What about payment?"

"You'll get your money."

"*All* of it?"

"Yes, Sweetie, every ruble."

"Excellent. And I will expect more if and when I'm needed."

"Money is not an issue."

"Will I hear from you or the Greek?"

"You haven't heard? The Greek is no longer among the living."

"Heart attack or stroke?" Sonia asked.

"Broken neck."

Cain.

"Then I will await your call."

Sonia closed the phone and dropped it on the seat next to the binoculars. Secretly, she was pleased with this recent turn of events. Killing the senator no longer held any interest for her. She now had a new and more challenging target.

And one infinitely more dangerous.

For specific reasons she had not bothered to inform Nick Marlow that Cain had met with the senator. Or that she suspected Cain of killing Dimitrios Sotirios. Perhaps she should have, but had she done so, it would only have gummed up her plans. Learning that Cain was involved, Nick Marlow and Lee Bartlett would, in all likelihood, order her to go ahead and eliminate the senator as planned. She didn't want that. She didn't want any obstacles standing in her way. She wanted no unnecessary distractions.

Her focus now was solely on one target, one man.

Cain.

CHAPTER TWENTY-FOUR

Dantzler wasn't surprised when Cain arrived at his house an hour before sunset. He figured Cain would show up at some point, if for no other reason than to have a comfortable and cheap place to crash for the night. What did surprise Dantzler, though, was that Cain knocked on the front door rather than enter via his standard cat-burglar method.

"Business all taken care of?" Dantzler asked, as he led Cain down the hallway and into the kitchen.

"Yes."

"Care for something to drink?"

"What are you drinking?"

Dantzler held up his empty glass. "Pernod and orange juice."

"I certainly don't want *that*. You have any beer?"

"Smithwick's."

"Yeah, Smithwick's sounds good."

Dantzler opened the refrigerator, retrieved a beer and handed it to Cain. After mixing another drink for himself, Dantzler said, "Let's go out on the deck."

"Nice place you have, Detective," Cain said. "How long have you lived here?"

"About fifteen years," Dantzler answered. "What about you? Where do you call home?"

"St. Augustine."

"Near the ocean?"

"*On* the ocean."

"Sweet. House or condo?"

Cain took a drink, said, "House. It's a little smaller than this one. But it's plenty roomy enough for one person."

"You ever been married?"

"No."

"Never found the right woman?"

"Never found the right time."

"Me neither. Maybe that's because we're both chasing ghosts."

"Or being chased by them." Cain picked up the photo of a young Dantzler standing in front of his parents. "Was this taken in Florida?"

"Yeah. About four months before my father was killed." Dantzler took a sip, then said, "How well did you know my father?"

"Very well."

"What was he like?"

Cain stared at the photo for a few more seconds before carefully placing it back on the table. "Tough, intelligent, brave, fearless. You father was a soldier's soldier and a man's man. I liked him a lot."

"Is that the truth, or are you saying it because you think that's what I want to hear?"

"I never lie about a man's abilities."

"Thanks for saying it." Dantzler pointed at Cain's beer. "Ready for a refill?"

"Not yet."

"I know who murdered my mother," Dantzler said.

"Oh, yeah? Who?"

"David Langley."

"And precisely how did you come by this information?"

"From Langley."

"You spoke with David Langley?"

"Yes."

"When?"

"Two days ago."

"And what? He confessed?"

"No. But when I asked him if he knew Lucas White, he hesitated for a split second before answering. It was a classic response, one I've seen from hundreds of suspects I've interrogated. They are trying to work out how best to answer. Continue with the lie or tell the truth."

"And what did Langley say?" Cain asked.

"That he knew *of* Lucas White, but didn't know him very well."

"You don't believe that's possible?"

Dantzler shook his head. "No, I don't. I am positive he was lying."

"Hesitation during a phone conversation? That's very thin evidence."

"The man was lying," Dantzler insisted. "You knew Lucas White. Don't you think it's possible that he knew David Langley on some level? Maybe even worked with him in some capacity?"

"Possible, I guess. Turns out Lucas did have his share of secrets, many of which I knew nothing about." Cain set the empty beer bottle on the table. "But you can't bring a man in for murder based solely on possibilities and silence. And so what if he did or didn't know Lucas? How does that connect Langley to your mother's murder? No, Detective, you need something more concrete. And after all these years, I don't know where you'll find genuine evidence."

"Well, for starters I'm going to pay David Langley a visit," Dantzler said.

"I want him to answer my questions face to face."

Cain shook his head. "You're not going anywhere near David Langley, Detective. For the time being, he's off limits."

"Wrong. This time I'm telling you how it's going to be. I'm going to question David Langley. End of story."

"Do so and you'll be making a big mistake. Maybe even a fatal mistake."

"Why are you suddenly so reluctant? Didn't you agree to help me find my mother's killer?"

"The situation has changed," Cain said. "It's Ray Dunlap's killer that I'm after. Finding the person who murdered your mother . . . that has to come later."

"I'm tired of waiting."

"Wait a little longer, Detective. Until I can help you."

"No. If you can't help me—or don't want to help me—that's fine," Dantzler said. "I'll go alone."

"You're a whole lot more stubborn than your father was, you know that? He understood when common sense came into play. I'm not sure you do. You're also forgetting what I told you the first time we met. You need to think like a cop, not like an aggrieved son."

"I'm a cop who simply wants to put a bad guy away, that's all. I would appreciate your help, but if you say no, that's okay. Like I said, I'll fly solo."

Cain picked up the empty beer bottle and handed it to Dantzler. "Get me another one of these and I'll give you some good news."

When Dantzler returned with the beer, he said, "Okay, let's hear the good news."

Taking the bottle, Cain said, "First, let me have your cell phone."

Dantzler handed the phone to Cain. He punched in the number and waited.

"Houdini. Yeah, Athens was fine. Everything went well. In Lexington, with Johnny's kid. Listen, I need you to get me some things. I need to know everything about the Apollo Enterprises compound. *Everything.* Aerial views, building layouts, wiring, security systems. I want to know where every single toilet is in that place. Also, personnel files on the top honchos. When? A couple of days at the most. I'll wait to hear from you."

Cain closed the phone and handed it to Dantzler.

"You were in Greece?" Dantzler said.

"Briefly."

"Achilles returned home."

"What does that mean?" Cain asked.

"Nothing." Dantzler took a drink. "The good news? I'm still waiting."

Cain said, "Ray Dunlap and Senator John Carlin were about to launch an investigation into Apollo Enterprises. It was in the early stages and was supposed to be top secret. But shit like that never stays secret. Not in

Washington, D.C. Too many leaks, too many spying eyes, too many people easily bought off. Had the investigation gone forward, Apollo Enterprises would have been put out of business and its leaders would have been indicted and sent to prison. Ray Dunlap was murdered because certain individuals want to shut down—or at the very least stall—the investigation."

"How do you know this?"

"I met with Carlin two days ago. He told me."

"Isn't he concerned about being the next target?" Dantzler said. "If he's running the show, he has to be in their crosshairs."

"Carlin's well-protected," Cain said. "And he's put the word out that the investigation will not go forward. That's not true, of course. It's still on-going. But very low key."

"Why was Apollo Enterprises being investigated?"

Cain took a drink of beer, set the bottle on the table and said, "Over the past quarter-century, more and more private security firms have been hired by our government to perform duties that once upon a time were strictly performed by our military and by government agencies like the CIA or FBI. Private firms were contracted by the U.S. to handle those duties because our military was being stretched so thin. With no military draft, there was a manpower shortage. In essence, because of this shortage, we created a paramilitary force comprised of civilians. These security firms provided a wide array of services, ranging from actual combat, to security, to transportation, to guarding and interrogating prisoners. Naturally, they didn't work on the cheap. They received billions of U.S. tax-funded dollars. It was a sweet deal for them in many ways. And what made it even sweeter was that they were subjected to very little oversight. They could act with almost complete impunity. They laughed at things like the Uniformed Code of Military Justice, or the protocols set forth by the Geneva Convention. They could be outlaws and get away with it. You with me so far?"

Dantzler smiled. "You keep talking and I'll do my best to keep up."

"Apollo Enterprises, being the first of these private security firms, has raked in untold billions of dollars. At its peak, Apollo employed about six-hundred men. Most were ex-military guys with combat experience. Some were mercenaries hired from foreign countries. Some were young guys looking for excitement and adventure. Some were thugs and goons with psychopathic or sociopathic tendencies. Wherever they were recruited from, they all eventually ended up at a training site in Virginia. It's located on land owned by Apollo, close to four-hundred acres, in fact. And . . ."

"That's what your conversation with Houdini pertained to, right?" Dantzler interrupted. "He's to secure the training site layout for you."

Cain nodded. "But Ray Dunlap discovered something very interesting about Apollo Enterprises, namely that the number of active personnel was now fewer than two-hundred. Yet, their most recent contract with the Pentagon was based on the original personnel figure of six-hundred. What Ray learned was that Apollo was receiving the same amount of money while performing far fewer duties. That didn't compute. But Ray didn't stop there. He also found out that Apollo Enterprises was using the excess funds to purchase guns, ammunition, grenades and other assorted weaponry, and then selling them at a huge profit to countries that are declared enemies of the United States. North Korea, Libya, Iran, to name a few."

Dantzler waited until he was certain Cain had finished his lecture. "All very interesting. But what you've given me is information, not good news."

"I shouldn't have to give it to you. By now, you should have figured it out."

"David Langley works for Apollo Enterprises."

"Bingo."

"How does that help me put Langley away for murder?" Dantzler said.

"Because I'm going to bring down Apollo Enterprises. When that happens, Langley goes down with it."

"Look, Cain, I don't care about the criminal activities of Apollo Enterprises. That's your concern, not mine. I want justice, and I won't have it until David Langley burns for murdering Sarah Elizabeth Dantzler."

"You want revenge, not justice, Detective."

"Revenge, justice . . . whatever. I am going to get David Langley."

"You're sure this is what you want to do?"

"Positive."

"You're willing to do this without me?"

"Yes."

Cain stood. "Be careful, Detective Dantzler. You are going after a dangerous man. Dangerous men."

"Let me worry about that."

"Trust me. You have reason to worry."

Dantzler silently watched Cain walk away.

CHAPTER TWENTY-FIVE

Kayce Clark stepped off the treadmill, grabbed her towel, bent at the waist and gasped for air. Her insides screamed with burning pain, like some invisible demon was raking her with a hot knife. Silently, she cursed herself for deciding to go all marathon distance rather than stick with her normal forty-five minute routine. For whatever insane reason, she tacked on an extra thirty minutes this morning. Plus, she upped the speed more than usual. A two-way mistake. No wonder her insides were on fire.

Ten minutes later, the pain having decreased from extreme to tolerable, she walked to the elevator and punched the number for her floor. While waiting, she checked her watch. Twelve-twenty. Plenty of time to shower and prepare for her two o'clock interview with Becky Shannon. Although she had no idea what to expect from her talk with Becky, her investigative instincts were feeling positive vibes. She felt the excitement that rides on the shoulders of possibility, just like she did after speaking with Ray Dunlap.

Back in her room, Kayce stripped off her workout clothes, and was about to step into the shower when her cell phone rang. Her first thought was, *Oh, shit, Becky has had a change of heart and is calling to cancel the interview*. But the call wasn't from Becky; it was from Andy Waltz.

"What's up, Andy?" Kayce asked.

"Funny, but those were the exact same words I was going to say to you."

"Nothing is up. Life's fairly dull at the present time."

"Can't imagine your life ever being dull."

"Trust me. It is."

"Where are you? I went by your apartment and they told me you had been gone for a couple of days."

"I'm in Boston, visiting my sister, her husband and their new baby. Obviously, you haven't heard the latest. You are now speaking to newly christened Aunt Kayce."

"Tell me, Aunt Kayce. Any lingering thoughts about pursuing the Ray Dunlap/John Carlin story?"

"Dead in the water, Andy. Strictly in the rear-view mirror. I'm moving forward."

"That's the most intelligent thing you've said to me in years, Kayce. I only hope you're telling me the truth."

"It's the truth, Andy. Listen, I hate to cut this short, but I've got to run. I've been working out and I smell like a sewer. The shower is beckoning me."

"Call me when you get back to New York. I'll spring for supper."

Kayce had not been truthful with Andy. Far from it. She had outright lied to the man, and felt no qualms about having done so. She wasn't at her sister's in Boston; she was in the Crowne Plaza Hotel in McLean, Virginia, which was located less than a mile from Becky Shannon's condo. Kayce offered to do the interview at the condo, but Becky, upon learning that Kayce was staying at the Crowne Plaza, suggested they meet at O'Malley's Pub in the hotel.

"How will I recognize you?" Kayce asked.

"You don't have to," Becky answered. "I'll recognize you. I've seen you on TV several times, and I read your book. It'll be like I'm meeting a famous celebrity."

Kayce had come across Becky's name during her preliminary research of Apollo Enterprises. She learned that Becky worked there from 1997 until sometime in 2011. Her job title was office manager, which could mean just about anything. She could have been an important cog in the wheel, or a gloried gofer. Maybe have important information to reveal, maybe not. Kayce wouldn't know until she spoke with Becky. Kayce's research did reveal one interesting tidbit about Becky: She was the only female to ever work for Apollo Enterprises.

At precisely two o'clock, standing outside the entrance to O'Malley's Pub, Kayce saw a tall, rather athletic woman walking straight toward her in long, confident strides. She was dressed in a pair of faded jeans, a white blouse and sneakers. Her hair, which was dark red, was pulled back into a ponytail. No jewelry, no make-up, nothing remotely fancy. *A woman without pretense*, Kayce decided. *I like her already*.

After exchanging hellos and handshakes, they went into O'Malley's. The place was virtually empty, which was not surprising for this early in the afternoon. The drinkers didn't begin to show up until Happy Hour, the diners an hour or so later. Typical for a bar/restaurant. A couple of elderly men sat at the bar, a family of four was at a table to the right of the front door, and a lone male was seated in a booth near the back wall.

Neither woman was hungry, so they each ordered a glass of iced tea. After the waitress brought the drinks, Kayce pulled a small tape recorder from her purse and placed it in the middle of the table. Next, she pulled out her reporter's notepad and flipped it open.

"This seems very official," Becky said. "Are you really investigating Apollo Enterprises?"

"To be perfectly honest with you, Becky, I'm not sure what I'm doing. I had a terrific source for a story, but that source is no longer available. So, unless I can come up with some credible information that will justify an investigation, I'm kind of blindly stumbling around in no-man's land."

Becky poured sugar into her tea, stirred and said, "Well, I'm not sure how much help I can be. I was only the office manager."

"What were your job duties?" Kayce asked, turning on the tape recorder.

"A little bit of everything, really. Answered the phones, scheduled appointments, typed and filed documents, did transcription, ran errands, made bank deposits . . . all the typical things an office manager does."

"Sounds like a pretty good job. Did they pay you okay?"

"Yes. I was making about thirty-five thousand when I left. And I had excellent benefits, too."

"Why did you leave?" Kayce said, scribbling in her notepad.

"I had saved some money, and I was only thirty-seven at the time, so I wanted to do something different. Maybe start my own business, which I did. I now do Billing and Coding, and I'm doing very well. Leaving Apollo was a gutsy move, but it turned out to be a smart one."

"Who was your supervisor at Apollo?"

"David Langley is listed as the Director of Operations, but the real boss is Nick Marlow. He's in charge of Security, but in truth, he runs the place."

"What were they like to work for?"

"David was very nice, easy to get along with, always flirting with me. I never had a problem with him. Nick . . . well, he wasn't always so pleasant. To be honest with you, Nick is a very scary individual. And dangerous. When I heard about what he did in Iraq, I made it a point to never, ever cross him."

"What did he do in Iraq?" Kayce said.

"He was over there—this was about nine years ago—when two of the Apollo guys were killed by a sniper. Nick and the rest of the men were certain the sniper had fired from a house across the street, so they went inside. There were about twenty people in the house, all of whom denied knowing anything about the sniper. Nick kept yelling at them, demanding that they give him the name of the shooter. They continued to say they had no idea what Nick was talking about. After a few more minutes, Nick lined them against the wall and shot them all dead. Old men, women, kids . . . he simply executed them. When I heard about that incident—and that was only one of several I heard about that involved him—I knew I didn't want to get on his bad side."

"How did Nick avoid punishment after committing an atrocity like that?"

"Simple. Mr. Bartlett made a few phone calls to friends in high places. Two days later Nick was back in the United States, the incident forgotten. To put it more accurately, the incident was covered up."

"*The* Lee Bartlett?"

Becky sipped at her tea. "Lee Bartlett."

"What connection does Lee Bartlett have to Apollo Enterprises?"

"He put up the money that helped launch Apollo Enterprises. This was back in the late sixties or early seventies. And it's through his connections in Washington that the money continues to roll in. I'm talking millions and millions of dollars. It's like a river of money that never stops flowing. Whatever Mr. Bartlett wants, he gets. No questions asked."

"Why would Lee Bartlett feel the need to help a man who could commit a crime like that?"

"To protect Apollo Enterprises, of course. Also, he's like a father to Nick. He practically raised Nick from the time he was a teen-ager."

"Did you ever meet Lee Bartlett?"

"No. Only spoke to him on the phone once or twice. Far as I know, he never came to the office."

"Did you ever visit the compound in Virginia?" Kayce said.

"Never."

"Looking back, did you ever get a sense that Apollo Enterprises was involved in any illegal or shady activities?"

Becky shook her head. "Everything I saw seemed to be above board. But like I said, I was just the office manager. I'm sure there were many things going on that I wasn't privy to."

"You said part of your job was making bank deposits. Did you ever handle any cash?"

"No. Always checks or money orders. And some of those checks. Wow! Quite a few were for incredible amounts of money."

"What about personnel files? Did you have access to them?"

"Oh, sure. When new guys were hired, I typed up all the forms. Then I would give them to David. He would check them over, then give them back to me to file away. I also had to fill out some forms when an employee was killed or wounded in action, which happened occasionally."

"How were the employees recruited?" Kayce said.

"Most were guys who had just left the military. They needed work, and Apollo pays extremely well, so they signed on board. Some of those men make really big bucks."

"Any employees from other countries?"

"There were a few. But most were our guys."

"Anything else you can think of that might be of interest?"

"Nothing comes to mind. Sorry."

Kayce picked up the tape recorder, turned it off and put it in her purse. "Thanks for speaking with me, Becky. You've given me some interesting things to chew over."

"Enough to continue with your investigation?"

"I'd say the jury is still out on that question. For sure, I'll need more than what you've given me if I hope to do a serious investigative story. But this is a start, so who knows what will happen?"

"Just promise me this," Becky said, standing. "If you do continue, please do not use my name. That would not go over well with the Apollo people. Secrecy is extremely important to them. Will you make me that promise?"

"You have my word," Kayce said.

*****

The lone customer sitting in the booth near the back wall was the man known as Jet. He had just paid his bill, and was about to leave when he saw Kayce and Becky enter the pub. He instantly recognized both women. The pretty one, whose name escaped him, he had seen several times on TV, hawking a book she had written. A big-time investigative journalist, that much he did remember. The tall, plain-looking lady was named Becky, who he recognized as a former employee of Apollo Enterprises. He recalled that on several occasions, during visits to the office, he had chatted briefly with her while waiting to meet with David Langley. Because of that, he had no doubt she would recognize him if she got a good look at his face. Fortunately, she never glanced in his direction, and when being seated she chose to sit in the chair facing away from him.

Why would a famous investigative reporter want to interview some nobody like Becky? Jet wondered. And clearly this was an interview, not a social outing. The tape recorder and reporter's notepad attested to that. There could only be one answer, Jet knew, and that was Apollo Enterprises. That had to be what they were talking about.

But what could Becky possibly tell the reporter? She worked in the outer office, and therefore didn't have access to what went on behind closed doors. Her knowledge of the inner workings of Apollo was limited to what she saw and heard in her primary work space. She couldn't have much useful information to offer.

Still . . .

She worked there a long time, so who knows what she might have overheard or seen? What important documents she might have been asked to file away or copy? What financial records she might have had access to? And God knows what information a loose-lip numbskull like David Langley might have shared with her? Langley would say anything to impress a woman, even if it meant giving away classified information. There was no telling what he might've told her.

Maybe this was cause for concern, maybe it wasn't. Either way, Jet wasn't about to take any chances. He would contact Lee Bartlett, tell him what he'd seen, and then let the old man handle it from there. That was always the smart move.

Smart because . . .

Lee had a unique gift for making potential problems disappear.

CHAPTER TWENTY-SIX

Nick Marlow sat across the desk from David Langley, silently waiting until the man he had little use for ended a phone call that had already lasted more than ten minutes. After suffering through another two minutes of what he judged to be inane chatter, Nick reached behind him, pulled out a .45 from his back pocket and waved it in Langley's direction. Then Nick took the pistol, raked the barrel across his throat, indicating that it was time for Langley to cut the call short.

Message received, Langley said good-bye to the other party and quickly closed his cell phone.

"You prattle on more than an old woman," Nick snapped. "No phone call should ever last more than a minute."

"Not everyone can be as concise and succinct as you, Nick." Langley leaned back in his chair. "Why are you here, anyway?"

"Lee wants to know if you spoke with the detective from Kentucky. And if you did, how did it go?"

"Yes, I did speak with him."

"And?"

"What can I say? He asked questions, I answered."

"Langley, if you don't give me more information right now, I'm going to point this pistol at your empty head and pull the trigger."

"You're a real prince, Nick. Anyone ever tell you that?"

Nick pointed the pistol at Langley. "Tell me what the detective said."

"He wanted to know if I was in Lexington, Kentucky, on February the fifth, nineteen seventy-eight," Langley said. "I assured him that I had not been in Lexington then, or ever."

"Is that when you allegedly eliminated his mother?"

"Yes."

"Did the detective believe you?" Nick asked.

"I was pretty convincing, so, yes, I think he did believe me. But I can't know that for certain."

"He's a cop, which means he has access to records and files. Is there any possible way he could trace your movements to Lexington?"

"Jesus, Nick, we're talking thirty-five years ago. There's no way he could locate records going back that far."

"Did you drive, or travel by plane?"

"Plane."

"Which company?"

"Delta, I think."

"That means you rented a car at the airport, right?"

"Yes."

"Which rental company?"

"Hertz."

"Stay in a hotel?"

"The Hyatt."

"Hate to tell you this, Langley, but those companies will have records going back thirty-five years. If this detective didn't believe you, and if he decides to really dig into the past, he'll have no trouble proving you were in Lexington, Kentucky."

"But why is he doing it now, after all these years?"

"Because it's his mother, you idiot. I'm surprised he's waited this long to come after you. If it had been my mother you killed, you would have been dead years ago."

"What are you going to tell Lee?" Langley said.

"The only thing I can tell him," Nick said, again pointing the pistol at Langley. "This is a dangerous situation that needs to be dealt with."

*****

"Did you have an uneventful flight from D.C.?" Lee Bartlett said, sipping scotch. "Those are always the best kind."

Nick opened a bottle of Heineken, sat in the chair across from Lee and said, "The flight was as smooth as Candace's ass."

"Yes, I'm sure Candace has a lovely ass. And I've no doubt that you have explored every inch of it. But that is not a subject for discussion."

The two men were alone on the veranda of Lee's Long Island estate. The night air was cool, the fireflies seemed to be working overtime to light up the surroundings, while off in the distance, the Atlantic's waves pounded relentlessly against the rocks.

Of all his properties, this was Lee's favorite.

"Did you chat with David?" Lee said.

"You mean, did I chat with the idiot? The answer is, yes, I did."

"Haven't I told you a thousand times that name calling is for individuals of a lesser intelligence? You are above calling someone an idiot."

Nick chuckled. "You've also told me a thousand times to tell the truth as I see it. Well, calling Langley an idiot is telling the truth . . . as I see it."

"No more debate on a subject so far beneath us. We have more important items to discuss. What did David tell you?"

"Langley spoke with the detective about a week ago. He thinks the detective bought his story about never having been to Lexington, Kentucky, but he isn't sure about it."

"What are your instincts telling you, Nick?"

"It all comes down to how aggressive this detective is. And since it's his mother's murder he's looking into, we need to assume he's going to be extremely aggressive. If that's the case, there could be trouble on the horizon."

"From an event that happened so long ago? How is this even possible?"

"Langley flew on a commercial flight. He also rented a car once he got to Lexington. Stayed in a downtown hotel. That means he left a paper trail a mile long. If this detective is any good at all, he can locate that stuff. Once he does, Langley is toast. If Langley goes down, so could we."

"You're right, Nick. This is a matter that must be addressed."

"Do you want me to take out the detective?"

"Let's not be in too big a hurry. I need to ponder this for a while before I make a decision as to how we should proceed." Lee finished his scotch and set his glass on the table. "On to a separate matter. This Sunday, Benjamin Parker will be here as my guest. I want you to join us. In anticipation of your protest, let me assure you that this will not be a big social affair. Only the three of us will be here."

"Are you really so certain he'll give you the list?" Nick said.

Lee smiled. "As certain as I am that the sun will rise out of the Atlantic tomorrow morning."

"Ben Parker hates you."

"And the feeling is mutual."

"I'm surprised he's agreed to be here."

"Ben Parker hates me, but he's also intelligent enough to fear me. He knows that in the long run, I wield far more power than he does. Hate aside, there is no way he'll risk getting on my bad side."

"What time do you want me here?"

"No later than three," Lee said, slowly rising from his chair. "We'll chat, have a drink, eat and then watch a movie."

"What are the odds you can find a movie that a right-wing zealot like Ben Parker will watch?"

"Oh, I'm sure I can come up with something that will hold his attention."

CHAPTER TWENTY-SEVEN

Houdini unfurled the large map of the Apollo Enterprises compound and spread it across the kitchen table, using salt and pepper shakers to weigh down the top corners. After securing the bottom corners with paper weights, he stepped back and looked at Cain.

"As you can easily detect, this place is more secure than most military posts," he said. They were in Houdini's Greenwich Village apartment on Bank Street. "That damn double fence is the big problem."

Cain nodded his agreement. From what he was looking at, the compound's interior was fairly typical. A main house, two buildings used as barracks, one used for a mess hall, a large circular building that housed a gym, swimming pool, running track, weight room, steam room and a sauna, and an even larger building where weapons, ammunition, vehicles and other supplies were kept. Directly behind the main house was a helipad. Beyond that was the firing range.

Cain also noted that there was a single entrance into the compound, a front gate that would undoubtedly be manned by armed guards 24/7.

While the front of the compound was protected by a sophisticated security system, nature had provided security at the rear in the form of deep woods that continued east until they bumped up against the base of a mountain. In Cain's experience, natural terrain invariably kicked man-made obstacles' ass by posing challenges that were virtually impossible to overcome. In matters of security, Mother Nature was the great defender.

"The men who built this compound were very smart," Cain said. "By backing it up against woods and a mountain they effectively eliminated any attack from the rear. The only way in is through the front gate."

"Well, we know who those men are," Houdini said, pointing at the three photos pinned to the wall. They were 8x10 close-ups face shots of Lee Bartlett, David Langley and Nick Marlow. "And, yes, they are smart."

"Men like them are never as smart or as clever as they like to believe. They almost always overrate their intelligence and their abilities. That's what leads to their downfall."

"Maybe so. But they aren't to be taken lightly."

"Tell me about the security system," Cain said.

Houdini pointed to the outer fence. "This one is twelve-feet high and it has a live electrical wire running across the top. High voltage, I'm assuming. The bells and whistles extend outward fifteen feet from the fence. Step anywhere within those fifteen feet and the place lights up like Times Square on New Year's Eve. There is a gap of three feet between the outer fence and the inner fence, which is also twelve-feet high. And as you might expect, those three feet are protected by a separate system. So, even if you could somehow manage to breach the outer system, you'd still face the challenge of getting past the second system. The way I see it, breaking into that place is damn near impossible."

"When faced with an impossible challenge, the best solution is always the simplest one," Cain said.

"And that is?"

"I'll enter through the front gate."

"And exactly how do you propose to do that?"

"Let them capture me."

*****

Sonia Ivanovna followed approximately twenty feet behind Cain and Houdini, the man her KGB teachers referred to as "the Magnificent Scrounger." She began trailing them the moment they emerged from the apartment, which she had been observing from a bench across the street. Their journey was the same as it had been for the three nights Cain stayed at Houdini's place—north up Bank Street, across Greenwich Street, a right turn on Hudson, and then one block to West 11th and their final destination, The White Horse Tavern.

Sonia had been on Cain's trail since he left Senator Carlin's townhouse in Georgetown. From there, Cain made a brief stop in Lexington, Kentucky, where he met with a man she later learned was a homicide detective. After that, he traveled to Manhattan and hooked up with Houdini. The quick stop in Kentucky was the only puzzling part for Sonia. Why had Cain met with a homicide cop? she wondered. How did he figure into any of this? *Did* he figure in, or was it a meeting totally unrelated to what was going on? Sonia had no answers to any of her questions.

As she followed the two men, Sonia occasionally glanced at her reflection in darkened store windows. She did this to check out her disguise. Seeing her "new" look, she couldn't help but smile. It was as if she was seeing a stranger, a woman she had never seen before. Her disguise was better than perfect, she concluded. She doubted her KGB handlers would recognize her.

The blond hair, parted in the middle, was the key. Real hair, too, the result of a professional dye job. She simply did not trust wigs, not when so much was at stake. She wore wire-rim glasses, a black sweater, black jeans and flat black shoes. This ensemble gave her the look of an actress, or maybe one of those 1950's Beat Generation chicks she had seen in American magazines. Either evaluation was okay with her. All that mattered was no one could possibly recognize her.

What she planned to do was, she acknowledged, a dangerous move. No doubt her KGB teachers would scold her for taking such an unnecessary risk. "Never allow your pride or your ego to interfere with the task at hand," they told her maybe a thousand times. "Never act in a foolish manner."

But tonight Sonia wasn't going to heed their advice. She felt bold and fearless and invincible. Certainly not foolish. Her confidence level was off the charts, so why not take advantage and do something entirely different? Something unexpected, maybe even a bit outrageous? On this night she was going to go one step further than she had on the previous three nights. Tonight, rather than wait outside the White Horse Tavern until the two men departed, she was going to follow Cain and Houdini into the legendary pub.

Insane, yes. But something I have to do.

Sonia waited until the two men had been in the bar ten minutes before entering. She went straight to the bar, ordered a drink and then casually looked around. Cain and Houdini were seated at a table near the back. Hovering above them like a disembodied ghost was a large portrait of Dylan Thomas, the Welsh poet who drank himself to death. Died in a gutter was how Sonia remembered the story. An inglorious but not unexpected ending for such a famous literary figure, she concluded.

Sonia had just finished her drink and was about to order another one when she felt a man's shoulder brush against her. She turned, looked up and found herself staring into the eyes of the world's greatest assassin.

Cain.

Even at this close distance, she couldn't tell if his eyes were blue or gray.

"Sorry for bumping into you like that," Cain said, smiling. "Hope I didn't cause you to spill any of your drink."

"I barely noticed it," Sonia said, giving him a 1000-watt smile. "And the drink was long gone before you showed up."

God, I can't believe I'm this calm, Sonia thought. *I'm in the presence of a lion, yet my nerves are like steel. I feel no fear whatsoever."*

"Then let me get you a refill," Cain said. He motioned to the bartender. "Two more pints of Guinness for me." He looked at Sonia, "What are you having?"

"Dirty martini, Stoli rather than gin, two olives." She pointed at Cain's hands. "You must be a pianist. Or maybe a professional athlete."

"Why would you say that?" Cain asked.

"Because your hands are huge."

"No. You're wrong on both counts."

"What line of work are you in, if you don't mind my asking?"

"I'm retired."

"That's a rather evasive answer," Sonia said, grinning. "There has to be more to it than that."

"Not really. How about you? What do you do for a living?"

"Photographer."

"A shooter."

Sonia's heart jumped up into her throat. A wave of ice raced down her spine. *What the hell is he saying? What can he possibly know?* "I'm a professional photographer," she repeated, praying her suddenly raw nerves hadn't betrayed her.

"Photographers are sometimes referred to as shooters. Or shutterbugs."

"Oh, I've never heard that before."

Cain paid the bartender and picked up the two pints. "Enjoy your drink," he said to Sonia. "And, again, I apologize for bumping into you."

"Stop apologizing . . . it was nothing. And thank you for the drink. Perhaps our paths will cross again somewhere along the way. If they do, I'll buy the next round."

"I look forward to it."

"In case you're interested, my name is Erin."

"Mickey."

"Pleased to meet you, Mickey."

"Same here, Erin."

Sonia kept her eyes on Cain as he walked away. Inwardly, she was filled with a sense of pride and excitement. And she had every right to feel this way. She had come face to face with the ultimate killer, and with the exception of a single brief instance she had handled herself like a true professional. She had not been overwhelmed by the lion. At this moment she felt as though she was Cain's equal.

She felt something else as well.

Killing Cain was going to be a piece of cake.

CHAPTER TWENTY-EIGHT

During his six terms as a United States senator, Benjamin Parker had become known as "Rector of the Righteous Right." And for the very reasons you might expect. He was their Joshua, a fearless warrior who charged into countless battles being waged by those who viewed big government as the enemy, and the poor as a drag on society. Not unexpectedly, he was something of a divisive figure. Neo-cons, Tea Party adherents and the Religious Right worshipped at his feet, seeing him as the one individual courageous enough to stand up against the evil forces of liberalism and progressive thinking. He was the defender of all things conservative.

Those on the Left had a decidedly different opinion of Ben Parker. To them, he was nothing less than an out-of-touch, self-righteous, bigoted Neanderthal.

On social issues, in particular, he was unbending in his beliefs. Hell, no, he would say when asked if he believed in gay rights, same-sex marriage, a woman's right to choose, immigration, universal health care, expanded oversight of Wall Street and the banking industry, or gun control. Hell, yes, to capital punishment, prayer in schools, continuing the wars in Iraq and Afghanistan, tax loopholes for the wealthy, and cutting funding for social programs that provide assistance to the poor and needy.

On the personal side, Ben Parker was viewed as a paragon of virtue. Married to the same woman for forty-five years ("the only woman I have known in a biblical sense"), he had four children, nine grandkids and three great-grandkids. He was a Baptist, a Mason, and as he proudly proclaimed during every speech he gave, "a humble man who has been born again in the name of our Lord Jesus Christ."

Despite his reputation as a divisive figure, during his long stint in the senate there was no denying the fact that Ben Parker had become a powerful force, particularly in the area of national defense. He chaired several important committees, including the highly influential Senate Committee on Armed Services, which was empowered with legislative oversight of the nation's military. He was known to have an open checkbook when it came to military affairs. If the Department of Defense or the Pentagon wanted additional money, Ben Parker made sure they received it. The word no was not in his vocabulary when it came to funding the military.

As a result, he was not only revered by the military, he was trusted. He was their go-to guy, an ally in every respect. Ben Parker was so trusted by the top brass that he was the only senator in the situation room watching along with the president and other top leaders as Operation Neptune Spear played out in real time. It was during this operation that SEAL Team 6 took out Osama bin Laden.

Like virtually all politicians, Ben Parker had a knack for twisting facts in such a way as to benefit his own image. It was his claim—one he pronounced often and with great enthusiasm—that he never accepted a penny from Lee Bartlett. This was more than twisting the facts; it was simply not true. On several occasions, when Ben Parker found himself in a heated battle for re-election, he had secretly dispatched an aide to meet with Lee for the purpose of securing campaign financing. Ben Parker would deny it, of course, arguing that he couldn't be held accountable for actions committed without his knowledge by certain members of his campaign staff. In politics, this was known as plausible deniability.

In the real world, it was known as an outright lie.

And yet, despite their differences, for several hours on a beautiful Sunday afternoon at the Long Island estate, Lee Bartlett and Ben Parker, two men who despised each other, managed to engage in a civil conversation. They did so by focusing on the one thing they wholeheartedly agreed on: doing what it takes by any means necessary to ensure that the United States has the best-equipped, best-trained and best-funded military on this planet.

Power in all forms meant everything to these two men.

As they chatted on the veranda, Lee drank single malt scotch, Nick Marlow had his usual Heineken, while Ben Parker, a self-professed teetotaler, slowly sipped Club Soda with a twist of lime.

Lee, breaking almost five minutes of silence, said, "Given our rather contentious relationship, I'm sure you are wondering why I invited you here."

"That thought had crossed my mind," Ben Parker answered.

"There is something I need, and you are going to get it for me."

"That sounds more like an order, not a request. And I don't take orders from you."

"See it in whichever light you choose. I don't care. I need something, and you are the one man who can make sure I get it."

"What is it that you want?" Ben Parker asked.

"A list of names and addresses."

"Names and addresses? That's it?"

"That's it."

"For what purpose do you need these names and addresses?"

"That's of no concern to you, Senator. You get the list, give it to me and you're out of the picture. Simple as that."

Ben Parker sipped his Club Soda, said, "Whose names and addresses?"
Lee told him.

Ben Parker slammed his drink down and recoiled as though he had come face to face with his own ghost. Shaking his finger at Lee, he said in a trembling voice, "There is absolutely no way on God's earth that I would ever give you that list. Never. You can forget it."

"You're sure about that?"

"Absolutely."

Lee stood. "Fair enough, Senator. You have a justly earned reputation as a man of stern principles, and you are to be respected for that. Now . . . let us move to the dining room, where we will enjoy a marvelous repast prepared for us by my chef. I'm positive you will be impressed."

The meal was eaten in virtual silence, in an atmosphere best described as chilly. Three men sitting at a long oak table, saying nothing, keeping their thoughts and opinions to themselves. They may as well have been dining in different galaxies. Occasionally, Lee would look up, his eyes flashing from Nick to Ben Parker, a wry smile playing on his lips.

Nick said nothing, but knowing Lee like he did, he knew something big was in the works.

When they finished eating, and the table was being cleared, Ben Parker said, "You were right . . . the meal was excellent. Give my compliments to the chef. Now, if you don't mind, I must be on my way. It's getting late, and I really don't like long drives after dark."

"No, you mustn't leave so soon, Senator. I have selected a movie I'm sure you will enjoy."

"I really don't care much for movies. They tend to bore me."

"I can promise you that this one will not bore you. However, if you don't like it, for whatever reason, we'll stop it and you can leave. I will not be offended."

"As you wish," Ben Parker said, reluctantly.

Lee led Nick and the senator down the hallway and into a room he had especially designed to resemble today's movie theaters—full-size screen, cushioned chairs, stadium seating, projector and sound system that were state of the art. In all, there were fifty seats. Lee loved this room and did, indeed, watch many movies here. On occasion, Lee's friends in the movie business would send him just-released movies, or sometimes soon-to-be-released movies, which he would screen for his friends and supporters, usually on the weekend. Those were always special evenings enjoyed by all who attended.

After Lee and the senator sat in front row seats, Lee said, "Nick, if you push the red button, the lights will go down. After that, push the blue one, and that will start the projector."

Nick followed Lee's instructions, and within seconds the huge screen came to life. The film was in color and extremely high in quality. There were no titles and no music. The opening scene showed a teen-age boy lying naked on a large bed. He had dark hair and dark skin, and was, in all probability, a Latino. His eyes were wide and bright, and the smile on his face was genuine. He seemed eager, even excited about what was going to happen.

Seconds later, a man, also naked, entered from the left side of the screen, moved slowly around the room, and eventually sat on the side of the bed. It was obvious from the man's body that he was much older than the boy. When he leaned down closer to the boy, for the first time his face came into view.

Benjamin Parker.

He leaned over and kissed the boy on the lips, letting his right hand move down the boy's chest until it touched his fully erect penis. Slowly, his hand began moving up and down.

"Stop this! Stop this now!" Ben Parker screamed. "For God's sake, stop it!"

"Are you sure?" Lee said, smiling. "It gets a lot better."

Ben Parker, red faced and trembling, said, "Where did you get this film?"

"That's a great question, Ben. But if I were in your shoes, that would've been my *second* question. My *first* question would be, what are you going to do with this film?"

Ben Parker looked at Nick. "Turn that off. Now!"

"Not just yet, Nick," Lee said, pointing to a yellow button. "Hit that one, please."

Nick hit the yellow button, causing the action on screen to pause, freezing the frame at the moment when Ben Parker's mouth was inches from the boy's penis.

"Here's how this is going to play out, Senator," Lee said. "You get me that list by noon next Sunday or this film will be given to CNN, MSNBC, Fox, ABC, CBS, NBC, the Huffington Post and every Internet site out there. When that happens, it goes . . . what's the term, Nick?"

"Viral."

"Yes, viral. That means it will spread across the world faster than the plague. And then everyone will know the real truth about Saint Benjamin Parker, the homosexual who railed against homosexuals for four decades. The anti-gay proponent who can't keep his paws off young boys. One can only wonder what your wife, your kids, your grandkids and your legions of admirers and followers will be thinking. I'm certain they will be crushed and disappointed to learn they have been worshipping a false idol all these years."

"If I give you the list, I want this film," Ben Parker ordered.

"Sorry, but it doesn't work that way, Senator. You see, if you are going to negotiate, you always want to do so from a position of power. Unfortunately, in this negotiation, you have no power. The film stays with me. And in case you are wondering, I also have three other films in which you have the starring role. I particularly enjoyed the one where you were with the two young oriental lads."

"You are an evil man, Lee."

"Yes, Senator, I am. But I'm not a hypocrite, a liar or a pedophile."

"I can't promise that I can get the list," Ben Parker said. "I'll do my best, but . . . I can't guarantee it."

"Well, I can *guarantee* this, Senator. If I don't have the list in hand by this time next Sunday, you'll be the most reviled man on the planet twenty-four hours later."

Lee walked to the door and opened it. "Nick, escort Saint Benjamin to his car." Turning to the senator, Lee said, "One more thing, Senator. Suicide is not an option. If you choose to go that route, the film will be released that very day. You'll be spared the fallout, but think about your family and supporters. They will be left to taste the ashes of your sins."

Ten minutes later Nick walked back into the room, a glass filled with scotch in one hand, a bottle of Heineken in the other hand. Handing the scotch to Lee, he said, "You are one ruthless bastard, old man."

"Thank you, Nick. That's a compliment I will proudly embrace."

CHAPTER TWENTY-NINE

During the three days since her interview with Becky Shannon, Kayce Clark continued her investigation into Apollo Enterprises. She wasn't sure what she was looking for, and the information provided by Becky amounted to almost nothing of consequence, but she knew—*felt*—that there was an important diamond yet to be uncovered. To find it, she simply had to keep digging.

For convenience, she kept her room at the Crowne Plaza rather than head back to her Manhattan apartment. Staying there made the most sense in a variety of ways. She had plenty of journalism cronies in the area who could be counted on for help, if needed. Also, she had several solid sources who worked in the Pentagon and in other high-level government offices, any of whom might come through for her in a pinch. Staying in close proximity to those potential allies was a strategically sound plan.

As it turned out, her decision proved to be the right one. Through a friend of a friend of a friend, Kayce was given the name of a young clerk who, after nearly an hour of haggling with Kayce, agreed to provide a list of Apollo Enterprises personnel. To get the clerk to agree, Kayce had to promise upon the death of her first born to never mention where or from whom she obtained the list. Under the circumstances it was an easy promise to make.

While waiting for the list to arrive, Kayce calculated that since Apollo Enterprises began operation in the early 1970s, perhaps as many as two-thousand men had been employed there. If that figure was even close to accurate, she knew it could take her days, perhaps weeks, to do a thorough investigation. Tracking down that many individuals, even if half were no longer living, would be a daunting task. Maybe even an impossible one. But, as Andy Waltz always reminded her, "a task is only impossible if you allow it to be."

An hour later, when the package arrived at her hotel room via private courier, Kayce was surprised—and disappointed—to find that it consisted of a single page with only twenty-nine names listed. This had to be a mistake, Kayce thought. There was no way in hell only twenty-nine men worked for Apollo Enterprises. She knew from her research that at its peak Apollo Enterprises employed up to six-hundred men. So, where were the rest of the names?

Opening her cell phone, Kayce was about the call the young clerk and inquire as to why he had sent so few names. However, just as she began punching in his number, she noticed something interesting about the list—it contained only the names of those either killed or wounded while employed by Apollo Enterprises. The first seven names were KIA, the next twenty-two were wounded in action.

Kayce studied the list of names for almost ten minutes. There wasn't a single name listed that she recognized. It was, as she expected, a list of complete strangers. In particular, she looked at the ones who had been killed, hoping one of those names might mean something to her. None did. Next, she slowly went through the names of the twenty-two who had been wounded, again finding nothing that jumped out at her. Her investigation was nowhere close to uncovering the diamond she desperately needed to find. And, she knew, it wasn't going to happen without a more detailed list of names.

But the young clerk, to his everlasting credit, had included an address for each man listed. She had no clue why he had done this; at first glance, it didn't seem to be particularly helpful. But she couldn't have been more wrong. The answer was right in front of her, and within a matter of seconds it became crystal clear to her why the clerk included those addresses.

Kayce's eyes carefully scanned the list, eventually stopping halfway down the page. There, listed among the wounded, was the name Todd Weaver. His address: McLean, Virginia.

Kayce's growing excitement was tempered by two realizations: Todd Weaver might have relocated to another city, and if he did still live in McLean, would she be able to track him down?

The phone book listed plenty of Weavers but none named Todd. This meant he probably had a cell phone and no landline. No surprise there; in today's technologically advanced world most folks seemed to be going in that direction. There were two T Weavers listed, so Kayce decided to give them a try, even though she would bet that both were females. The first one was. Her name was Terry, and she wasn't familiar with a Todd Weaver. The second T Weaver was also female, Toni, and she was quick to say she knew Todd very well. According to Toni, she and Todd were first cousins.

"Todd is head of security for a large finance company," Toni said. "He's been there for five or six years. Makes serious money, too."

"What's the name of the company?" Kayce asked.

"Ford and Maddox."

"Thanks for the info, Toni," Kayce said, hanging up before Toni could ask any questions.

Kayce's call to Ford and Maddox was answered by a honey-voiced woman named Amy, who, in another life could easily have been an opera diva. She wasted no time putting Kayce through to Todd Weaver's extension.

"Todd Weaver . . . how may I help you?"

Kayce introduced herself and told him the reason for the call. There was more than a minute of silence before Todd Weaver responded.

"Why are you calling me?" Todd finally said. "I haven't worked for Apollo Enterprises since I was wounded. That was seven years ago. I have no information to give you."

"Well, then, just tell me a little about yourself. Where you were stationed, your duties, how you were wounded."

"That's ancient history, lady. And damn sure none of your business. If you want to know about me, you'll have to get your information from another source. I never talk about my time with Apollo Enterprises."

"Fair enough," Kayce said. "But I would like to ask you one question, and I would really appreciate an honest answer."

"You ask, then I'll decide if I answer or if I slam this phone down."

"What can you tell me about Nick Marlow?"

"Nick's a tough guy, a real bad ass," Todd said. "Certainly not someone you want as an enemy, that's for sure. But he's also good with his men, treats them fairly, really looks out for them. He cares about their well-being. I wouldn't hesitate to go into combat with Nick anytime, anywhere."

"What about the story of him lining up men, women and children, and then executing them?"

"I've heard that story, but I was stationed down in Gitmo at the time. So, I don't know if it happened, or if it's fantasy. But if it did happen, I say, so what? We were in a war, and war is an ugly, brutal business. Shit happens, and most of it ain't pretty. If you're expecting me to pass judgment on Nick Marlow's actions during combat situations, you're talking to the wrong guy."

"What about Lee Bartlett?" Kayce said.

"You've had your one question, Miss Clark. I don't mean to be rude, but this conversation is over."

"Well, screw you, too, pal," Kayce muttered, after closing her cell phone. Taking the list of names, she once again scanned addresses, hoping to find another ex-Apollo employee living within close proximity to McLean. She didn't. The next closest one resided in Atlanta.

Kayce's cell phone buzzed. She looked at the caller ID but didn't recognize the number.

"Hello," Kayce said.

"Kayce, this is Becky Shannon. I hope I'm not bothering you. If I am, I can call back later."

"No, Becky, you're not bothering me at all. What's up? You sound worried."

"More embarrassed than worried, I think."

"Why are you embarrassed?"

"Because . . . well, I wasn't completely forthcoming with you when we spoke the other day."

"How do you mean?"

"There are some things I didn't share with you about Apollo Enterprises. Some facts you might find interesting, especially if you do decide to continue with your investigation."

Grabbing her pen and notepad, Kayce said, "What things? What facts?"

"If it's okay with you, I would rather not discuss this over the phone," Becky said. "I know I'm asking a lot, you living in New York City and all, but would it be possible for you to come to my condo within the next few days?"

"Becky, I'm still at the Crowne Plaza."

"You are? That's good . . . we can meet tonight. Can you make it at seven or seven-thirty?"

"I can come right now, if you'd prefer."

"I can't do it now. I'm in the middle of something and won't be finished until five-thirty or six."

"Okay, I'll see you at seven," Kayce said.

The next three hours, which she spent pacing her room, seemed like an eternity to Kayce. Patience may be a virtue, but it was never part of her makeup, as anyone who really knew her would confirm. For her, waiting, especially if something potentially big was at the end of the wait, was barely tolerable. The slower time passed, the more anxious she became.

By seven-ten, when the cab dropped her off in front of Becky Shannon's condo, Kayce's energy and excitement levels were higher than Mount Everest. She had that feeling deep in her gut that something huge was about to happen, that the deeply buried diamond was soon to be discovered. Moments like this were what she lived for.

That Becky's front door was slightly ajar caused no concern for Kayce. After all, Becky was expecting her. It was, she felt, Becky's way of saying, "the door's open, come on in."

Kayce called out Becky's name as she pushed the door open and entered the condo. There was no reply. From a room off to her left, Kayce could hear the television, which, she felt, was being played at an unusually high volume. No doubt that's the reason why Becky hadn't answered, Kayce thought. She couldn't hear me calling. Kayce went in the direction of the noise, into the small den, and that's when she saw Becky sitting on a couch, facing the TV. Kayce called out to Becky, again getting no response.

Something was not right, and she felt it in her bones. Slowly, and with a growing sense of unease, she moved around to the front of the couch. Looking down, she gasped when she realized what she was seeing. Becky Shannon was sitting upright, her eyes were open and staring at nothing, and there was a thin red necklace around her neck. It didn't take Kayce long to determine that the necklace was blood.

Over the years Kayce had seen plenty of dead bodies, including many that were the victim of a homicide. But never had she seen one *before* the police and medical examiner gave their okay to view the body. Never before had she stumbled upon a murder victim. And clearly this was a homicide. Becky Shannon had definitely been murdered. Someone had strangled her to death.

As Kayce reached into her purse to take out her cell phone, she felt something nudge against her back.

"That's a gun, Miss Clark," a man whispered in her ear. "Walk quietly out the front door, down the steps and toward the black SUV parked to the right. Don't do anything foolish. If you do, I will not hesitate to kill you."

CHAPTER THIRTY

Jack Dantzler walked off the court after having played three sets of tennis against Randall Dennis. As always, each set ended in the usual six-love score. After taking a sip of water, Dennis, ever the optimist, stated (again) that a new day was on the horizon, meaning that at some point in the future he would take a set from Dantzler, who, since his teen-age years, had been considered the best tennis player in Lexington.

"A set?" Dantzler said, picking up his racket and gym bag. "You might want to establish lower, more realistic goals for yourself, Randall. Like maybe trying to win a *game*. A set is about a thousand miles beyond your reach."

"Whatever, you cocky prick." Dennis put an arm around Dantzler. "Let's go upstairs, get something to eat. To prove I'm not a sore loser, it'll be my treat."

"A very Christian offer, Randall, but I'm going to take a pass. I'm working on some things, so I need to get home. Maybe next time."

"Maybe next time I'll take that set from you."

"A game, Randall, first try winning a game. Don't dream beyond your capabilities."

"Yeah, yeah, I hear you."

Dantzler tossed his racket and gym bag into the backseat of his car, and then settled in behind the wheel. He was about to start up the engine when his cell phone began to vibrate. This meant he had either missed a call or someone had sent a text message. Since he rarely ever received a text, his money was on a missed call. Snapping it open, he saw that someone had left a voice mail. He dialed, punched in his code and listened.

"Detective Dantzler, this is David Langley. Since we last spoke, I have been so troubled by your obvious belief that I had something to do with your mother's murder that I've been looking into the matter on my own. And just as I expected, my effort has not been a waste of time. Approximately an hour ago, I came across information relating to her death. To be more precise, I have uncovered evidence that will exonerate me. This same evidence will offer conclusive proof as to who did kill her. I will not discuss this over the phone. If you desire to see the evidence, you will have to meet me tomorrow evening, seven o'clock, at this address."

Dantzler opened the glove compartment, grabbed a pen and an old envelope, replayed the message and wrote down the address. After tossing the pen back into the glove compartment and closing it, he listened to the message a third time. Closing his eyes, he let Langley's words sink in.

As he replayed the message mentally, he had no doubt that what he had heard was nothing but pure BS. Langley was lying. Of that, Dantzler had no doubt. The message itself was the tipoff. It came across as something penned by a screenwriter or novelist. *Exonerate, conclusive proof . . . who says shit like that?* It was nothing less than pure fiction. And not very clever fiction, at that. Dantzler knew in his heart of hearts where the so-called evidence was heading. It didn't take a genius to figure out this plot. Langley was going to lay the blame for Sarah Dantzler's murder on the only person he could—Lucas White. Because Lucas White's name was mentioned in the murder book, he had to be the culprit. What other route could Langley possibly take?

And wasn't it all just a little too damn convenient? How did Langley come up with this information so quickly? And where did he find it? There's no feasible way he could have.

It was, Dantzler knew, total bullshit.

The address, a street in Arlington, Virginia, was further proof that Langley was not only a bad liar, he was also an arrogant jerk. Did Langley really believe he could dissuade Dantzler from showing up by giving him less than a day to make a rather lengthy trip? Could Langley be that foolish? That misguided?

It didn't matter . . . Dantzler was going to Arlington, an eight-to-ten-hour drive from Lexington. A lengthy but easily manageable trip. Also, having played in several tennis tournaments there, he was vaguely familiar with the area, which meant he should be able to find the location without much trouble. Since Langley set the meeting for seven o'clock in the evening, Dantzler could leave early in the morning and still make it in plenty of time.

Nothing was going to keep him away from this meeting. Not time, not distance. He would be there if the meeting was in Los Angeles in four hours. He would be there because he wanted to see Langley face to face, to look into this asshole's eyes as he attempted to lay the blame on Lucas White, a dead man who could not defend himself. He wanted to hear the lies tumble out of this coward's mouth.

Dantzler wanted to smell the stink of mendacity.

*****

Sonia Ivanovna was tired, stiff, bored and—what was the word she heard Americans use?—grimy. Yes, grimy was exactly how she felt. Her clothes were, she feared, beginning to smell, her hair needed to be washed, her legs and underarms pleaded for a razor, and the discomfort in her back and her butt were reminders that she had been living a sedentary existence for far too long.

Three days and three nights, in fact. That's how long Sonia had been sitting in a rented car on Bank Street, twenty feet from the front door to Andy Waltz's apartment. She was beginning to wonder if killing the world's top assassin was worth this much effort. Was it a mission worth such personal and physical discomfort? Did she really need to do this? Her answer to those questions was, yes, it's worth it. After all, she wasn't going after Cain to simply enhance her own reputation. No, she had personal reasons for wanting Cain dead. For what he had done to her beloved aunt Nastasia three years ago. He had executed her. For that, Cain had to die.

She would gladly suffer any degree of discomfort to make this happen.

Were it not for the French bistro across the street, the past seventy-two hours would have been intolerable. She would have smelled like a three-day-old corpse, and likely would have looked like one as well. Thankfully, the small bistro was her salvation. The food, which she judged to be quite good and affordable, provided nourishment that fueled the tank. Water and an occasional beverage kept her hydrated. Of equal importance was the bistro's restroom, where she could use the facilities and do some personal grooming. She had been on her share of dreary assignments in the past, living in tents, or oftentimes on the cold, hard ground, but not until now did she realize how refreshing a splash of warm water on the face could be. Sometimes the simplest things have the most meaning.

During the three days' surveillance she had only seen Cain one time. The first evening, around six-thirty, he and Waltz left the apartment and walked to the Minetta Tavern, where they had supper. They stayed for just over an hour, then walked straight back to Waltz's apartment. After that, no subsequent sightings of the man she was going to kill.

While Cain remained inside, Waltz followed a different routine, leaving the apartment once each day at a little past noon. He flagged down a taxi, and was gone for approximately two hours. Each time he returned, he was carrying a large brown envelope.

Today, at eleven a.m., a black sedan pulled up in front of the apartment and double-parked. A man ran from the vehicle to the front door, where he was promptly met by Waltz, who accepted an envelope from the man. They engaged in no conversation, no small talk. The man handed the package to Waltz, got back in his car and drove off.

Sonia had no clue what was going on behind closed doors. Nor did she much care. Her concern was Cain, and having not laid eyes on the man for two full days was beginning to worry her. Was it possible he had slipped out during the night, when Sonia had briefly dozed off? She quickly discarded that possibility, since she was never asleep for more than ten to twenty minutes at a time. Was there a back way out of Waltz's apartment? Did he leave when she was in the bistro, either while she was ordering food or washing up in the restroom? Was it possible she let the great Cain slip away? If so, she would never forgive herself.

Great assassins don't lose their quarry.

Sonia's fears of having let Cain slip past her proved to be unwarranted. At four-thirty, another black sedan pulled up in front of Waltz's apartment. Seconds later, Cain emerged and hopped into the front seat. The sedan then pulled away and headed uptown. Sonia started her car and began following.

She smiled, relieved to know she had not let her target slip away.

Cain was still in her sights.

And Sonia had never failed to score a kill when a target was in sight.

CHAPTER THIRTY-ONE

The address David Langley had given Jack Dantzler was on a narrow tree-shaded street lined on both sides by small and what appeared to be very old houses. The houses were probably owned by retirees or first-time home owners. The neighborhood had that kind of feel to it. The old waiting to die, the young looking to move upward. There was a park at the end of the street that, at five-fifteen in the evening, was being enjoyed by several dozen small children and their mothers or nannies. Only a few of the kids were attended to by a male figure.

Dantzler made a special point of arriving early for the meeting. He wanted to scout the surroundings, to make sure he wasn't walking into some kind of trap. Langley's house—if this was Langley's house—was the last one of the left side of the street. It was dark inside, and looked to be empty. Dantzler thought about going up to the house and looking through a front window, but decided that wasn't a good idea. Someone could be inside, and even if the house was empty, a vigilant neighbor might be inclined to call the police and report seeing an intruder. Dantzler didn't need that kind of a hassle.

Dantzler had dozed off when his cell phone buzzed. He snapped it open and answered. The caller was David Langley.

"How close are you to Arlington, Detective Dantzler?"

"I'm already here. In fact, I'm parked in front of your house. It is your house, right?"

"Yes, it is. And I'm not surprised you are early for the meeting. Unfortunately, our original plan is no longer an option. I'm tied up at the moment, working on some inventory issues, and won't be done until much later tonight. However, I'm not very far from where you are, so if you still want to meet, we can do it here."

"Will your 'evidence' also be there?" Dantzler said.

"Most assuredly. And don't think I failed to catch the sarcasm in your reply, Detective."

"It wasn't sarcasm, it was doubt."

"Once you see the evidence, you'll have no more doubts."

"We'll see," Dantzler said. "How do I get to where you are?"

"Very simple. Turn around, go to the end of the street and make a right. Go through three stoplights, then make another right. Once you've done that, look off to your left. There is a large warehouse maybe one-hundred yards away. You can't miss it. Come through the gate and park at the front door. I'll be to your left, in a small office."

"And the evidence is in that office with you?"

"Yes, Detective Dantzler. The evidence is here."

Dantzler had no trouble finding the warehouse, even though his car was not equipped with a GPS or any navigation system. The trip took less than twenty minutes. He drove past the unmanned gate, parked slightly to the right of the front entrance and went inside.

David Langley didn't come close to fitting the image Dantzler had of him. In Dantzler's mind, Langley was short, stocky and either completely bald or had thinning hair. Dantzler was wrong on all counts. Langley was tall and thin, had a head full of solid white hair, and wore black horn-rimmed glasses. He was dressed in a pinstripe suit, the pants held up by suspenders, white shirt, red tie and black shoes. The man looked and dressed like a scientist. All that was missing, Dantzler concluded, was a pipe.

But Langley wasn't a scientist. He was a murderer. Of that, Dantzler had no doubt.

Langley wasn't alone, a fact that troubled Dantzler. He had expected the two men to discuss the Sarah Dantzler "evidence" in private. Maybe they would. Maybe the other man would leave once he and Langley concluded their business. Dantzler hoped so. He had no intention of discussing private matters or sharing information with a stranger in the room.

He also didn't want Langley to have a confederate to help him smooth out the tangle of lies he was sure to tell.

Langley spoke without standing. "Detective Dantzler, it is good to finally put a face to the voice of the man who is certain I murdered his mother. Please, have a seat."

"I never said I was certain you murdered by mother," Dantzler said, sitting in the chair across from the metal desk.

"You didn't say it, but that's what I heard." Langley nodded at the man sitting to his right. "This is Nick Marlow. He's head of Security at Apollo Enterprises."

Marlow looked at Dantzler but didn't speak. Dantzler decided to match Marlow's silence.

Langley said, "If you will give us ten or fifteen minutes, that should be ample time for us to conclude the initial stages of our task. Nick and I can take a break, then you and I can take a look at the evidence I've uncovered. Is that acceptable to you?"

"Do I have a choice?" Dantzler said.

"Not really." Langley pointed to a pitcher sitting on a table to his left. "In the meantime, would you like some lemonade? As you can see, Nick and I are having some, and I must say it is quite refreshing. Let me pour you some."

Langley reached across, picked up the pitcher and a paper cup, and poured the lemonade. "Here, try this," he said, handing the cup to Dantzler. "It's very good."

Dantzler hadn't eaten or had anything to drink since before noon. He was hungry and thirsty. Taking the cup from Langley, he quickly drank the lemonade. Langley had been right; it was refreshing.

For about thirty seconds.

Then Dantzler began to feel a slight tingling sensation in his head. His eyes began to burn, and his vision became fuzzy. Suddenly, there were two David Langleys and two Nick Marlows sitting across from him. His heart was racing, and his breathing was quick and shallow. Perspiration beaded on his forehead.

Even though he was only seconds away from losing consciousness, he was aware of one simple fact—he had been drugged.

The last thing he remembered before passing out was Nick Marlow removing the Glock from its holster.

CHAPTER THIRTY-TWO

The Olympus Club was the oldest and most-exclusive private men's club in the D.C. area. Its doors opened in 1887, and the man who founded the club was Amos Bartlett, Lee Bartlett's grandfather. Old Amos, who by all accounts was a cantankerous and racist individual, was dead serious about the club being exclusive. Jews, Catholics and men of color need not apply. This was strictly meant to be a sanctuary for wealthy, powerful white Protestants. It was, as one critic famously called the club, "The WASP Nest."

The club was housed in a three-story red brick building two blocks north of Lafayette Park. This was the original site, but not the original building, which had been a log cabin. The ground floor served as a meet-and-greet area, where members could mingle, chat, order drinks from the bar or a nice meal from the kitchen. The second floor, with its leather chairs, oak tables and large portraits of former members hanging on every wall, was the conversation room, where these men of great wealth and even greater egos spoke in a language most Americans could not comprehend.

But it was the third level that was most special, the most private. This was where the truly powerful members gathered, old men whose bodies had been ravaged by time, and yet their minds had remained clear, their thoughts sharper than a razor blade. A man had to be a club member in good standing for twenty-five years before he was allowed to venture into what was known as "The Upper Room." Here, the oldest club members recalled the grand old times, while lamenting how the world—and the United States in particular— was quickly going to hell. A Black president, too many immigrants, multiculturalism, an excess of entitlement programs . . . those were but a handful of clear indications that the country these men revered, an America once ruled by towering giants like Rockefeller, Vanderbilt, Carnegie and J.P. Morgan, had long since lost its way and was now traveling in a downward spiral.

To these men, America's greatness was a thing of the past, having died along with those old giants they worshipped as gods.

Lee Bartlett had belonged to the club since his early twenties, and was by consensus, the most-powerful and most-feared member. Also, the most-hated. Every club member bowed in his presence and smiled to his face, but away from the man, few kind words were ever spoken about him. Power generated fear, but seldom did it generate love or respect. This was especially true for Lee Bartlett.

Although a five-man board ruled on matters ranging from finances to which applicants were to be included or excluded, it was understood that the final vote belonged to Lee. Always. If he disagreed with the board's decision, the ruling was quickly changed. Without argument, without debate. No one dared challenge Lee Bartlett. Who in his right mind would argue with God?

On this beautiful sunny afternoon, Lee was sitting at his own private table near the back, an area long-ago christened "Bartlett's Cove." No one was allowed to sit at this table unless invited by Lee. Even though every member hated Lee, each one considered it an honor to be beckoned to his table. The status of sitting with Lee was stronger than their hatred of the man.

Today, Lee was sitting with the man known as Jet. According to strict club rules, a non-member like Jet should not have been allowed inside the building, much less sitting at a table in The Upper Room. But Jet was with Lee, which was not much different from being with Jesus Christ. While club members might not like the way Lee bent the rules whenever he pleased, they protested in silence. To do otherwise would be disastrous.

Lee and Jet had been at the table for close to an hour. Lee was drinking scotch, Jet a gin and tonic. They were waiting for Nick Marlow.

Stirring his drink, Jet said, "I would have given a year's salary to see Ben Parker's face when that movie came on. I can only imagine how he must have reacted."

"Oh, it was priceless," Lee said. "I have never seen blood drain from a man's face faster than it did when those first images appeared. He went white faster than Michael Jackson. I was almost certain he was going to stroke out on me."

"Too bad he didn't. The world would be better off without a sorry scumbag like him."

"Don't worry. He'll die soon enough. And when he does, there'll be a special place in hell reserved for him."

"How long have you known he was bent?" Jet said.

"Oh, a long time. Twenty-five years, maybe longer."

"You really should leak those movies to the press."

"If Nick arrives without the list, that's precisely what I'll do."

Jet took a drink and shook his head. "No, I think you should give them to the press, even if you have the list in hand."

"Can't do it, Jet. Although I truly detest Ben Parker and everything he stands for, I did give the man my word. My word counts, even when given to my enemies. If he fulfills his end of the bargain, then so will I. If he doesn't, then all bets are off."

Across the large room, the rickety elevator came to a stop and its doors opened. A white-haired man who had to be close to the century mark age-wise maneuvered his motorized wheelchair off the elevator, made a sharp left and headed toward a group of four men playing cards at a table beneath a large portrait of Amos Bartlett. The men, all of whom looked to be close to his age, cheerfully greeted the new arrival as "General."

Nick Marlow stepped off the elevator, looked around the room until he located Lee, and moved quickly to the table. Like Jet, Nick was not a club member. But, again, everyone knew Nick was "Lee's boy," so they wisely kept their thoughts to themselves.

Arriving at the table, Nick pulled a large envelope from his briefcase and handed it to Lee.

"Did we get what we ask for?" Lee said.

"There are a couple of names and addresses missing, but that's to be expected. Those folks move around a lot, as we all know. But there is more than enough to make Abdul-Aziz happy. It should keep him and his men busy for a long time."

"Well, as long as we get our money, I couldn't care less what that lunatic does," Lee said.

Nick scooted a chair back, sat and stared at Jet. "What's he doing here?"

"Nick, this is Jet," Lee answered.

Nick, confused by what he was hearing, said, "*You're* Jet? Why didn't I know this?"

Lee snapped his fingers and a maitre d' was at the table in two seconds. "Bring Nick a Heineken," Lee barked. "And make sure it's cold."

"I've seen you a million times. Why didn't I know you were Jet?" Nick repeated after the maitre d' was gone.

"To be honest with you, Nick, I'm surprised you didn't figure it out years ago," Lee said.

"Damn, I had no clue." Nick waited until his beer arrived before continuing. "Changing the subject to more pressing matters, I'm sure you are aware of the two 'guests' we have recently taken in."

"I am. And I see it as a most troubling problem in many ways."

"What guests?" Jet said, leaning forward.

"Seems a detective and an investigative reporter have been sniffing into areas that do not concern them," Lee said. "Areas involving Apollo Enterprises."

"Do you have them at the compound?" Jet said.

Lee sipped his scotch and nodded.

"Then what's the problem? Make them disappear."

"I'm afraid it's not quite that simple," Lee said. "We have no idea if they are working solo or if they had shared their itinerary with bosses or fellow workers. I wouldn't chance eliminating an investigative reporter, only to later learn that one of the paper's editors was aware of what was going on. As for killing a cop, well, that's always a risky thing to do, especially if we're unsure who knows what he's up to. That could open a whole new can of worms, bring on serious heat, which we don't need. No, we need answers before doing anything drastic."

"Were they working together?" Jet said.

"No, they were looking into entirely different matters," Nick answered. "The detective, I suspect, was acting alone. But like Lee said, with the reporter, I'm not so sure. She's the wild card in all this."

"The reporter is female?" Jet said. "Hell, leave me alone with her for five minutes and I'll guarantee you we'll know for certain if she's working solo or not. As for the detective, if you think he's flying solo, put a bullet in his brain."

"Let's move with caution and not do anything hasty." Lee turned to Nick, "When are we handing off the list to Abdul-Aziz's man?"

"I'm not sure yet," Nick said. "I'll phone Abdul-Aziz and let him set up the time and place for the meeting. It should happen within the next forty-eight hours. When I know, I'll pass along the information to Jet."

"Before it does happen, make sure we have our money," Lee pointed out. "Abdul-Aziz is a wacko, and I tend to not trust unstable men."

"You got it," Nick said, standing. "As for our guests, how do you want us to handle that?"

"You and Jet go to the compound sometime tomorrow. Let Jet have his time alone with the female reporter. If he ascertains that she is acting alone, we eliminate her. If Jet wishes to question the detective, he can do so, although I remain convinced that, given the circumstances, he is acting alone. Once Jet gets the information he needs, and if he is positive we're in the clear, kill them. Then burn the bodies and scatter the ashes. Remember, gentlemen, loose ends can hang you as quickly as a rope. That's why you always make sure there are no loose ends."

Tom Wallace

CHAPTER THIRTY-THREE

The two sentries manning the Apollo Enterprises guard shack were definitely not well-trained, professional soldiers. They were beginners, rookies, and nothing in their actions or behavior indicated otherwise. Cain came to this conclusion after observing them for less than fifteen minutes. He recognized a good soldier when he saw one, and these guys were nowhere close to being good. Even calling them soldiers was a stretch. One was sitting in a chair, head back against the wall, mouth open, sound asleep. His partner was standing by the window, paperback in one hand, a can of soda in the other hand. Good soldiers on guard do not behave in such an unprofessional manner.

Cain figured them to be in their late teens or early twenties, two young men seeking excitement and adventure, looking to prove their manhood and to show everyone how tough they were. For them, carrying a M16 rifle, having a pistol strapped to the hip and wearing a military-style uniform was all the proof they needed. Sadly, they had no idea what it meant to be a real man. Cain had seen plenty of young soldiers like these two, wannabes who invariably take photos of themselves dressed in full battle gear, and then send the photos back home to their buddies. *We're tough guys now* was the message they wanted to convey. To a pro like Cain, what the message conveyed was how misguided and naïve they were.

Ironically, their inexperience made Cain's mission that much more dangerous.

The plan devised by Cain and Houdini was simple enough, although to call it a plan was to grant it an undeserved status. It was more a ploy than a plan. Cain would stroll down the road in front of the compound, stop, take out his cell phone and begin taking pictures. Even if the guards were only half awake, this should be enough to get their attention. Once that happened, they would confront him, ask questions, pat him down and take him to the main house.

At least, that's what professional guards would do. With these two young knuckleheads, there was no way to predict how they would react. They might shoot first, then do the pat down later.

Cain would have to tread carefully, never taking his eyes off the men at any time. If either or both made a let's-kill-him-first-and-ask-questions-later move, he would have to react accordingly. He had no desire to kill these young

141

guys, but he wouldn't hesitate to take them out if it came down to his life or theirs. Staying alive was rule number one.

Cain parked a quarter mile from the compound's entrance, walked to within a few yards of the gate, and found a huge maple tree that provided good cover. He had been here since a few minutes before four o'clock. At four, the two young guys came on duty, replacing a pair of older, more grizzled men, neither of whom looked to be much more professional than their youthful replacements. This was almost an hour ago. Based on the lack of energy displayed by the young guys after only one hour on duty, Cain was convinced they would be virtually comatose by the time their shift ended, most likely around midnight. If things went according to plan, he wouldn't be around to find out.

Cain quietly backed away from the tree, and staying in the woods, he headed back toward his car. Once he was a safe enough distance away from the guard shack, he got back on the main road and began walking toward the compound. Less than ten minutes later, he passed by the front gate, stopped, took out his cell phone and began taking pictures of the main house.

Now came the most dangerous moment. What would the guards do? Would they confront him or start firing? Given this uncertainty, his senses and instincts were on high alert.

The guard who was standing put down his book and can of soda, nudged his partner awake and pointed at Cain. Both men quickly grabbed their M16s and bolted from the guard shack. Within a matter of seconds they were standing in front of Cain, weapons pointing at him. Cain was impressed. They might not be competent soldiers, he concluded, but they had more than enough speed to be track stars.

"You can't do that," the smaller of the two guards barked, pointing at Cain's cell phone. "Photos aren't allowed."

"You mean, I can't take a few pictures?" Cain asked, giving his best innocent tourist impersonation. "The main house is probably an historic structure. I'd bet it's almost two-hundred years old."

"I can't speak to that," the kid said. "All I know is, photos are verboten. So . . . put your phone away and skedaddle on down the road."

Cain realized these guys were content to simply let him walk away without checking the photos, questioning him, or patting him down. Getting captured shouldn't be this difficult, he thought. But with these two young mutts in charge, it was clear he was going to have to make things happen.

"Look, I'm not bothering anyone," Cain argued. "I'm simply taking a few pictures, that's all. Where's the harm in that? Anyway, this is America. I have rights, and one of my rights is that I'm free to do what I please, so long as I'm not hurting someone else. And I don't believe I am."

The second guard, the one who had been sleeping, moved closer to Cain.

"Dude, we know this is America. We're not stupid. But you're standing on private property, which means America or not, your precious rights just got fucked. So make like Elvis and leave the building."

What do I have to do to get these clowns to do their job? "I don't think so, *Dude*," Cain said. "I'm standing on a state road, and last time I checked, state roads are not private property."

Cain wasn't sure if this was true or not, but it sure sounded good. And he'd said it with the authority and conviction of someone who knew what he was talking about. Not that it mattered much either way. He was trying to goad them into taking him prisoner, not give them a lesson on privacy laws.

"Dude, you're like a pimple on my ass that just won't go away," the guard said, pointing his weapon at Cain's face. "We don't want to get rough with you, but we will if we have to."

It was all Cain could do to keep from laughing at that statement. "Like I said, *Dude*, I'm not bothering anyone, so I'm not going anywhere."

"What's your name, asshole?" the smaller guard said.

"You don't know me, so what difference does it make what my name is?" Cain said. "Dude or asshole works for me."

"Throw in wise ass while you're at it."

"Look, guys, this is a big misunderstanding," Cain said. "I mean no harm. You can frisk me, pat me down, whatever, and you won't find anything incriminating."

It took a few seconds before the guard caught the hint

"Okay, asshole, hand me the phone, turn around, spread your legs and hold your arms straight out like airplane wings."

Now we're getting somewhere. "Whatever you say." Cain handed his phone to the guard and turned around. "I never argue with a man holding a rifle."

The taller guard looked at the photos on the phone, said, "There's nothing worthwhile here. Check his wallet for ID."

"I don't carry a wallet," Cain said.

"Every man carries a wallet," the guard replied.

"Not this man," Cain said.

"Turn around . . . slowly," the guard said to Cain. Then to his partner, "Check his pockets."

Once again the guard showed his inexperience by only checking Cain's pants pockets, front and back. Cain's upper torso, legs, ankles and back were not checked. He could've had five weapons on him and they would have gone undetected. These guys really were in the wrong line of work.

If he was going to be taken prisoner, he was going to have to do everything but put the handcuffs on.

"Are you satisfied that I'm not a terrorist?" Cain said, holding out his right hand. "If you don't mind, I'd like my phone back."

The two young men looked at each other, shrugged as if to say *why not*, and then the guard with the phone handed it to Cain. He started to put the phone into his shirt pocket, hesitated, and after making a big show that the pocket was full, pulled out a folded piece of paper, and dropped the phone into the now-empty pocket.

"What's on that piece of paper?" the taller guard asked.

"Nothing that would interest you," Cain said.

This was a lie. In fact, it was his entry into the compound. It was what they should have found ten minutes ago, and would have if they were the least bit competent. On the paper was a detailed sketch of the compound's grounds and buildings that had been drawn up by one of Houdini's artist pals.

"That's for us to decide," the guard said, yanking the paper from Cain's hand. He unfolded it, studied it briefly and then handed it to his partner.

"Holy shit, this fuckin' guy is some kind of spy," the smaller guard said. "This is a map of the compound. They need to know about him inside."

The taller guard shoved Cain forward. "Come on, *Dude*. You're coming with us."

Finally, Cain said to himself.

CHAPTER THIRTY-FOUR

Based on aerial photos of the compound, Cain knew the main house was exactly twenty-eight yards from the guard shack. Walking briskly along a stone pathway, he and the young guard reached the house in less than forty-five seconds. Once again, the guard demonstrated his inexperience by keeping the barrel of his M16 pressed against Cain's back every step of the way. It was a move only an amateur would make. No professionally trained guard escorting a prisoner would ever be that close. Distance was a safety valve. Had Cain wanted to disarm the guard, he could have done so without breaking a sweat. By executing a quick spin move to his left, using his left arm to force the weapon away from his back, followed by a right-handed judo chop to the guard's carotid artery and a snap of the neck would have done the trick. The guard would have been dead in five seconds.

They walked up the steps onto a huge veranda, where, following the guard's command, Cain opened the front door. Entering the house was not unlike entering a decent-size hotel, maybe one you might have visited in a city like San Francisco or Chicago in the late 19th century. It was a grand and glamorous structure modeled after the great mansions of England and France. A house meant to advertise wealth and privilege. The foyer, with its hardwood floor, was fifteen feet wide and extended at least half the length of a basketball court. At the end of the foyer was a staircase that wound upward to the second floor. There were three doors on the right, two on the left. A row of lights on the arched ceiling were so bright they generated heat as well as light.

The guard shoved Cain down the hallway several feet, and then ordered him to enter the first door on the left.

There were six people in the large room, four to Cain's left, two to the right. The two on his right were Jack Dantzler and Kayce Clark. They were standing in front of a large sofa. Kayce had a darkening bruise under her left eye, and blood was dripping from her nose. It was obvious she had recently been worked over by someone serious about inflicting real pain.

Cain shifted his attention to Dantzler, rolled his eyes and shook his head like an exasperated father does when confronting a disobedient child. He was not the least bit surprised that Dantzler had not heeded his advice to stay away from these people. Given the fact that Sarah Dantzler's murderer was probably in this very room, Cain couldn't blame Dantzler for refusing to follow orders.

Were he in Dantzler's shoes, he would have been equally disobedient.

Looking at the four men to his left, Cain only recognized the two standing in the middle. He recognized them from the photos Houdini secured. The tall one with white hair and black horn-rimmed glasses was David Langley. The smaller man was Nick Marlow, who, according to Houdini's research, was "volatile and extremely dangerous." They were flanked on both sides by uniformed men with M16s pointed at Kayce and Dantzler.

"Who do we have here?" Langley said to the young guard who brought Cain to the house.

"Don't know," the guard answered. "He had no ID on him."

"Cain."

The word seemed to float into the room like it was riding on a cloud, or drifting on the wind. Like a beam of light had suddenly penetrated a vast expanse of darkness. It was not there, and then it was.

All heads turned to see the man known as Jet standing in a rear doorway.

"His name is Cain."

"How do you know him?" Nick Marlow asked.

"Oh, we go back a long way, don't we, Cain? Of course, I'm assuming you still remember me."

The man who walked slowly into the room needn't have had his doubts. Cain recognized him the instant he heard the man's voice. Seeing him in the flesh only confirmed the man's identity. This was a man and a voice he would never forget. It could have been a hundred years since he last saw the man, but he would always remember the face and the voice.

The man known as Jet was now completely bald, the face had earned a few wrinkles along the way, the stomach a little thicker. Other than that, not much had changed. The same dark eyes, the all-white suit, with the bulge on his right side, where he holstered his pistol, the same smugness, the ever-present arrogant and condescending attitude that said I'm superior to you and we all know it.

Jeff Toland.

The CIA operative who shot and killed Doctor Ducky all those years ago.

"Put cuffs on him," Toland said to one of the two older guards. "Hands behind his back."

The guard leaned his M16 against the wall, grabbed Cain's arms, pulled them behind his back and slapped on the handcuffs.

"Gentlemen, are you aware that we are now in the presence of a living legend?" Toland said, looking at Langley and Marlow. "This man is reputed to be the world's greatest assassin. They say the number he has killed could go as high as five-hundred. Personally, I've always considered him to be vastly overrated, and the numbers to be greatly inflated."

Langley said, "So this is Cain. I've heard about him."

"What have you heard, David?" Toland said. "Enlighten me."

"What you just said . . . that he's the best."

"Don't believe everything you hear, David." Toland moved closer to Cain, said, "I should have killed you in Kontum when I had the chance. Not taking you out was a grave error on my part."

Cain smiled and nodded. "You're right about that. But you didn't, and now it's too late."

"It's never too late to rid the world of a pest."

"Listen to what I'm about to say, Toland. And pay close attention, because what I'm about to tell you is serious."

"I'm all ears, Cain."

"I'm going to make you a promise."

"What are you going to promise me?"

"That before this night is over you'll be a dead man."

"And who is going to make me a dead man?"

"You're looking at him."

"A man with his hands cuffed behind him and surrounded by armed guards shouldn't make brash promises like that," Toland said. "Makes you look bad when you fail to keep them."

"This is a promise I'll keep. You can count on that."

Toland drove his right fist into Cain's stomach, pushed him aside, and walked closer to Dantzler. He studied Dantzler's face for almost a minute.

"You look familiar to me," Toland said. "Where do I know you from? I'm positive we've met."

"Never happened," Dantzler said.

Toland looked at Marlow, said, "Who is this guy?"

"He's the detective I told you about," Marlow answered. "Jack Dantzler."

Toland reacted at though he was seeing a ghost from his past. His face came alive with sudden recognition. "Johnny Dantzler's kid? Sure, you have to be. You're the spitting image of your old man."

"Did you know my father?" Dantzler said.

"*Know* him? I killed him. Shot him right in the heart. You should have seen the surprised look on your father's face when that bullet slammed into his chest. He couldn't believe what was happening. Went down like he'd been dropped from an airplane."

Dantzler was stung by the words, but he had to be sure Toland was telling the truth. "You killed my father in Vietnam?"

"Johnny Dantzler died in the rain on a muddy road in Laos."

"Why did you kill him?"

"I was protecting my assets."

"What assets?"

"We were running an operation that was making us millions of dollars.

Your father showed up and started asking too many questions. At a certain point, he was close to finding some answers. His aim was to shut us down. I couldn't let that happen."

"What about my mother? Why did you kill her?" Dantzler asked.

Toland shook his head. "Don't know anything about your mother. If she was murdered, it was by someone's hand other than mine."

"That would be my hand," Langley said, stepping closer to Dantzler. "She was a very beautiful woman, lovely in every way. I regretted having to eliminate her, but she, like your father, was simply too inquisitive for her own good. She was a voice that had to be silenced."

Dantzler glared at Langley but chose to remain quiet. Anyway, what could he say? He now had the answer to the one question that had haunted him since he was fourteen years old: The name of the man who murdered Sarah Elizabeth Dantzler. He also knew who killed his father. But what good did it do him to have those answers? Under the present circumstances no good at all. Unless taking them to the grave counted for something.

Nick Marlow took an envelope from his briefcase and handed it to Toland. "That's the list," he said. "You know the time and place, right?"

"It's all been arranged," Toland said, taking the envelope. "Dispose of the detective and our lady friend if you so desire. But keep Cain alive until I get back. He's all mine."

After Toland was gone, Marlow said to the two older guards, "Take Cain and Dantzler down to the basement and lock them in the storage room. There are two locks; use both of them. And make sure one of you stays outside the door at all times. If they try anything, shoot to kill."

"What about the girl?" Langley said. "What's your plan for her?"

"Put her in one of the upstairs bedrooms. After what she's been through, she's no threat to go anywhere." Marlow nodded to the guards. "Get these two clowns downstairs."

"This way," one of the guards said, pointing to the doorway where Toland entered.

Dantzler left the room first, followed by Cain.

CHAPTER THIRTY-FIVE

Judging by the heavy steel door and the two big locks, Cain suspected the only thing that had been stored in this room were human beings. It was nothing less than a cage meant for confinement. Most likely, the original prisoners were slaves kept here by their masters. Those who attempted to escape or disobeyed orders were probably kept here until they could be taken outside and severely beaten. Others, those who were about to be sold or traded, were locked up in this cage until the deal was finalized. In this relatively small space, men and women had been subjected to treatment that was cruel, inhumane and evil.

The room had the definite look and feel of a jail cell, although it was in fact only a storage room. The walls were bare, a single light bulb dangled from the ceiling, and the only furnishings consisted of a wooden bench and two wrought-iron chairs. There was no toilet, no wash basin. It was a room that reeked of sweat, fear, desperation. And death. No doubt, many had died in this small enclosure.

Cain had no intention of joining that list of the dead.

Turning to Dantzler, Cain said, "You just couldn't stay away, could you, Detective?"

"Did you really think I would? I wanted answers, and I wasn't going to find them unless I went looking for them. They weren't going to fall into my lap."

"Well, now you have your answers. You're also a prisoner who'll likely be dead by morning. The question you have to ask yourself is, were finding those answers worth it?"

"Save the lecture for later on down the road, Cain. Right now, I'm in no mood to hear it."

"No, I don't imagine you are."

Dantzler said, "I'm surprised these Apollo guys were cagey enough to capture you."

"Get real, Detective. These guys couldn't catch a lightning bug. I'm here because I let them take me."

"That doesn't strike me as a sound strategy."

"Maybe not, but it was the easiest way in. What I've seen thus far of Apollo Enterprises personnel isn't all that impressive, but their security system is excellent. I'll give them credit for that. There was no way I could have breached it. So, I let them grab me."

"Okay. Now what are we going to do?" Dantzler said.

"I can't speak for you, but I plan on getting out of here."

"Exactly how does your plan work?"

"First, I'm going to kill the two guys guarding us. Then I'm going to kill anyone upstairs who gets in my way. Does that plan meet with your approval, Detective?"

"I like it. But . . . how do you execute the plan when your hands are cuffed behind your back?"

"The cuffs are coming off."

"Who's going to remove them?"

"Who do you think? One of the guards."

"Just like that?"

"Yeah."

"How are you going to persuade him to do it?"

"In about two minutes I'm going to tell the guard that I need to take a leak. When I do, it is going to put him in a very delicate situation. He's going to have an extremely difficult decision to make. He'll have two clear-cut choices. He can remove the cuffs and let me do my business, or he can unzip my pants, reach in, take out my pecker and hold it while I piss. My hunch is, he sees himself as the real macho type. Guys like him always do. And macho guys have no desire to handle another man's package. So . . . he'll opt for plan A. When he removes the handcuffs, he will have signed his own death certificate."

"Sounds simple enough," Dantzler said, adding, "provided you can make it work."

"Detective, I wouldn't try it unless I was sure it was going to work."

Cain went to the steel door and yelled to the guard that he needed to hit the latrine. After several seconds of silence, Cain heard the sound of metal against metal. The guard inserted the key, unlocked the two locks and pulled the door open. Stepping back, his M16 pointed at Cain, the guard said the latrine was at the end of the hallway to the right.

Before heading toward the restroom Cain assessed the situation, focusing primarily on the actions and behavior of the two guards. Based on how they were handling this situation, he judged them to be only slightly superior to the two young men he encountered at the gate. These two were older and more experienced, but they were miles away from being thoroughly professional. Everything they were doing was wrong.

For starters, the guard standing at the foot of the stairway should have left his post and locked the door to the storage room. That should have been his first order of business. Then he should have followed his partner and Cain to the restroom, keeping his weapon pointed at Cain while the handcuffs were being removed and Cain emptied his bladder. But none of this happened. The guard chose to remain at the bottom of the stairs, apparently unconcerned that the storage door remained open and unlocked. Nor did he show much concern for his partner, who had the task of escorting Cain without appropriate backup.

Although they had no way of knowing it at the time, these blunders would cost both men their lives.

Killing the guard escorting him would be easy enough. It could be done in a matter of seconds. The only issue confronting Cain was that it had to be done silently. If the guard made a loud noise, or managed to fire off a shot, it would alert his partner at the far end of the hallway. Then things could get tricky and complicated. Both he and Dantzler could find themselves in real danger.

Inside the small restroom, Cain positioned himself in front of the toilet and waited until he heard the rattling of keys. He was now only seconds away from making his move. Cain knew the guard would need both hands to unlock the cuffs, and that he would have to secure his M16 by tucking it under his arm. This meant the guard's finger would be a good distance from the trigger, which greatly increased Cain's chances of a silent kill.

At the precise moment when Cain felt the cuff on his right wrist fall off, he went into action, first by yanking the weapon away from the guard, then by spinning around and landing a hard judo chop to the guard's throat. The blow not only stunned the guard, it rendered him unable to speak or make a sound. Next, Cain moved behind the guard, forced him to his knees, bent him over and pushed his head into the toilet bowl. Three minutes later the guard was dead. Suffocation by drowning. Cain had always heard drowning was an easy death. After seeing the guard go out this way, he wasn't sure he agreed. It seemed like a pretty damn unpleasant way to die.

Cain picked up the M16, went to the door and peered down the hallway. The guard at the steps had not moved, meaning Cain had accomplished his goal of killing in silence. Phase one was easy and had gone as planned. Phase two could be trickier. But given this set of circumstances, Cain only had a single option, and that option played to his advantage. He couldn't attack the guard— to run twenty feet down the hallway would be an insane move that would get him shot—so he had to bring the guard to him. How best to make that happen? Simple. By remaining silent. Human beings tend to be naturally nosy, so at some point, the guard, not seeing or hearing from his partner, would be compelled to investigate, to see what was happening. Being aware of what was going on was part of his job.

It took almost five minutes before the guard called out his partner's name and asked what was going on. His question was met by silence, which only increased his curiosity. Slowly, he began moving down the hallway toward the restroom. Cain backed against the wall and waited, knowing the guard would have his weapon pointed straight ahead. This meant Cain would see the barrel of the M16 before he saw the guard. When the barrel came into view, he grabbed it, and jerked the weapon out of the guard's hands. He then stepped in front of the stunned guard and hit him hard in the face with the butt of the weapon, driving him against the wall. Cain took the guard's head in both hands and gave a savage twist, snapping the man's neck.

After dragging the guard's body into the restroom and positioning it alongside his partner, Cain went through their pockets until he found a set of keys. It took him two tries before he found the one that unlocked his handcuffs. Once both cuffs were off his wrists, he quickly raced down the hallway and into the storage room, where Dantzler was sitting in one of the chairs.

"Maybe you are as good as they say you are," Dantzler said. "As good as *you* say you are."

"Did you have your doubts, Detective?"

"To be perfectly honest, yes, I did."

"A cynic . . . no wonder you're a good cop," Cain said, adding, "stand up and turn around."

After removing the handcuffs from Dantzler, Cain handed him the M16. "You know how to use one of these?"

"This may come as a surprise, but I'm pretty good with a rifle."

Cain laughed. "So was your old man."

Cain led them down the hallway to the foot of the steps. Using his hands, he signaled that he would go up first, check out the situation and then give Dantzler the okay to follow. Dantzler understood and nodded his consent.

When Cain reached the top of the stairs and looked into the big room, he was surprised to find it occupied by only one person. David Langley was standing with his back to Cain, and was holding a drink in his right hand. Cain motioned to Dantzler that it was time to move.

As Cain and Dantzler burst into the room, two things happened simultaneously. First, Langley spun around, and upon seeing his assailants, he dropped his glass and fell onto the sofa. Second, a back door slammed shut, and there were footsteps on the hard wooden porch.

"Who's leaving?" Cain said to Langley.

"Nick Marlow."

"You stay with Langley," Cain said to Dantzler. "I'm going after Marlow. And don't kill him, Detective. Not yet, anyway. Not until he answers some questions."

With that, Cain was out the door.

CHAPTER THIRTY-SIX

Cain had no doubt that he would kill Nick Marlow. This was a given. Marlow was the enemy, part of the team that paid an assassin to murder Ray Dunlap. Therefore, Marlow had to die. But Cain needed information, namely what was on the list Marlow handed to Toland, and where the exchange was taking place. This meant Cain had to keep Marlow alive long enough—and inflict enough pain—to extract the information.

Killing a man was easy. Subduing him and forcing him to talk presented an entirely different set of problems. This was especially true if the man was, as Marlow was reported to be, "volatile and extremely dangerous." Cain never took an opponent lightly, not even those he judged to be inferior. Against a foe like Marlow, a man familiar with combat and killing, Cain would have to be sharp, precise and ruthless.

Cain saw Marlow walking briskly toward one of the outer buildings. He was approximately twenty-five feet ahead of Cain, and fewer than ten paces from the building. Cain had to move fast.

Marlow heard movement coming behind him, turned and saw Cain running toward him with the speed of a jungle cat. Marlow may have been startled to see Cain approaching, but he didn't panic. Cain had to give him kudos for remaining calm under pressure. Finally, Cain thought, an Apollo guy who knows how to handle himself.

As Cain shortened the distance between him and Marlow, and as Marlow reached behind him to get the pistol from his back pocket, a sharp crack rang out from the wooded area to Cain's right. Realizing the shot came from a high-powered rifle, Cain ducked down, but never stopped moving toward Marlow. His first priority was simple: secure Marlow before the pistol came into play.

Cain needn't have worried.

A split-second after the shot rang out, the top of Marlow's head came apart, a huge chunk of his skull flying off into the dark, followed by a heavy spray consisting of blood, bone and brain matter. Miraculously, Marlow, though obviously dead, remained standing, his eyes open but unfocused. Moments later, a second shot hit him in the throat, driving him backward and to the ground.

Cain eyed the pistol next to Marlow's body. He grabbed the weapon, tucked it into his waistband and, keeping low, headed back toward the main house. He'd only traveled a few feet when he saw a figure moving slowly in his direction. It was the young guard from the front gate. And once again, the guy was doing everything wrong, this time committing a tactical error that could get him killed. He was moving toward a man recently killed by sniper fire. Even worse, he was moving at a snail's pace, making him a sitting duck if the sniper chose to take him out.

But, Cain knew, neither he nor the young guard were targets for the shooter.

Staying in the shadows, Cain eased his way toward the young guard. When he was even with him, Cain punched him in the stomach. The blow wasn't hard, but it served two purposes. The guard bent over, gasping for air, and he dropped his M16. Cain stood behind the guard, wrapped his arms around him, and carefully lowered him to the ground, keeping a knee in the guard's back and a forearm on his neck.

"Are you going to kill me," the guard moaned.

"If I were going to kill you, you wouldn't be alive to ask that question," Cain whispered into the guard's ear. "Okay, here's the deal. You are going to remain in this exact position for the next fifteen minutes. When those fifteen minutes have passed, you get up, go around to the guard shack and collect your partner. Then the two of you get the hell away from this place as fast as you can. Leave your weapons behind, along with anything else issued to you by Apollo Enterprises. Apollo Enterprises is going down, and so are the men who run it. If you're anywhere near this place, or have any obvious connection to it, you'll go down with them. Trust me. You don't want to end up behind bars for those guys. If you agree to do what I've said, nod your head. If you disagree, tell me and I will kill you."

The young guard vigorously nodded his head.

"Excellent," Cain said. He tapped the watch on the guard's left wrist. "Stay the full fifteen minutes. Leave earlier and I'll know it. The clock starts now."

Cain left the young guard and went back into the main house. David Langley was sitting on the sofa, head down, looking almost like he was in shock. Dantzler was standing a few feet away, the M16 aimed at Langley. Kayce Clark was to Dantzler's left. She had an icepack pressed against her left eye.

"Who did this to you?" Cain asked.

"Toland."

Cain nodded. "Do you have your cell phone with you?"

"Yes."

"Call Houdini, and tell him . . ." Seeing the confused look on Kayce's face, he said, "Call Andy Waltz. Tell him where you are and what's happened. He'll know what to do."

Cain stepped in front of Dantzler, took Marlow's pistol from his pocket and placed the end of the barrel against Langley's forehead. The fear of being shot had the effect of snapping Langley back to life. He bolted upright, eyes wide behind those large, thick black glasses. He looked like a frightened owl.

Cain said, "I'm going to ask you a series of questions, Langley, and you are going to answer each one quickly and honestly. If I so much as smell a lie, I'm going to turn your head into a taco shell. Do you understand?"

"I understand," Langley whispered.

"The list Marlow gave to Toland. What's on it?"

"Names and addresses."

"Whose names and addresses?"

"I don't know. Why don't you ask Marlow?"

"He's in no position to answer. So why don't you tell me?"

"I don't know. Really, I don't."

"I'm beginning to smell a lie, Langley."

"No, no, I'm not lying. They never told me any details about what was on the list. I swear. What I can tell you is that we're being paid fifty-million dollars for those names and addresses."

"Who's paying?"

"Sheikh Abdul-Aziz."

"Who gave you the list?" Cain said.

"No one gave it to me. Senator Ben Parker gave it to Nick Marlow and Lee Bartlett."

"Is Toland meeting with Abdul-Aziz?"

Langley shook his head. "He's meeting with one of Abdul-Aziz's cousins. His name is Ahmad. I think he works at the U.N."

"Where is the meeting taking place?"

"The Vietnam Memorial."

"The Wall?"

"Yes."

"When?"

"Two-thirty."

Cain was convinced that Langley had told the truth. He was too afraid of dying to lie. However, Cain wanted to make sure.

Pressing the pistol even harder against Langley's forehead, Cain said, "Is everything you've told me the absolute truth?"

"Yes, yes, I swear. Do you think I would lie if it meant being killed? I'm not stupid."

Handing the pistol to Dantzler, Cain said, "He's all yours, Detective. Do with him as you please."

Cain had one final hurdle to clear before he could get to his car and begin the journey to D.C. He had to take care of the young guy manning the guard shack. Not a hard task, but a time-consuming one. And right now, time was not on his side. He had to get to the Wall before Toland or Abdul-Aziz's cousin arrived. If he didn't, the handoff would likely take place. Worse, he would miss the chance to kill Toland.

That was unacceptable.

Cain left the main house through the back door, eased to his left, and staying in the shadows, slowly made his way to the guard shack. The guard, having heard shots fired, was nervous, on edge, high on adrenaline and clearly very agitated. A guy this jumpy would fire at anything, even a shadow. Cain was aware that he had to move with extreme caution. The slightest mistake could prove fatal.

He kept moving forward, deep in the shadows, until he was almost even with the young guard. Cain waited for the right moment before beginning his attack. It came almost a minute later, when the guard turned his back to Cain. In less than a heartbeat, Cain disarmed the guard, had his arms around him, and carefully forced him to the ground. Following the same routine as before, he placed a knee in the guard's back and a forearm against his neck.

"About ten minutes from now your buddy is going to show up," Cain said. "When he does, the two of you get the hell out of Dodge. If you have questions, ask him. He'll have the answers. But until he arrives, you stay exactly as you are now. Got it?"

"Come on, Dude. Can't I at least sit up? Maybe have a smoke?"

Cain fought hard to suppress a laugh. "No. Your buddy is on his belly, you stay on your belly. What's good for him is good for you. And one final thing: You two guys look for another way to make a buck. You're not cut out for this line of work."

Cain gently patted the young guard on the shoulder, stood, went through the gate, made a right and began running toward his car.

His destination: The holy of holies for all Vietnam vets.

CHAPTER THIRTY-SEVEN

When Cain first laid eyes on the Vietnam Memorial Wall in 1982, his initial thought was, "My country has finally paid a fitting tribute to the more than fifty-eight thousand men and women who lost their lives in that faraway place."

Men and women who, as Lincoln so eloquently stated in his Gettysburg Address, "gave the last full measure of devotion" while fighting in a questionable war poorly managed by our so-called best and brightest leaders. Turns out, the best weren't all that good, and the brightest weren't all that smart. But then, they seldom are.

For Cain, as with most surviving Vietnam vets and their families, the Wall was considered a sacred place. Controversial at first—some critics loathed the design, labeling it "nihilistic" and a "black gash of shame"—it has since become one of the most-visited sites in D.C. Each year more than three-million visitors walk along the pathway that runs parallel to the Wall, some in search of a single name, others there to pay tribute to all the fallen heroes. Some visitors leave small flags, flowers, photos or other personal mementoes at the base of the Wall, while others will take pencil and paper and etch the name of their loved one. Many are content to simply reach up and touch the name of their departed family member, friend or fellow soldier.

Using rare black granite to construct the Wall was, Cain felt, nothing less than an inspired choice. The reflective quality of black granite was the reason why it was chosen in the first place. It was intended to symbolically bind past and present. While achieving that goal, it also did much more—it connected the visitor to the past. Standing in front of the Wall, a person was confronted by his or her own image staring out from the black granite stone, giving the person the sensation of being inside the Wall with the dead.

Cain was familiar with more than a dozen of the men whose names were listed on the Wall, and he felt a deep sadness when thinking about the sacrifice each man made. They died too soon, too young, years before they should have. They died far from home, far away from loved ones. And like countless other soldiers who fought in wars dating back to antiquity, they died a violent death.

Of all the names on the Wall, there was one that haunted him most—Johnny Dantzler. Cain had encountered many soldiers over the decades, the majority of whom were dedicated, brave, selfless and tough. But none of those men, not even the very best, were equal to Johnny Dantzler. None were braver, more intelligent or more dependable. From Cain's perspective, Johnny Dantzler was superior in every way.

But Johnny Dantzler did not die in combat with the enemy; rather, he had been gunned down in cold blood on a muddy path somewhere in Laos. Shot dead at the age of twenty-six by Jeff Toland. His life snuffed out by a coward. Toland, like all men of great arrogance, believed himself to be above such judgments as retribution or accountability. And, of course, in the end, those men are always wrong. At some point, every individual must answer for past crimes committed. Toland had no way of knowing it, but in a very short time he was going to pay for his sins. Pay the supreme penalty . . . with his life.

Johnny Dantzler's death would be avenged.

And Cain would be the avenger.

The Vietnam Memorial Wall remains open to the public twenty-four hours a day. However, from 11:30 p.m. until 9:30 a.m., no Rangers or other personal are on duty to answer questions or give directions. Toland surely knew this. That's why he scheduled the meeting for this time of night. He wanted no one around who might ask questions or interfere with the planned exchange.

Cain's big concern was that a handful of late-night visitors might be present. If they were, it would dictate a change of plan. Killing two men while a host of witnesses looked on was never an acceptable tactic. If visitors were there, he would be forced to make the necessary adjustment, and that would mean acting on the fly, when variables that can't always be foreseen or controlled can jeopardize the mission. Failure's favorite hiding place is in the unknown.

Cain arrived at the Wall a few minutes before two o'clock. After positioning himself at the east end, the end pointing toward the Washington Monument, he looked out of the shadows to see if he could spot any night-owl visitors. There were two—a man in a wheelchair and the person who accompanied him—and they were no more than twenty to twenty-five feet away. Cain had no idea how long they had been at the Wall, or how long they intended to stay. He could only hope they departed before Toland or Abdul-Aziz's cousin showed up.

He got lucky; the two men left ten minutes later, heading in a westward direction, away from him. As he watched them disappear into the darkness, he couldn't help but to wonder if he'd made a mistake by positioning himself at the end of such an extended structure. From end to end, the length of the Wall was just shy of two-hundred-fifty feet. If Toland and Abdul-Aziz's cousin met at the opposite end, Cain might not see the exchange take place. Nor would he be able to get to them before they got away. Maybe, Cain thought, a more strategic location would have been in those trees straight across from the Wall's center. Being positioned there would give him a clear view of the entire Wall.

As he pondered making the move, he saw a lone figure walking slowly in his direction. The man was small, dressed in an expensive-looking suit, and he appeared to be scared and very nervous. Based on his Middle East features, he was obviously Abdul-Aziz's cousin and not a visitor. It was also obvious that he was not happy to be here. He continuously looked behind him, as though he were expecting to be attacked from the rear. This man, Cain assessed, was not accustomed to late-night clandestine meetings.

What Cain didn't know was whether or not this man had ever met Jeff Toland. He doubted it, calculating the odds to be fifty-fifty at best. But even if they had met at some point, Cain figured the odds to be a more favorable seventy-thirty that the man would not recognize Toland's voice in the dark. Given those odds, he would take the risk.

The man continued moving forward until he was no more than twenty feet from Cain. He hesitated, looked behind him once again, made a slight turn, and with Toland nowhere in sight, he started to hurry away.

"Up here, Ahmad," Cain said, his voice barely above a whisper. "I'm up here."

Startled, Ahmad turned quickly, said, "Is that you, Toland?"

"Yes."

"Do you have the list?"

"Do you have the fifty million?"

"Of course I have it," Ahmad said, sounding hurt that such a question was asked. "When we make a deal, we honor it."

"Excellent. Then let's get this over with."

Ahmad hurried forward, no doubt eager to make the trade and get the hell away from a situation he wanted no part of. Cain waited until the man reached the end of the Wall, grabbed him by the shoulders and threw him to the ground. Ahmad was a diplomat, not a warrior, so killing him was easy. Cain snapped the man's neck, dragged the body behind the Wall and began rummaging through his pockets. He found the envelope and carefully opened it. Inside was a check for fifty-million dollars made out to Apollo Enterprises, Inc.

Cramming the envelope into his pants pocket, Cain stood, returned to the shadows at the end of the Wall, and began the wait for Jeff Toland. Cain had already made the decision to inflict as much pain as possible before ending Toland's life. Allowing emotion to enter into his mindset was something Cain had never done before. It was his belief that emotion was not only useless, it was dangerous. Being emotional led to mistakes, and mistakes got you killed. That's why he never felt emotion when eliminating an opponent. For him, opponents were nothing more than obstacles that had to be cleared away, and emotion wasn't required when removing an obstacle.

But Toland was more than an obstacle. He was the man who gunned down Johnny Dantzler in cold blood. He was one of the men willing to make a deal with an individual who was proud to call himself a sworn enemy of the United States. Toland was not only a coward and a murderer, he was a traitor.

Jeff Toland deserved to suffer.

And Cain would make sure he did.

Toland, true to form, was late for the meeting. Two-thirty came and went. So did three o'clock. Cain was beginning to wonder if Toland had arrived early, found a place to hide in the darkness, and then waited to see if it was safe for the meeting to take place. Perhaps after witnessing Cain kill Abdul-Aziz's, Toland, deciding now was not the time for a fight, eased back to his car and drove away. Perhaps it happened that way, but Cain didn't think so. Toland wasn't that intelligent, that cagey. He was not a strategic planner.

At three-twenty, Cain saw a man emerge from the darkness, walking in his direction. It was Jeff Toland. The all-white attire was the giveaway. Toland moved quickly, his head turning in all directions, looking for the man he was expecting to meet. His left hand was positioned on his chest, inches away from the .45 he carried there.

Toland was less than ten feet away when Cain stepped out of the shadows. Toland stopped dead in his tracks, stared hard at Cain, doing his best to give the impression he wasn't surprised or shocked. He even managed a slight grin, his vain attempt to show that he wasn't afraid or intimidated. It didn't work. Cain saw fear dancing in the man's eyes.

Toland had reacted the way any normal man would when suddenly overwhelmed by the hard, cold realization that he had come face to face with Cain. Face to face with certain death.

The desire to stay alive is our most basic primal instinct, and Toland felt it to the very core of his being. But desire alone won't keep death at bay. To stay among the living, especially when squared off against a proven killer like Cain, requires clear thinking and bold action. Toland let his mind run through a checklist of possible moves, finally settling on the one he felt would give him the best chance of surviving. The best chance to stay alive.

Cain waited for Toland to make his move. But rather than go for the .45, Toland did something totally unexpected. He dove to his right, landed in the grass, rolled, did a complete somersault and came up on his knees, his left hand reaching for the pistol. It wasn't a bad opening gambit, and had it been made by a more worthy opponent it might have had a chance of succeeding. But Toland was far from being a worthy opponent, and the move he executed proved it.

Toland made the crucial mistake of diving to his right, thus landing hard on the side of his body where the .45 was holstered. At some point, probably while executing the somersault, the .45 became dislodged and fell to the ground. When Toland reached into the holster, his hand found nothing but empty space.

Not that securing the pistol would have mattered. Cain had encountered too many superior opponents to ever be fooled by any move a guy like Toland would make. Toland probably thought his move was daring and unexpected, and that it would take Cain by surprise. But what Toland never factored in was the likelihood that Cain would not only anticipate the move, he would also know precisely when it was going to happen, and in which direction. Nothing Toland could possibly conjure up was going to surprise Cain.

And as a consequence, there was nothing Toland could do that would save his life.

Cain slammed his right fist hard into Toland's chest, knocking the air from his lungs and sending him flying backward into the grass. Next, after pulling Toland to a standing position, Cain drove his right foot into Toland's left knee, bending the leg inward at such an extreme angle that every bone, ligament and joint were shattered beyond repair. Toland's scream echoed throughout Constitution Gardens.

But Cain wasn't through inflicting pain, not by a long shot. For the first time in his life, he was acting out of pure hatred. And he felt no qualms about doing so. For what Toland had done, he deserved to be severely punished.

As Toland tried to crawl away, Cain reached down and pulled him to his feet. Within three seconds, Cain landed judo chops to Toland's throat and nose. The first blow silenced the screams, the second blow broke Toland's nose and sent blood flying in all directions. Toland crumbled to the ground, groaning and whimpering. Cain kicked him twice in the ribs and once in the face.

Looking up at the Wall, knowing Johnny Dantzler's name was listed among the dead, Cain decided that Jeff Toland did not deserve to die in the presence of genuine heroes. A coward wasn't worthy of dying among the honored, so Cain dragged Toland's battered body behind the Wall, to the top of a small ridge maybe twenty yards away.

Leaning down, putting those huge hands on either side of Toland's head, Cain whispered, "See you in hell, Toland."

Then he ended it by breaking Toland's neck.

Cain searched through Toland's pockets, quickly finding the envelope that contained a single piece of paper. On the paper was a list of names a crazy Saudi Sheikh was willing to cough up fifty-million dollars to obtain. Cain was eager to learn whose names were worth that kind of money, but now was not the time to find out. That would have to come later. First, he had to do something with Toland.

After putting the envelope in his pocket, Cain gave Toland a push, sending him rolling down a fifteen-foot embankment. Toland's body ended up wedged between a concrete wall and the ground, but it was still clearly visible. There was nothing Cain could do about that. Nor was there anything he could do about the body of Abdul-Aziz's unlucky cousin he left behind the Wall. Making them disappear was out of the question. He couldn't take the chance of being seen carrying two bodies to his car. Even he would have a difficult time explaining that to the authorities. So, the two men he killed would remain where they were. Early morning visitors to the area would surely be shocked to find a pair of dead bodies littering the grounds. They had come to honor the dead, not stumble upon real corpses.

Cain returned to the place where he fought Toland, located the .45, and tucked it into his waistband. While using a handkerchief to wipe Toland's blood from his hands and face, he walked quickly past the Wall, toward his car. Once he was inside, he started the engine, turned on the overhead light, took out the envelope with the list of names, opened it and began reading.

After seeing what was on the list, Cain was left with but one thought:

Jeff Toland did not suffer nearly enough.

CHAPTER THIRTY-EIGHT

Lee Bartlett sat in a swank Manhattan restaurant, drinking scotch and reading *The Wall Street Journal*. Sitting across the booth from him was a much younger man, maybe twenty-five, who was bored stiff but trying not to let it show. At this hour, almost midnight, the dining area was empty. All the action was congregated around the bar, where about two dozen late-night imbibers were enjoying themselves to the fullest.

Cain had been standing just inside the front door for ten minutes, observing Lee and his companion. His main focus was on the younger man, who was dressed in a black skin-tight T-shirt, chinos and loafers. Judging by the man's massive upper torso, enormous biceps and thick neck, he was either a serious bodybuilder or a big-time steroid user. Cain figured the man fell into both categories, neither of which caused Cain to break out in a nervous sweat. Pure strength was one thing, but the will to use it in a physical confrontation with another man was something else entirely. Cain doubted the young guy possessed the will to risk life and limb for the man he was being paid to protect. If he did, well, too bad for him.

Only one way to find out what the young guy was made of, and that was to confront him head on.

Weaving his way through the dining area, Cain eased to his right, came up behind the young man and put a hand on his shoulder. The young man spun around, looked up at Cain, and started to stand. Cain pushed him back down into his seat.

"What the hell?" the kid barked. "Get your paws off me."

"You need to take a hike, Schwarzenegger," Cain said. "I want to have a chat with your boss, and nothing I say to him is going to interest you. Stand up, don't make a fuss, and find the nearest exit. Now. "

"Screw you, pal. I take orders from Mr. Bartlett, not you."

"Forget Mr. Bartlett. You're dealing with me now. And I'm telling you to get lost."

"And what if I don't? What if I decide to kick your ancient ass all across this restaurant?"

"Then it will be the last decision you ever make."

"I doubt it."

"No. You can take it to the bank."

"Man, you sure talk tough for an ancient fuck."

"What's your name, kid?" Cain said.

"Dale. And I'm not a kid."

"Well, Dale, here's the situation. In ten seconds you can be gone, or in ten seconds you can be dead. Your call."

"I'm half your age and twice your size," Dale said. "Do you think I'm scared of you?"

"I know you're scared of me. I can see it in your eyes. You see, Dale. Steroids may give you strength, but they don't give you courage."

"I have courage, and you'd be a dumb ass to think otherwise."

"You sure about that?"

"Damn straight, I'm sure about it."

"I'm standing right here. Go for it."

"Who the hell are you, anyway?" Dale said.

"I'm the guy who is counting down from ten . . . nine . . . eight . . . seven."

"Wait, wait . . . let me think."

"Think about this, Dale," Cain said, pointing at Lee Bartlett. "Do you really want to die for this old man? Are the paychecks he gives you worth your life? Remember, Dale. Once they plant you in the ground, there are no more paychecks."

Dale was silent for several moments, stood, eased past Cain and said, "Fuck it. I don't need this shit. Sorry, Mr. Bartlett, but I'm out of here."

"Wise move, Dale," Cain said. "You're much smarter than you look."

After Dale was gone, Cain slid into the booth next to Lee Bartlett. "Where'd you get that guy? The yellow pages? I can't help but believe a man of your means could do a lot better than that."

Lee sipped his scotch and shrugged.

"Do you know who I am?" Cain said.

"I have a pretty good idea."

"Good. Then we can skip the introductions." Cain looked around the restaurant. "This is a very nice place. Do you come here often?"

"I own the joint. I come here whenever it pleases me."

"Must be nice, owning your own restaurant. Never having to pay for a meal. You can't beat free food."

"This is just one of dozens of business establishments I own."

"Tell me, Lee. How much money are you worth? You don't have to give me an exact number, just a ballpark figure."

"That's none of your damn business, Cain."

"Come on. Just for fun, give me a figure."

"State your business, Cain, and then go away."

"Let's say I have a billion dollars. Would I have more money than you, less money than you, or would we be about equal?"

"If a billion was all you had, I could buy you twenty times over," Lee said.

"Okay, so you're worth twenty billion. That wasn't so hard to say, was it? My question is, what happens to all that money when you die?"

"I don't plan on dying anytime soon, so I haven't given it much thought."

"No one plans on dying, but it happens. Sometimes it happens when we least expect it. When the old heart decides to close shop, the final curtain comes down."

"Will you get to the point, Cain? You are really starting to bore me."

"The last thing I would ever want to do is bore an important and celebrated citizen like you."

"Well, you are."

"You are one lucky, lucky man, Lee. You know that?"

"Why am I a lucky man?"

"Because I'm not going to kill you, that's why." Cain reached across the table and grabbed Lee's paper-thin wrists. "I came here with every intention of ending your miserable life, Lee. For what you had done to Ray Dunlap, and for assisting Abdul-Aziz in the absurd plan he concocted. But you know what? I've decided to let you live. And that not only makes you lucky, it also makes you unique. Know why? Because not once have I ever let an intended target off the hook. Never. This time, I am. But I'm still going to hurt you, Lee. I'm going to hurt you by passing along some very interesting news."

"I seriously doubt that anything you say will be of interest to me."

"Well, see how this rates on your interest scale. Nick Marlow is dead. Jeff Toland is dead. David Langley has been arrested and will soon be spilling his guts to a half-dozen government committees and federal agencies. The end time has arrived, Lee. Your Apollo Enterprises empire is about to come crashing down faster than a straw house in a hurricane."

Cain waited several beats, and then said, "Now, be honest, Lee. Didn't you find that bit of news to be somewhat interesting?"

"Nick is dead?" Lee said, more to himself than to Cain. "Are you sure?"

"He's already in hell, Lee," Cain said, releasing the old man's wrists. "Down there with Jeff Toland. And they're both eagerly waiting for you to join them."

Cain scooted out of the booth and stood. "Have a nice rest of the evening, Mr. Bartlett. Have a nice rest of your life."

Leaving the restaurant, Cain kept an eye out for Dale. The young man was nowhere in sight. Cain smiled. The kid *was* smarter than he looked.

CHAPTER THIRTY-NINE

Cain spent the next five days at his St. Augustine ocean-front house, essentially living the life of a bum. The majority of his time was spent divided among jogging on the beach, swimming in his pool, sitting on his deck staring out at the ocean or simply relaxing. Not once did he read a newspaper, turn on the television or fire up his computer. For all he cared, the outside world could go to hell.

He did, however, have a keen interest in what was happening with the Apollo Enterprises investigation. Although he would play no role in the investigation, nor would he be interviewed or questioned about his own actions, he wanted to be kept in the loop. For that, he didn't need the outside media; he had his own source. Houdini phoned three or four times each day with further updates on what was transpiring in regards to the investigative process.

According to Houdini, David Langley was singing longer and louder than Bruce Springsteen, providing exact and minute details relating to all aspects of Apollo Enterprises activities, both in this country and abroad. Langley was like a rubber ball being bounced from building to building, from room to room. Everyone, it seems, was interested in the tale he had to tell. Among those questioning him were Senator John Carlin's committee, the CIA, FBI, Justice Department and the State Department.

Langley told the investigators everything, no doubt hoping full cooperation would result in a reduced sentence somewhere down the road. He gave up details concerning money transactions, the names and location of banks where the accounts were held, and the companies through which money was laundered. He told them about contracts with foreign governments, how Apollo Enterprises was in bed with several defense contractors, how the financial books were cooked, and for good measure, he identified three U.S. diplomats who took money to help facilitate those transactions. He said Nick Marlow and Jeff Toland were the primary forces who engineered the evil. And, of course, he identified Lee Bartlett as the man who bankrolled the operation.

What David Langley detailed was the story of greed and corruption run amok, the story of an organization that began with good intentions but ended up being a traitor to its own country. It was the all-too-familiar and sordid saga of a few men whose desire to make huge sums of money trumped loyalty to the United States. Not the first time this had happened, nor would it be the last.

During his most recent call, Houdini informed Cain that sometime late last night two well-known and prominent American citizens committed suicide. In his Manhattan penthouse apartment, Lee Bartlett went into the den, sat in a big leather chair, drank half a bottle of expensive scotch, put a German Lugar to his temple and blew his brains all over a six-million-dollar painting. In Falls Church, Virginia, Senator Benjamin Parker closed the garage door, rigged a hose to his car's exhaust pipe, ran the hose into the front seat, got behind the wheel and started the engine. An hour later he was fast asleep . . . forever.

Cain wasn't surprised by this news. Men like Lee Bartlett and Ben Parker, both of whom had been subpoenaed to testify before the Carlin Committee, were never going to allow themselves to be put through the ringer. Public humiliation, even more than the fear of being sent to prison, was the one thing they could never accept. Their pride was too great for them to let that happen. So, they chose to avoid being humbled and embarrassed by taking their own lives. In the end, when it came down to crunch time, they revealed themselves to be nothing more than cowards.

During his five days as a beach bum, Cain pretty much followed the same routine. He mostly snacked during the morning and afternoon, and then threw together a light meal for dinner, usually a sandwich or a bowl of clam chowder. After eating, he would drive off the island and head into town. His destination was a small pub located across the highway from Castillo de San Marcos, the old Spanish fort that dated back to 1672.

The pub was home to a core group of regulars, all of whom knew him only as Mickey, the retired college professor. Cain did not exist in this place. Along with the regulars, there were always a few fresh faces, usually tourist who happened to see the pub and decided to pay a visit. Most never came back, but a few did, popping in each evening to mingle with the regulars until their vacation ended and they had to leave for home.

Because the owner's name was Kelly, everyone assumed this was an Irish pub. It didn't seem to matter that Kelly's last name was Roth, or that he wore a Star of David rather than a Cross or a St. Christopher's medal around his neck. With his reddish hair and ruddy complexion, Kelly *looked* Irish. This was more than enough to convince the regulars that they were frequenting an Irish pub. It also didn't hurt that he served great Guinness, arguably Ireland's most popular export prior to U2.

Cain always sat on the same stool, located at the far end of the bar, facing the front entrance. The regulars knew of this quirk, and if one of them was sitting on the stool when Cain arrived, he respectfully relocated. No questions, no complaints. Every king has his throne, and this one was Cain's. One of the bar's oldest regulars dubbed the stool "Mickey's Monument."

Tonight, sitting at the opposite end of the bar was one of the most gorgeous women Cain had ever seen. She was breathtaking in every way.

Movie star beautiful. She had red hair, hazel eyes, full lips and firm skin more smooth than silk. She was dressed in shorts, a sleeveless top and sandals. No make-up, not that any was required. She was a natural beauty, one of those women with a face and body that would tempt a saint.

Cain couldn't remember the last time he'd seen a woman this stunning.

On several occasions Cain tried to make eye contact, but she never let her eyes meet his. Being rejected by a beautiful woman was nothing new. Every man, including Cain, had experienced it countless times. Failure went with the territory. Most times, Cain accepted it and moved on to the next beautiful woman. Sooner or later, if he was persistent enough, he usually got lucky. The mating game, like the Lottery, was all about numbers.

But with this beautiful creature, he wasn't ready to throw in the towel. Not yet, anyway. Not before giving it his best shot. If he struck out, so be it. At least he'd been in the batter's box. At least he'd tried to hit a home run.

Summoning Kelly, Cain said, "Give the gorgeous redhead a drink and put it on my tab."

"What's this I'm feeling, Mickey?" Kelly said. "Could it be kismet?"

"What are you talking about?"

"The lady just gave me the exact same directive. 'Buy the handsome guy at the end of the bar a drink and put it on my tab.' I'm thinking something special is in the air tonight."

"I'm thinking you're full of shit, Kelly. But I'm also thinking I need to walk down there and introduce myself. I can't let her buy a drink for a complete stranger."

"Go for it, Mick," Kelly said, smiling. "The only thing you have to lose is your dignity. And we've all been there before."

Cain strolled to the front of the bar, pulled back a stool next to hers, sat and said, "There seems to be some confusion about who's buying the next round. You have any thoughts on how to settle the issue?"

"As a matter of fact, I do," she said.

"Okay. How?"

"You pay."

"Well, that was certainly easy enough," Cain said. He motioned for Kelly. "Give me another pint of Guinness, and give the lady another . . ."

"Dirty martini, Stoli rather than gin, two olives," she said, extending her hand. "My name is Samantha. And unless the bartender was being untruthful, your name is Mickey."

"Mickey, it is. Do your friends call you Sam?"

"Not if they want to remain friends and keep their front teeth."

"Ouch." Cain waited until their drinks were served, then said, "Are you a tourist or a local making your first visit to our friendly little pub?"

"I fall into the tourist category."

"Visiting us from . . . ?"

"Los Angeles."

"Last time I checked, Los Angeles has its own ocean. Why travel all the way across country to see our little pond?"

Samantha stirred her drink and then took a sip. "I work in real estate. Each year the top realtors hold a big convention. It just happens to be in St. Augustine this year."

"Isn't selling real estate in this economy a tough gig?"

"I work with very high-end clients," Samantha said. "The Malibu, Beverly Hills crowd. You know the ones, people with more money than they know what to do with. The lucky stiffs who aren't affected by the economy."

"Sounds like you have a good thing going."

Samantha nodded. "What do you do, other than drink Guinness at night?"

"I'm a retired college professor."

"What did you teach?"

"Literature."

"Never one of my favorite subjects."

"Unfortunately, a lot of people feel the same way. They don't know what they're missing. There is a lot of truth and beauty in great books."

Samantha took another drink, said, "And now you live near the ocean, the fulfillment of a life-long dream, yes?"

"Actually, I live on the ocean."

"House or condo?"

"House."

Samantha said, "This is a terribly nosy question, but how much did you pay for your place?"

"Slightly more than a million."

"I can assure you that if your house was on the beach in Malibu, it would be worth five times that much. And that's a conservative estimate."

Cain finished his Guinness. "Tell you what. Why don't we leave here and go to my place. That way, you can judge for yourself what it might be worth."

"Uh, you're moving a little too fast, cowboy. You need to slow down."

"Relax. I'm only asking you to pay a quick visit, nothing more," Cain said.

"Plenty of bad things can happen during what you call a quick visit."

"Nothing bad is going to happen. I don't have much alcohol in the house, but I do have one bottle of a very nice red zinfandel. You can inspect the place, or walk on the beach if you prefer. Stay as long as you want. When you're ready to leave, I'll bring you back here."

"No harm, no foul. Is that what you're telling me?"

"Exactly. You'll be as safe as if you were wrapped in God's arms."

"My mother's advice was, always be wary of strangers."

"Well, I would never ask a lady to ignore her mother's words of wisdom. So . . . we'll stay here and drink."

Samantha frowned. "Suppose I did agree to go with you. How do I know I can trust you to be a perfect gentleman?"

"Ask Kelly. He's a bartender. Everyone knows bartenders are the ones to ask if you want an honest assessment of a person's character."

Samantha waved to Kelly. "Can I trust this man to do me no harm?" she asked, putting a hand on Cain's shoulder.

"You can trust him with your life," Kelly said. "You can, but I wouldn't."

His deep bellowing laugh rattled the walls.

"That's not exactly a ringing endorsement," Samantha said. "But . . . I'm a gambler, so I'll take my chances."

Cain put two twenties on the bar, stood and said, "Is this enough to keep me in your good graces?"

"More than enough," Kelly answered. "You are a prince among men, Mick."

Cain led Samantha out of the bar and into the parking lot. "The white Lexus LX to your right," he said.

"Nice ride."

"It gets me from here to there."

After both had buckled up, Cain started the engine, pulled out of the parking lot, made a right onto the highway and headed toward the island.

CHAPTER FORTY

Cain drove off the mainland onto the island and made a right on A1A Beach Boulevard. He drove slowly, passing mostly motels and condominiums on the left, and restaurants, bars and a residential area on the right. His house was approximately three miles away, on the left, located behind an iron fence. As he approached the house, he hit the remote that opened the gate. After driving past the gate, he parked and they got out of the Lexus. Two minutes later he and Samantha were inside the house.

"Give me a minute while I open the wine," Cain said. "In the meantime, make yourself comfortable."

There was no kitchen table, only an island with two bar stools on one side. Samantha put her purse on the island and sat on one of the stools.

Cain said, "Do you want to look around, give the place a serious assessment? Decide for yourself what it would be worth in Malibu? Or would you rather take a walk on the beach? You name it, we'll do it."

"No. I'd prefer to just sit here, drink the wine and talk. We can do all that other stuff after we've gotten to know each other a little better."

"Oh, I think we already know each other pretty well."

"How can you say that? We met less than two hours ago."

Cain leaned against the wall, a big grin on his face.

"Why are you grinning like that?" Samantha asked.

Cain was silent for several seconds, and then said, "I thought you would be better than this."

"Better? What are you talking about?"

"Come on. You know exactly what I'm talking about."

"No, I don't."

"I'd heard you were a real pro, that you were one of the best. Turns out those reports weren't accurate."

"I haven't a clue what you are referring to," Samantha said. "But this talk is making me very uncomfortable."

"Ordering the same exotic drink twice," Cain said, shaking his head. "Dirty martini, Stoli rather than gin, two olives. I couldn't believe it. No half-assed amateur would make that mistake. And yet, the great Sonia Ivanovna did."

Setting her glass of wine on the island, she said, "So . . . a dirty martini gave me away?"

"No. I recognized you the moment you walked into the White Horse Tavern. You really need to work on your disguises, Sonia. They leave a lot to be desired. But I must admit, I like you better as a redhead than a blonde. The Marilyn Monroe look doesn't work for you."

"I'll keep that in mind."

Cain said, "You should have taken a pass on the Ray Dunlap job. You had to know that at some point it was going to come back and bite you on the ass."

"That one shot to the back of his head earned me a half-million dollar payoff," Sonia said. "There is no way I would ever pass on that much money."

"You've been following me for several weeks, so I can only assume your plan is to eliminate me. Are you doing it for the bounty? Ten million is a lot more than five-hundred grand."

"I couldn't care less about the money," Sonia said. "I'm doing it for revenge. You murdered my aunt Nastasia."

Nastasia Ivanovna was a famed KGB agent who had spent much of her adult life working against the interests of the United States during the Cold War. Cain learned that Seneca, one of his former colleagues, was plotting to assassinate the U.S. president and three Middle East leaders. Seneca was living with Nastasia in her Manhattan apartment, where Cain confronted her concerning Seneca's whereabouts.

"You need to get your facts straight, Sonia. I didn't kill Nastasia. She checked herself out by swallowing a cyanide capsule."

"But you would have killed her, yes?"

Cain nodded, said, "And thoroughly enjoyed doing it."

"You Americans are so arrogant," Sonia said.

"Nastasia said the same thing. Must be something about me that pisses off you Russians."

"And to think I saved your life. I never should have done that."

"Don't flatter yourself, Sonia. The only thing killing Nick Marlow did was save me about thirty seconds of time and energy. Because that's about how long it would have taken me to turn out his lights."

Sonia said, "So, what happens now?"

"Simple. I'm going to kill you."

"Unless I kill you first."

Cain laughed. "We both know that's not going to happen."

"I'm as good as you," Sonia said, her eyes now filled with hate. "Maybe I'm even better than you."

"Only one way to find out."

When teaching close quarter combat, most instructors tell their students to always keep their focus on an opponent's hands. When the hands move, the encounter has begun. And by following the direction of your opponent's hands, you'll have a good idea what his plan is, or where his weapon of choice might be located. According to those instructors, watching your opponent's hands was the key to victory.

Cain never bought into that theory. For him, it was all about the eyes, not the hands. He always focused on an opponent's eyes, knowing the slightest movement, usually no more than a flicker, provided him with all the information required for assessing the situation. It was as though he had been given access to his opponent's battle plan. That quick glance told him the action was about to begin, and in which direction his opponent was heading. For the greatest assassin of them all, this was more than enough to ensure success.

Sonia cut her eyes to the left. In that split-second Cain knew Sonia was going for her purse, which was approximately eighteen inches from her hands. Eighteen inches is a relatively short distance, but for Sonia it must have seemed like five miles. With Cain, the fiercest lion standing so close, even two inches would have been too far away. Yet, she had no other choice. Her weapon was in the purse, and without the weapon she had no chance against Cain. She had to go for it.

Sonia reached for the purse with her right hand. As she did, Cain closed in, grabbed her wrist with his right hand, stood her up, wrapped his left arm around her throat and began applying extreme pressure. It was the classic choke hold, a maneuver meant to close the carotid arteries, thus cutting off blood flow to the brain. Depriving an individual's brain of blood and oxygen for a certain length of time will result in that person passing out. Keep the pressure on for a longer period and the person dies.

Sonia struggled, and although she was a strong and well-trained fighter, she was no match for Cain. He handled her as though he was handling a paper doll.

Cain had no intention of killing Sonia. Not yet, anyway. Her death would come later in the night, and not too far from Cain's house. And it would be something special, a unique death he knew Ray Dunlap would appreciate.

Cain wanted her unconscious but alive, so he had to apply pressure for just the right amount of time. He had done this many times in the past, but never with any intention other than killing the opponent. Using the choke hold for the purpose of putting an opponent to sleep was new territory for him. Therefore, he had to be careful not to keep the pressure on too long.

It took almost two minutes before Sonia passed out. Wanting to ensure that she would be out for a while, Cain kept the pressure on for another fifteen seconds. When he was satisfied that she was in a deep sleep, he laid her on the floor, went to a kitchen drawer and found a roll of duct tape. Kneeling, he rolled her onto her stomach and bound her ankles. Pulling her arms behind her, he then bound her wrists. Next, he ripped off a small piece of tape and put it across her mouth.

Standing, he went through Sonia's purse, removing a SigArms P239, which he guessed was likely the same gun used to execute Ray Dunlap, and a switchblade knife. He tossed the pistol onto a chair and put the switchblade in his hip pocket. Bending down, he picked up Sonia and carried her outside to the Lexus. He opened the back door and laid her across the floorboard. After closing the door, he climbed into the front seat, started the engine, drove past the gate, made a right onto AIA Ocean Boulevard and headed back toward town.

After leaving the island, Cain got on Anastasia Boulevard and drove several more miles before finally reaching his destination, an empty parking lot that fronted several white Spanish-style buildings. He swung the Lexus around so the passenger-side door was parallel to the front entrance. Before exiting the Lexus he checked his watch. It was just past midnight, maybe a little too early for what he had planned, but at this point, none of that mattered. He was here, and he would take his chances that he could pull it off without being seen.

The next minute was critical. He had to gain access to the building within those sixty ticks of the clock, or risk being spotted by a passerby who might be inclined to call the police. Or he might even be seen by a member of law enforcement. Those guys were notorious for patrolling the area with great regularity. Trying to explain his intentions to a cop, especially with a bound and unconscious female in the back seat, would likely fall on deaf ears.

Success or failure hinged on a single key given to him more than five years ago by a retired Marine veteran who was once employed here. Whether the key still worked, Cain had no way of knowing. If it didn't, he would have to alter the plan he had concocted for Sonia. There would be no other choice but to punt. And that would be greatly disappointing. This was one mission that he desperately wanted to succeed.

He inserted the key, turned it and the lock fell open. Seems Lady Luck was on his side tonight. He silently offered her his thanks. Returning to the Lexus, he opened the back door, pulled Sonia out, lifted her onto his shoulder and quickly carried her inside the building. There was enough light for him to easily see where he was going. He carried Sonia past the front desk, through a second room, and out into open air. Following a wooden pathway, he kept going until he came to a small bridge. This was as far as he needed to go.

Setting Sonia down, he took her by the shoulders and gently shook her. She came to, looked around through groggy eyes, obviously confused by where she was. She tried to speak, but the tape muffled her words.

"Did you have a nice nap?" Cain asked. "I hope so. Sleep builds energy, and believe me when I say you are going to need all the energy you can get."

Cain picked Sonia up and laid her body across a narrow wooden railing. He positioned her so that she was facing away from him. This was done for the dual purpose of letting her see the future, and for instilling maximum fear.

"Do you know where you are?" Cain asked. "No? Well, let me tell you. You are in St. Augustine's world-famous alligator farm. See all those bright lights in the water? Those are alligator eyes. There must be at least three dozen gators down there. And you'll be joining them very shortly."

Panicked and fear-stricken, Sonia began to struggle against Cain like a wild animal. But with her hands and feet bound, and being balanced so precariously on a slim wooden railing, where the slightest tilt forward would send her plunging into the dark waters below, she was in no position to put up much of a struggle. She was at Cain's mercy in every way, and unless he made a mistake, she was going to die.

And, she knew, Cain never made mistakes.

"Here's the way this is going to play out, Sonia," Cain whispered in her ear. "In less than a minute you're hitting the water. But I'm going to do something for you that you didn't do for Ray Dunlap—I'm going to give you a fighting chance. I'm going to free your feet, then I'm going to free your hands. That way, you'll at least be able to swim. Most of the gators are on the other side, so if you swim toward this area to the left, and if you can climb over that fence, you just might survive this. But you're going to have to swim fast. Are you ready?"

Sonia vigorously shook her head while pushing back harder against Cain's body. A flood of tears flowed down her cheeks and dripped into the water below. Her pleas, muted by the duct tape, sounded like the moaning of a wounded animal.

"Let me offer a word of advice, Sonia. Don't try anything foolish when I free your legs. If you do, I'll send you over with your hands still bound. And I would think it nearly impossible to swim without the use of your arms."

Taking the switchblade from his hip pocket, he flicked it open, leaned over and cut the tape binding Sonia's legs together. He fully expected her to try some type of attacking move, maybe swing her legs around in an effort to trip him, or kick him in the groin, but she remained perfectly still. He wasn't sure if she was contemplating another way to attack him, or if she had given up hope and resigned herself to certain death. It didn't much matter to him either way. What did matter was that in a few seconds, Ray Dunlap's death would be avenged.

Without saying another word, Cain cut the tape that bound Sonia's wrists, gave her a push, then watched as she fell off the railing and into the water ten feet below. Sonia's head popped up above the water for a brief moment, and then she was gone, pulled under by one of the alligators. Within seconds, every gator was moving in her direction, hoping to get in on the action. Watching from above, Cain thought they resembled a fleet of nightmarish submarines moving rapidly toward what they recognized as live prey.

With tails thrashing and jaws snapping, the gators fought among themselves in an effort to get at Sonia. The water roiled and soon turned blood red as the gators bit into her body, went into the classic death roll, ripping off huge chunks of flesh, devouring it and then going back for more. It was a feeding frenzy, where primal instincts perfected by millions of years of evolution drove the gators toward the food source. Nothing or nobody was going to slow their relentless onslaught.

In less than the time it takes to tie your shoe laces, it was all over.

Sonia Ivanovna was gone forever.

Cain couldn't help but smile when recalling that hot afternoon he and Ray Dunlap fed Hank to Samson and Hercules. At the time, Cain adamantly opposed the plan, arguing instead that he should kill Hank rather than feed him to a pair of alligators. But General Lucas White, Cain's commanding officer, insisted otherwise. Cain followed orders, hooked up with Ray Dunlap, and together they provided Samson and Hercules with a perfectly nice mid-day meal.

Feeding Sonia Ivanovna to alligators seemed like the right and proper method for avenging Ray Dunlap's death. Cain had dozens of ways he could have ended her life, some quick, some slow and painful, but none of those appealed to him. This was one of those situations that cried out for something special, something truly unique, a death with meaning and symbolism. The only method that met his criteria was the one he chose. And he had no doubt he'd chosen wisely.

Of course, there was always the option of handing Sonia over to the authorities and letting the justice system mete out punishment. But Cain dismissed that possibility outright. He had no interest in seeing Sonia get lost in legal wrangling and bureaucratic red tape, becoming a pawn battled over by a half-dozen countries. And that's exactly what would happen. She would eventually be sentenced to death, but it might take decades before she was executed. Cain saw no need for waiting that long. Anyway, who needs a gas chamber or a hangman's noose when three dozen hungry gators can get the job done in a short time and with no hassles?

He also had no doubt that Ray Dunlap would have agreed.

"This one was for you, old friend," Cain said. "Hope you enjoyed it."

Somewhere, Cain knew, Ray Dunlap was nodding his approval.

CHAPTER FORTY-ONE

Few sites anywhere are more beautiful than the Lexington Cemetery at dusk. As the sun slowly eased its way west, its last rays filtered through the canopy of trees, creating the perfect blend of light and shadow on the sacred ground below. For a few final minutes, the east side would be bathed in sunlight, while the western portion of the grounds remained in shadows. In less than an hour, the entire cemetery would be blanketed in darkness.

Jack Dantzler always preferred coming to the cemetery at this time of day. He wasn't sure why he chose to visit his parents at dusk, but he did. Maybe it was because fewer people were here. Maybe it was because he appreciated those final moments before daylight yielded to darkness. Or maybe there was no underlying reason. Perhaps it was nothing more than habit.

Dantzler was on his knees cleaning dead leaves and twigs from his mother's grave when he heard a sound coming from behind him. Standing and turning, he was surprised to see Cain walking in his direction. This was the first time he'd laid eyes on the man since leaving Virginia almost three weeks ago.

"You're losing your touch," Dantzler said, grinning.

"Oh, yeah? How so?"

"I heard you coming. You're not as stealthy as you once were."

"Did you ever consider that I might've wanted you to hear me? That I didn't want you to spin around and gun me down?"

Dantzler slapped his right hip. "You're safe . . . I'm not armed."

"Lucky me." Cain came forward until he was standing shoulder to shoulder with Dantzler. Looking down at Johnny Dantzler's headstone, Cain said, "Your father would have been proud of you, Detective. He would've been proud of the way you handled the David Langley situation. For arresting Langley and turning him over to the authorities rather than executing him yourself, which I know was what you wanted to do. And you would have had every right to do it. But you showed restraint, and for that your father would have been proud of you."

"Is that how my father would have handled it?"

Cain laughed. "No. Your father would have put two bullets in his heart."

"Then how can you say he would've been proud of the way I handled things?"

"You're a cop, a sworn member of law enforcement. You handled it the way a cop should. Your father was a soldier; he would have acted the way a soldier should. You were both bound by a strict set of rules. What you did was right and proper, and your father's way would also have been right and proper. Simple as that."

"Was my father like you?"

"No one is like me."

Dantzler thought he detected a note of sadness in Cain's response.

"In retrospect, knowing what is probably taking place in Washington, I should have killed the bastard," Dantzler said.

"What do you think is happening in Washington?"

"Come on, Cain, we both know how this shit works. The first thing Langley did was hire some slick attorney. The attorney meets with the people wanting to interview his client, and together they hammer out a deal that satisfies all parties involved. Langley will give them what they're looking for in exchange for a reduced sentence. Or maybe he'll receive no sentence at all. I wouldn't be all that shocked to see him walk out of there a free man."

"You can forget that, Detective. David Langley is going to prison for the rest of his natural life. He'll never be a free man again. Unfortunately, his natural life probably won't last too long. Guys like him don't do very well behind bars."

"But no matter what happens, he'll never stand trial for murdering my mother."

"No, probably not."

"Like I said, Cain, I should have killed him. And I should have been the one to kill Jeff Toland. He deserved a bullet from my gun for what he did to my father."

"Toland was mine, Detective. There was no way anyone other than me was going to kill him."

"What about Nick Marlow? Was he all yours, too?"

"I didn't kill Marlow," Cain said.

"Who did?"

"A Russian assassin named Sonia Ivanovna."

"Any chance she'll come for you?"

"Sonia has retired from the business. Taken a permanent leave of absence is a better way of putting it."

"In other words, she's no longer with us."

"That would be correct."

Dantzler said, "The list Marlow gave to Toland. What was on it?"

"The names and home addresses of the SEAL 6 team members who took out bin Laden."

"Who would want that list? And why?"

"Sheikh Abdul-Aziz. Why? He planned to have them all killed, which was, of course, an insane idea. He was also going to have their families killed, an even more insane idea. By now, I hope you're getting the picture, Detective. Abdul-Aziz is a certifiable nut job."

"Would it be wrong of me to assume that you'll soon be paying him a visit?"

"Maybe later, I will. But for now the situation is being handled through diplomatic channels. Abdul-Aziz's father has many business interests in our country, and he doesn't want anything to interfere with those interests, which, if things went sour, could cost him billions of dollars. He also doesn't want to be publicly humiliated. The top honchos in our State Department will give him a choice—either get your idiot son under control, or risk losing untold amounts of money *and* be humiliated throughout the world. He is a proud man who is not about to allow his nutty son to cause those kinds of personal or financial catastrophes. He'll have Abdul-Aziz locked up, never to be heard from again. If he doesn't, then at some point in the future, I will pay him a visit."

"Tell me, Cain. How does this end for a guy like you?"

"What do you mean, 'a guy like me'?"

"An assassin."

"I've never considered myself an assassin."

"What do you consider yourself?"

"I'm a soldier. I'm given orders to track down and eliminate the enemy. And that's what I do."

"We will always have enemies," Dantzler said. "That's never going to change. But you can't keep doing this forever. Let's face it, you aren't getting any younger."

Cain laughed. "You got that right. Who knows? Maybe I'll get back down to Florida and the phone will never ring again."

"Would it please you if there were no more calls?"

"Honestly, I don't know." Cain dug into his pants pocket, came out with a small cassette, and handed it to Dantzler. "Here, take this. You might have need for it in the future."

"What's on it?"

"David Langley confessing to the murder of your mother."

"Where did you get this?" Dantzler asked.

"Seems our intrepid reporter, Kayce Clark, had a tape recorder in her purse. It was on the entire time we were together in that room. She got everything, including Langley admitting to killing your mother. Hang onto it, on the off chance that Langley does get out of prison early. There is no statute of limitations on murder, so you could have him arrested and tried for what he did to Sarah Dantzler. This tape is all the evidence you would ever need to convict him."

"Thanks, Cain. I really appreciate this."

"Johnny Dantzler was a good man, one of the best I've ever known. And you are your father's son, Detective. That's about the highest compliment I can pay you."

"I wish I could have known him as well as you did."

Cain nodded, gave Dantzler a gentle tap on the shoulder and started to walk away. After taking a few steps, he turned back around.

"One more thing, Detective," he said. "Your father was shot in the back, not the chest. There is no way a guy like Jeff Toland could ever get the best of your father face to face. That simply never would have happened."

"Once again, I have to ask. Is that the truth, or are you just saying it to make me feel better?"

"Like I said, Detective. I only tell the truth. I'm just careful who I tell it to."

Dantzler watched Cain walk away for a few seconds, then knelt between his parents' graves and whispered a soft "It's all over now. You can both rest in peace."

We can all rest in peace.

Remembering a question he wanted to ask Cain, Dantzler stood, turned and looked off across the cemetery grounds, his eyes searching for the man who saved his life. The man who helped him find answers to the two mysteries that haunted him his entire life. The man he now considered a friend.

But Cain was gone, lost in the shadows, among the dead.

Acknowledgments

As always, I want to thank by small band of friends who have stuck with me and encouraged me throughout the years. This special group includes Julie Watson, Ed Watson, Wanda Underwood, Denny Slinker, Suzanne Slinker, Christina Young, Scott Boggs, Chris Boggs, Jimmie Nell Jenkins, Grant Sparks and my aunt Bobbie Watkins. Thanks to Kayce Ireland for loaning me her name. I also want to thank Annie Leckenby for her advice concerning exotic drinks. Two superb and enlightening books by Joseph J. Trento—*The Secret History of the CIA* and *Prelude to Terror: The Rogue CIA and the Legacy of America's Private Intelligence Network*—provided valuable insight into the darker involvement of the CIA during the Vietnam War. Lastly, the biggest thanks of all go to Marilyn Underwood. She's the first reader, the first critic and the glue that holds it all together.

About the Author

Tom Wallace is the award-winning author of four previous novels, including *Gnosis*, *Heirs of Cain*, *What Matters Blood* and *The Devil's Racket*.

Tom is also the author of five sports-related books, including the highly successful *Kentucky Basketball Encyclopedia*. He earned his B.A. in journalism in 1982 from Western Kentucky University, then became sports editor for the Henderson *Gleaner*, where he was twice honored by The Kentucky Press Association for writing the best sports story in the state. After leaving the *Gleaner*, he became editor for Cawood Ledford Productions in Lexington.

He is an active member of Mystery Writers of America and The Author's Guild. Tom, a Vietnam veteran, currently lives in Lexington, Kentucky.